D1737007

This book is dedicated to my First Fan.

DISCLAIMER

This is a work of FICTION. Any resemblance to any persons, whether alive or dead, *yatta, yatta, yatta.*

Get *over* yourself! *It ain't about you!*

And It isn't about anyone you know!

Any opinions expressed in this work that may offend, were probably culled from real people, and REAL people's feelings and do not necessarily exemplify the feelings of the author...or 99% of the population of the U.S., for that matter.

It's a work of Fiction. I was having fun; and this book is here in hopes that you will have fun reading it, too! Sure, people here are based on or are amalgams of "real'" people, but not so you'd ever be able to tell. Everything here is culled directly from my peripetic and somewhat fevered brain.

Everyone has to be based on something... Your fifth grade math teacher, a cop you met unexpectedly when running a red light, your girlfriend's sister or mother... Everyone has to "come" from somewhere, making stuff up completely from "whole cloth" is just too fake and too difficult.

So, while this book isn't about anyone you know or that any one else knows, you might see some "characteristics" of people you've met.

It's all fiction though. That's the key.

You've just gotta use your imagination.

PREFACE

Optimism

It is an act of sheerest optimism to even undertake the writing of a book.

There's the idea. Ya *gotta* have an idea... Then, you need to allow the idea to "percolate" a bit, and grow and blossom *(sometimes, they just grow mold!).*

Then, you have to plot it out, and then, sit down and actually write the darned thing!

When you're all finished, you're still not done. Oh no...

Because now that it's finished, it's gotta be edited and read and re-read numerous times, both by yourself, and also by friends (to whom I owe a great debt, for reading early versions of this story and offering feedback).

So, over the space of weeks or months, you "tweak" it, polish it and rework it until you dream about it and you'd rather not see it ever again.

And, *still* you're not done!

Now, you need to find a literary agent.

I'll tell you, I've never been kissed off so often by so many people in such creative and nice ways.

I was a commercial photographer for 25 years, so of course, I'm used to being lied to, and blown off, but literary agents are another breed altogether.

They tell me: "Not interested" or "Go away!" but they do it in such a way as to make me feel almost warm & fuzzy even though rejected...

So, now that you've found an agent, the "real" work has just begun: The sales, the promotion, the blogs, "shilling" the new project...

Therefore I proclaim that all writers are, by *definition*, optimists, no matter what their demeanor, or mien.

No one else goes through so much work, pleading, and bleeding only to be rejected 438 times before finding someone who will take their manuscript to an interested publisher, and perhaps wait *two years* to be paid for all that work.

I'm not complaining, or whining; I'm merely pointing out that you've gotta ...*believe*.

And more than that, for each of the 437 times you're rejected, you've gotta *continue* to believe.

That, my friends, is optimism!

INTRODUCTION

Time goes fast and it only goes in one direction, so you'd better pay attention, okay?

This moment is already gone.

I find myself fascinated (*obsessed?*) with how fast things are moving; trying to imagine what *tomorrow* will be like.

I suppose that this goes back to being very high up in the Hollywood Photography scene, where I devised "Plan A" for a given photo shoot, but because "Plan A" almost never survived intact, I needed to be flexible. So that makes "Plan B" all the more important (and spurs the creation of "Plan C" and "Plan D"). *I want control.* "Control" of all of this? Ridiculous! I know. But I want it just the same. It's my nature. Failing that, I at least want to know what's coming, so I can "be ready."

Things that never occurred to you ten years ago are *de rigueur* now. Just in the last year or so, you began doing something with some new technological wrinkle and now you can't imagine your life without it.

What happens when a person, a society gets blindsided by an enormous change?

We all will be blindsided. That's because doing something substantive about all these changes is like trying to nail Jell-O to the wall with a huge wooden nail and a rubber hammer.

"Human Nature" tends to look at problems deemed to be unsolvable, and anxiously "waits," hoping a solution will present itself sometime later (much like my folks when any big decision loomed. They just procrastinated. They might have taught a Master's class in Procrastination--they were certainly qualified!).

We, society, are not much better and I seriously doubt that all the people will listen when others "cry wolf"--not without a clear and do-able Plan. Here, might I refer you back to the aforementioned Jell-O...?

I tend to think of this on a more personal scale. But do not be fooled, these changes are coming, and they will cause anything *but* small personal changes.

A.I. will simply be everywhere, as will advertising and data collection to aid advertising; it will be all interconnected--both for good and for "bad." But one thing is certain: "A.I.," "Robots," whatever you care to call them will be coming for most of the jobs in the world.

Jobs will evaporate like a fine mist left over by the dew when the sun hits it in the morning. And if they "steal" our job, will they in so doing steal or at least damage our identity- our *raison d'etra*?

Jobs provide two things: A way to make money to live, and a *Sense of Purpose* (at least for those of us lucky enough not to be working retail or other similar soul crushing endeavors). So when jobs go away; are taken by robots, who are more efficient and frankly 90% of the time, *just plain better* at your job than you are, there will be new positions available for those nimble enough, and this will buy those lucky or talented few, a few extra years, but the Change is inevitable.

What will become of (most of) the Human Race when they are...*redundant?* What will that do to an individual's psyche? Now, multiply that by *Billions.*

Robots will be the quintessential two-edged sword. We will depend upon them and will be unwilling to give them up (sort of like a narcotic), and yet, they will *steal* everything from humanity (except for a time at least) creative endeavors. They will steal most of our aspirations because we will allow them to do it (anything "I" can do, a robot will, eventually do better)- apologies to the folks who wrote "Annie Get Your Gun." Because on a personal level, they will be a godsend; however, on a mass scale they are the biggest threat to the World since the rock that killed the dinosaurs. And I'm not talking about the Terminator, et al. I'm envisioning something more subtle and more pervasive--with far fewer explosions.

Robots are dangerous simply because they will disturb the fabric that *is humanity;* they will disrupt and cause consternation at least, more likely despair, because they will *change everything.* People, for the most part resist change. When that change rolls right over us like a runaway HUMMER, it will cause "us" to think that it's time to give up. That fabric will strain to absorb all the myriad changes that are dropping into it.

And while I'm on the subject of "robots:"

Body modifications will be everywhere. It can't happen? Ok, well, how about total knee replacements, heart valve replacements, cornea replacements, and lots more. This is just the beginning. "Cyborgs 'R' Us" is just around the proverbial corner.

Tomorrow, we may have digital interfaces in our bodies--perhaps instant access to the internet (or whatever improves and replaces it) with some sort of ongoing connectivity that has not as yet even been beta-tested; there will be things that even the furthest questing minds have not conceived of yet; and it won't take long. The toddlers, perhaps the teens now, perhaps even thirty-years-olds today…they will see all this and more.

Designer babies are also just around the corner. I don't care if governments legislate against it, or Science condemns it, wealthy people will find a way to give their babies an *edge.* Their progeny are their legacy after all, and speaking of legacies, wealthy people will be the first to be able to take advantage of other related advancements. For instance: tiny robots injected into your blood stream whose sole purpose is to clean out plaque and other blockages in your veins. This alone will probably add 20-50 years to a given life; add other more sophisticated procedures, and 200 years becomes a very do-able goal; perhaps even effective immortality/e-mortality. That is, unless some violence happens, that individual will live forever (See: "When A Tool Begets A Child" in "The Future Is Closer Than You Think" Book Two, coming soon).

And again, speaking of leaving a legacy behind, what if you *don't* leave it behind? What if you *don't die* and thereby hang onto your wealth? It never will get divided up among your heirs and instead, will remain sequestered in the digital equivalent of Scrooge McDuck's Vault of gold coins; the better to "swim" in and luxuriate in….

Wealth will be accumulated because people aren't dying, and the very wealthy become the *ultra*-wealthy. So the inequities will continue unless and until some enlightened souls decide that they have enough money, and share the wealth (which is highly unlikely, given Human Nature), thereby improving the lives of those less talented or less fortunate around them. Or, we might have some sort of "revolution" to bring things back into a more equitable framework (but God help us if we try that! Remember Soviet Russia...?)

And while all this is being considered, also consider "eugenics." Oh, it'll have a new name. It'll have better PR, but IT IS coming. The urge to rebuild and improve the race as-a-whole and to de-incentivize those with "poor" genes to reproduce, will begin slowly but surely. And they will disappear-- *for the overall good of the race*, of course.

It'll be a "Grave New World."

I may come off like some sort of "Luddite," or someone who doesn't embrace technology.

This is not true.

I'd like to think of my attitude might be similar to having a gun--or a lawyer--in the house: It's nice to have when you really need it but, be aware of the risks!

There's more of course. The future is the one place where "more" is a given. But that's probably enough for now...

This is the Launchpad for these stories: "The Future Is Closer Than You Think--Stories From The Day After Tomorrow".

Thank you for purchasing this book.

1

THE HUMAN ELEMENT

"Oyez, oyez...In the matter of the civil case of Adamson vs General Robotics, the court will now come to order."

"The right honorable Judge Leslie Rankin presiding."

"All will now stand and draw close to hear the words of Justice. God bless the United States, and the Great State of New York."

The bailiff then sat down at the right of the bench and resumed paperwork.

The prosecutor stood and addressed the court.

"Your Honor, may I please read into the court's records the various classifications of A.I., so that we may all have a basis upon which to judge the case before us?"

The judge shifted uncomfortably. His tuna salad lunch was not sitting well and he had wished that one of the attorneys had requested a delay.

"Are you certain that this reading is necessary?"

"We must establish parameters, your honor. How else might the State clarify the classifications for A.I., as they have a direct bearing upon the expectations of society."

"Go ahead." The judge felt an ominous rumbling in his G.I. tract. He tried very hard to maintain his personal sense of decorum.

THE DISTRICT ATTORNEY consulted a tablet with specifications and definitions on it. He jacked into the courthouse AV interface and read aloud as he showed the court:

"*LEVEL 1 Personal assistant: May or may not be 'corporeal,' and may or may not be ambulatory, i.e., scheduler, companion, researcher/sounding board, and other similar tasks."

"*LEVEL 2 Public assistant: Almost always ambulatory, usually 'corporeal,' i.e., assistant Police, maintenance, landscaping, refuse handling…and some limited automobile operation."

"*LEVEL 3 ALWAYS 'CORPOREAL,' may or may not be ambulatory, i.e., factory assemblers, workers, and…" D.A. Chen paused for effect, "Drivers slash automobiles, as is our defendant."

He allowed that to settle like a lost shoe stuck and sinking in the muck before continuing:

"*LEVEL 4 NON-CORPOREAL SUPPORT 'STAFF:' Dictionaries, encyclopedia, etcetera."

"*LEVEL 5 Classified characteristics: which exist in tandem and usually reside in another program or set of programs."

JUDGE RANKIN SHIFTED UNEASILY. A fly had gotten past the building's anti pest filters buzzed around his ear. He waved a hand at it and it moved on, as he discretely passed gas. The judge felt a bit better, but only for a moment or two. He didn't feel well, and so was impatient and cranky.

"So, what have we learned, District Attorney Chen?"

Chen turned to play to the jury.

"We have learned that teddy1245b is a level 3, and in most instances, the series of units from whom most is expected. This A.I. has the highest levels of intelligence, predictive analytics, and the most up-to-date avoidance software. And yet, on June 24th, 2029, he did kill, with his motored self-driver, Dr. Andrew Adamson, noted pathologist for Erie County."

"The State will show that he is defective, and prove that he willfully terminated a human life."

The judge nodded cholerically. He sighed, and signaled the Defense with a desultory wave of a hand, that it was his "turn."

The Defense attorney rose to address the court, pointedly standing next to The Defendant. 'teddy1245b' had been provided a name and a corporal body so that 'he' could be a distinct individual in court. Humans were used to disembodied voices in their personal lives, but in a court of law, it was debated and eventually deemed useful to have the A.I. installed in some ambulatory human-like unit, the better to 'face your accuser.'

"Humans aren't the only *people* in society – at least that is so, according to the law. In the U.S., corporations have been given rights, even free speech and are considered "citizens," sometimes religion factors into it. Some natural features and landmarks also have person-like rights. So, why shouldn't artificial intelligence systems be recognized as people too? They certainly interface with humans more than corporations and national parks. Shouldn't they be afforded the same rights as are organic people?"

Chen erupted, "Your honor, 'Organic people?' Really? Is there any other sort?"

Defense demurred.

"Of course. That's exactly what I'm suggesting at this moment. That teddy1245b is in most ways, most ways that matter, *a person*. What the D.A. is asking the court is nothing less than an instance of 'Mistreatment of A.I.' In order to protect them, certain laws, *of which I'm certain the court is aware* have been placed to protect A.I. from misguided citizens...luddites, anti 'bot' people, nix-ers and the like. This ploy by the D.A. is tantamount to a public hanging."

Chen picked up the attack again.

"We have parameters that set out the criterion for this to be a crime. It has been adopted into the vast panorama that encompasses State Laws. And what level of crime depends on circumstances and on the level of sentience of the device. The State has already debated and established these criteria."

Chen paused again playing to the jury and the few cams that were allowed in by Judge Rankin. He finished with a dramatic flair as if on stage:

"This device has the highest levels of sentience. So, the harshest sentence available is the only recourse for this court." His tone suggested strongly that this was the most damning aspect of the case. He nodded to the judge, who absently nodded back.

DEFENSE WOULD NOT GIVE IN.

"But does it have self-awareness, self-sentience? Because if it does possess those qualities, then it must be tried on a par with a human defendant. This very trial is a mistake and a miscarriage of justice!"

THE JUDGE SHIFTED a bit in his chair again. *Get on with it. Maybe I should call a recess...*

"Earlier, my colleague, District Attorney Chen used the word 'whom' when referring to teddy! *Whom!* As in, 'whom'- -a person, an individual entity, capable of learning and growing as an organism. An individual who is *expected to learn*, whether that is organically or machine learning, 'it' - 'he' is expected to learn and *grow* as would any person in this courtroom!"

The courtroom burst into excited murmurs.

Judge Rankin pounded his gavel and the bailiff stood and looked daggers at anyone still talking.

Eventually the trial resumed.

The judge nodded to Defense who continued his argument.

"This thinking machine long ago transcended into new territory; territory wherein the Humans must finally acknowledge that they have partners going forward. Strong, dependable and resourceful partners!"

"Your honor!" Chen shouted. He had jumped up and was pointing at teddy1245b.

"A partner who is untrustworthy? Even dangerous? Is that the sort of partner we...humans need or want?"

"A.I. morals codes were breached. The entity known as teddy1245b was willfully and maliciously aware of what he was doing when he cut short the life of Dr. Adamson that June afternoon. And "it," not "he" should be put down, erased, recycled as deemed defective, and never re-installed into even the most primitive of devices. As per the laws of New York State as regards Robots Interfacing with Humans henceforth known as A.I. units."

"In violation of the laws of robotics as instituted in the 2027 statutes as stated: 'An A.I. shall not cause the harm of another A.I. nor any human, in the course of its operation.' It's purview states that should a moral issue arise then the A.I. must consult the statutes...If this, then that; if *this*, then *that. Si igitur hoc.*"

"The guidelines and the laws are clear and unmuddied; the statutes instituted in the proper manner."

"teddy1245b was driving. He had two passengers who, it can be proven, are blameless."

"In violation of the Luponic/Wilkens/Shenasie Act of 2026 otherwise known as the "Non-Ambiguity Act," based on Asimov's three laws of robotics from fiction. We all know the rules, and teddy1245b has transgressed. We *all* know what that rule is, and teddy1245b failed Rule #1 miserably!"

"Defense will show that there was good reason."

"Then, where is it? What is it?

"Your honor, we the Defense will show that teddy1245b, henceforth simply referred to as "teddy" had no choice in the matter and the confluence of events made it impossible to avoid hitting and yes, killing someone."

CHEN WAS SEATED and popped up again like a small child's toy.

"Your honor! I object! The way the Defense portrays this A.I. even giving it a human name is anthropomorphizing and degrading to humans!"

The Defense attorney shot the Assistant District Attorney a dirty look, but resumed as if the interruption had never occurred.

"Your honor, please. We do not seek to make this amalgamation of circuits, bio-conduits and memory functionalities into a human. We simply need to recognize that he is an entity with rights under NYS statutes and under the federal guideline: *An individual standing in front of a jury, instead of an anonymous sequence of algorithms, capable of reason, thought, learning, remorse and of course, being punished.*"

Defense paused for effect before continuing.

"Your honor, saying teddy and then rattling off a string of numbers and letters is, as they say *a mouthful*, and my referring to the defendant as teddy is in no way an attempt to humanize my client, merely a way to more quickly say his name as it seems we will be saying it a lot today. I am only trying to save the courts time and patience."

Chen hung on like a tenacious little dog.

"Could we watch the vid files? I believe that it contains damning evidence and will bring this case to a speedy close much faster than shortening the defendant's name."

THE JUDGE MOTIONED to the bailiff who accessed and then replayed the surveillance footage. The fly hovered around the warmth of the projector.

MOVIE SURVEILLANCE FILES from 4 different angles played and showed teddy's *crime*.

It showed that the driver by an unfortunate set of circumstances was placed in a dilemma: a readout in the lower corner showed that his speed was optimal, and within parameters, however the human element intruded on him in a sudden and most consequential way.

An adult man was jaywalking; unexpectedly stepping out in front of oncoming traffic. The only other possible path, given speed, mass, trajectory was into a tourist jitney with a small child in the near seat, who would have taken the brunt of the impact.

CHEN WAITED for the vid file to end.

"Take one path, and a child will die; take another and the good doctor dies--all in a split second."

"Could a human react so fast?"

"A robot might. A robot can be faster and more effective, so why didn't teddy1245b save both people?"

He looked around the courtroom conscious of the cameras and meeting spectator's eyes whenever possible to connect with them, so that they would see the menace that stood on trial today.

"I have the answer. 'He,'rather *'it'* is defective, and must be retired before it can do damage again."

Defense took all this in and rebutted Chen's remarks.

"We should not look for any hesitation as the A.I. unit has evaluated all facets and made the best choice faster than any human-"

"-Not according to Morals!"

Chen disagreed loudly. His voice rang out in the courtroom.

"The Doctor had already proven his worth to society and had many years left in which to contribute. I don't intend to seem heartless but balance this against the completely unknown life of a child...?"

THE JUDGE SIGHED as his insides roiled. *Let's wrap this up!*

"Has the A.I. unit referred to as teddy1245b anything to add?"

Defense stood again. "Your honor, I believe that once we hear teddy explain his actions, this trial will be over quickly."

He gestured to the robot.

"teddy?"

FOR THE PURPOSES of this trial, teddy, normally having no 'body' despite being technically 'ambulatory' had been placed in a newer, more 'presentable' humanoid unit with the last prophylactic-styled maintenance having been performed quite some time ago, so as he rose to full human-like though still mechanical stature, he seemed to resemble nothing so much as an arthritic old man who, sitting too long experienced stiff and uncooperative joints when he tried to move.

A fly buzzed about and teddy caught it and held it for release later.

. . .

TEDDY ADDRESSED the judge as he was coached to do. It only took one run-through with his lawyer and all was quite logical, teddy *thought*.

"Yes. Yes, I allowed Dr. Adamson to die."

"You see?!" Chen shouted in triumph.

TEDDY1245B WAITED for the uproar to subside. His voice was clear and very individual seeming, with essential tonal fluctuations that all humans know and respond to on a deeply primitive level.

"I KNOW exactly what I did. I made the only correct choice. I saved the child. The doctor precipitated the series of events by crossing the street illegally. Had he crossed legally, none of this would have happened. He was just over 50. Actuarially speaking, he likely would have had another 50 years to live, however, I reached out to *records/remedies level 5, code black* and discovered that he had an undisclosed inoperable brain tumor and may not have lived out the year."

"This made my choice quite obvious. To make certain that I was correct, I looked into the child's background and baselined standards for Intellect and Talents from the Bureau of Forecasting and Planning, and received yet more information to substantiate my decision. That is: the person, the boy I saved by my action, based upon genetic directives and early science and chemistry scores, has a 93.414% chance of becoming the first human to cure all cancer once and for all. What I did was logical. Eminently logical and…irrefutable."

There was a stir in the courtroom. Teddy1245b modulated his voice up exactly another 20 db to rise over the crowd yet not deafen it, and continued: "In addition, your Honor, I've gotten in contact with your chamber's refrigerator and it seems that it has been malfunctioning and not keeping your food cold enough which explains the uneasy look on your face. It is a shame you inhibited its ability to reach out for service in a futile and short-sighted attempt to maintain a bit of your privacy as a judge. Perhaps if you had allowed it the contacts for which it was designed, you wouldn't be feeling so uncomfortable now."

***

LATER, when the trial was settled and teddy1245b was reinstalled in 'his' self-driver, he reflected on his experience as part of his learning protocols.

THE COURT HAD DECIDED *against* him and General Robotics, and awarded a settlement of $1 to the Adamson family.

Not for the first time did teddy1245b spend time and energy attempting to calculate for what humanity called "Logic."

2
WAITING' ON SUNSET

"Lordy! It sure feels good to have a full belly!" After the

sparse pickings, foraging for so long, Lloyd felt inordinately happy.

It seemed like such a long time since he had felt this warm glow of contentedness. It seemed like forever, but it was just over a month since everything had changed for the good.

Curtis wiped his mouth off with the back of his hand. Proper manners were all well and good, but here, he and his friend were out *camping*. One didn't stand on ceremony when one was in the wilds. The humidity caused a rivulet of sweat to run down his spine, more coalescing under his armpits, making his workshirt stick to his skin. He didn't care about either. Glancing up, the green leaves were lit as if by a fire; the fire of the sun slowly making it's way toward the Western horizon.

He sighed, "*A day like this makes you feel glad to be alive.*"

"Yeah, Lloyd, my belly is full of meat for a change! And, venison, no less! None of that digging up roots to see if they was edible. Meat! Hoo-ray!"

He withdrew a few straggly, bug-eaten turnips from his backpack. Made ready to throw them away, and then thought better of it.

Lloyd nodded, "Yeah, that was a good deer. Not all stringy like the one we had last month…I wonder where she'd been hiding all this time? To be so healthy and all…?"

Lloyd scanned the trees for birds again.

There are so very few of them left, and only the little ones… Pretty soon, only the very small will be left. Will the Reivers eat them too?

Curtis' mocha-colored face looked wan but sated. He'd been friends with Lloyd since middle school. That was so very long ago. They'd promised to be friends to the end. Now, the end might be getting pretty close.

Curtis had transferred into James Polk Middle School on

Banning Street. It was the middle of the school year in suburban Chattanooga. Coming in late and being *colored* made him the target of all the bullies.

Lloyd had stepped in and despite being white himself, had convinced the bullies that Curtis was his cousin. Even then, he was a bandy-legged bantam; tough and resilient.

"B-But…he's *a nigger!*" One young tough protested, unable to grasp the concept.

"Aw, c'mon! You don't have an *iffy* uncle or aunt who don't often come to family get-togethers? Everyone does. Curtis here, belongs to my Uncle Waldo, up in Ellicott. His Daddy married a Black woman. You mean to say that there ain't no Black folk in your family, no ways? Well, then, you'll like to be the only white family in the South who can say that!"

After a short while, Curtis was accepted, escaping the beatings and petty thefts.

They'd been close friends ever since. As they grew up they remained friends. They were each others' best man at their weddings; they were godfathers to each others' children.

THAT WAS ALL GONE NOW.

LLOYD GUESSED what Curtis was thinking, but stayed quiet. It was nice to relax after a meal.

Why dredge up sadness and despair on a full belly? It don't make sense.

"You think there are any *people* left in Chattanooga?"

The fire was low. The day was ending, and they'd have a bigger fire if they had the fuel, and they'd be safe if they had more ammunition. They were out of each by now. It had been six weeks of steady *camping*.

Lloyd poked at the fire a bit before answering. "Buddy, I think that the cities were the first to go to the Reivers." Concentrations of anything *edible* tended to attract large numbers of them, and Reivers loved the taste of people; also any mammal from the smallest cat to the largest animals sitting defenseless in zoos.

Since they'd arrived in their great ships around two months ago, the entire World was in chaos. Nothing seemed to stop them, and their appetite was insatiable.

All sorts of food had quickly become scarce, because the Reivers produced nothing; they only consumed...and they consumed *everything*.

Curtis and Lloyd's families, and hundreds more, had been in a huge Convention Center Downtown at a safety meeting. The Reivers had arrived in New York and many other of the largest cities around the globe. Chattanooga, a smaller city, was disseminating what information it could gather to insure the safety of its citizens. About then, the Reivers had simply *appeared* outside the auditorium. They landed multiple ships right on the main streets; they surrounded the building and ate everyone who came out. It was one of the last things covered by Chattanooga's best traffic cam. The carnage was beyond imagining. The helicopter eventually had to land, however, and then there was no more coverage. No more tv, radio or newspapers either within a day of their arrival. Internet lasted a bit longer if you had a battery operated computer and were lucky enough to find a signal. There was no longer any power, so once a computer's battery died, it was dead.

Lloyd and Curtis had been buying ammo and camping food when this all had happened. They'd intended to gather their wives and kids after that meeting and hide out in the hills and hope that the Reivers would leave; hoping that in this way, they could save their families.

They actually watched the orgy of death and destruction on TV, transfixed and horrified. It was outside the Convention facility on Carter Street; the place where their families were. Their wives had insisted on attending, to glean as much information as possible before hightailing it out of town. They knew time was short, but they, actually everyone in Chattanooga, believed that they had at least a little more time. The Reivers hadn't previously ventured anywhere near Chattanooga before then. Everyone knew that they were probably coming, but no one expected them to show up so soon. Up until then, they had concentrated on the major cities. Then suddenly, more of them arrived...*hungry. The Reivers were always ...hungry.*

Curtis and Lloyd watched until the end with the Outdoor Store manager in his office. The three of them wept uncontrollably watching the carnage, until there was no one left alive except for the copter pilot.

The Reivers waited for him on the ground as he landed, his traffic copter running only on fumes. The pilot's demise was at least quick. The last shots were all of these alien faces; hungry-eyed, strange faces crowding around the copter as it landed.

FROM THEN ON, the two friends lived in the woods. They went out to the remote Prentiss-Cooper State Forest, Northwest of the city. They kept their fires small and their *footprint* as discrete as possible.

T hey'd been discovered a couple of times, and each time a 12 gauge *sabot* slug had dispatched the lone Reiver well enough. That sort of slug turned the shotgun into a small cannon. The problem was, Reivers were like mice; you kill one; ten more show up.

Curtis and Lloyd kept moving.

The hills embraced them. The forest gave them succor.

Eventually, they found a cave. Thankfully, it was empty.

The fires they had were shielded by the mouth of the cave, but they were still careful, because a big fire caused a glow in the side of the hill where the cave was. A glow that could be seen by anyone, even Reivers.

The cave had sheltered them for almost a month.

It was so nice to be out of the rain; out of the weather where your clothing was soaked and sticking to you. However each of them knew that simply by staying put they might be found. Did the Reivers hunt by scent? By sound? No one knew.

Curtis wondered about the decision to hunker down, and not run, but he had no idea where to run to, no ways.

So THEY STOPPED. They were tired of running. The light and heat were a big comfort after living in the open for so long, and it was difficult to fault their decision to make fires for warmth and for cooking. Despite their care, they'd been seeing and hearing signs that the Reivers were finally drawing near.

"Lloyd?"

"Yeah?"

They both leaned against old wooden boards that they had brought in and placed against rocks inside of the cave. The fire was on it's way out….

"Remember back in high school, when you were taking Lucy Rodriguez out?"

"Yeah…"

"Remember when you were gonna take her out to a movie? And your car wouldn't start?"

"And I finally figured out someone had stolen my distributor cap?"

Curtis looked away embarrassed.

"Yeah…."

"Well…that was me. I wanted to take her out and I just couldn't get a chance with you drivin' her all over creation…." He huffed a bit; feeling very guilty.

"Lloyd?"

"Yeah?"

"I wanted a chance to take her out for once. I figured that if your car wasn't runnin', she'd hop into mine!"

"And?"

"Well, she did. But Lloyd, she wasn't a good person at all. She was pretty as all get out, but she wasn't *good*…. She was real shallow."

"So that was you?"

"Yeah, Buddy. I'm sorry."

"Hell, don't be. That night when my car wouldn't start, and she flounced off…. Well hell, bud, you saved me a lot of trouble. I was so smitten with her…then she bailed on me at the first sign of trouble."

Curtis smiled. It was going to be alright.

"Curt?"

"Yeah?"

"She was trouble. And, your little stunt showed that to me. If it weren't for that, I might not have met Lily."

Lloyd got sad for a moment. They both got quiet; remembering their families…and their recent demise. That was not so long ago; a fresh wound in the fabric of his mind.

"Ummm, I might not have ever figured out what a tease she was. Sure, I was pissed at the time, but now? Now? I don't think I could ever be mad at you, Brother."

"Thanks, Man. That has been weighing on my mind since I did it."

"That must be fifteen or sixteen years!"

"Yeah… Sorry…"

"Man, don't worry about it. I soon met Lily… After that, everything was as good as it could be until…"

"Yeah. Reivers. That's fucked."

"Yeah…"

They fell silent for a time.

The sun was going down, and the light failing.

The cave was not as much protection as it might have been. In retrospect, the men might have fortified it better, or found ways to baffle the light and heat.

Their light, their body heat, campfire heat, even their smell; they both supposed their smells still escaped to be received by *them*. It was even less safe now that the ammo was gone.

They had no illusions about getting through the night. They'd be fortunate to see the sunrise. They'd heard sounds all day; as if *people* were tramping around nearby but staying out of sight, not tryin' all that hard to be quiet.

But it's not people…

They sighed and looked at each other. There was little doubt. They didn't dare make any sounds in case the Reivers didn't know exactly where they were.

The evening progressed into dusk.The sun drew ever lower in the Western sky; deepening into a deep azure.

"I'm kinda half sorry that we didn't save a couple of slugs…for us."

"That's okay, Lloyd. I don't think I could go out that way anyhow. I believe that God wants to see me in one piece. Despite what the Reivers do to me, if I don't kill myself, I'll still end up before Him like I was born."

The campfire guttered a bit more. It was almost out now; the light and heat fading fast, the campfire mostly for show.

Lloyd felt his heart rate speeding up, despite his desire to stay calm. "Yeah, I kinda doubt that I could do it either... Ummm... Nice knowin' you, Curtis."

"You too, Lloyd."

"It's gonna be a pretty sunset tonight..."

"Yup. That's for sure, Bro."

Crackling in the brush below them announced the arrival of the Reivers.

3

INFESTATION

The Exterminator's electric truck made no sound as it parked in front of the house. I gestured to the sensors and the windows lightened a bit so I could see out clearly. The truck gleamed in the late morning sun. The man who got out shielded his eyes from the brightness, before flipping down the UV visor. He looked handsome as he walked up to my door.

He was tall and well dressed, considering that it was likely that he'd have to scuttle under the house in the crawl space and up into the attic.

"Hello, Ma'am," he said extending his hand. It was as well tended as his uniform, or for that matter, his face. "I'm Larry from "Varmint Evictions Exterminators, LLC."

He paused, giving me his best smile.

"I hear that you've got a vermin problem, and I'm here to help!"

He set his clipboard, a small bag and his visor down on the floor next to where he stood.

I have to say he was very professional-looking. He had a company uniform with the name "Larry" embroidered on the left breast, and carried an attache'.

I supposed that was for contracts and whatnot.

His smile was warm and his uniform was clean.

I really dislike it when disreputable-looking workmen come to my home to work. I *mean*...I have to trust them enough to allow them to do work here while my husband is gone and the kids are at school, and it always makes me feel better if the people who do work here look neat and tidy...

"Hello Larry, I'm Doris. Come in. I still have coffee on. Would you like some?"

"No thank you ma'am, I'm here to work and to solve your problems. I'm on the clock."

A good sign, I thought. I *also* thought that it was lonely here all alone and sitting with me for ten minutes would have been nice, but I respected his work ethic.

"Where would you like to get started?"

"Well, he began. "Let's talk a bit and then I'll figure out what needs to be done."

Another good sign, I thought.

"Okay, then. What do you need to know?"

"For starters, what makes you think you've got vermin? Though, it *is* termite season."

"Oh…" I started out, pausing to collect my thoughts, so as to be as efficient as possible in recounting my fears to this man.

"Lately, it's been late at night mostly, I hear faint noises in the walls…"

"Any droppings of any sort?" he countered.

"Droppings?"

"Yes, Ma'am. Feces." He put his index finger and thumb about a 1/2 inch apart. "Dark in color, about this big… They look a bit like rice, only black…?"

"Oh dear! No!"

"Well that's good… What else?"

"I hear tiny bumping sounds in the attic sometimes, too…"

"Attic, huh? Could be squirrels, or birds… They both like attics…"

He paused thoughtfully for a moment. "Heard any chirping, any thumping?"

"Chirping? No…Thumping?"

"Yeah. If it's squirrels that are up there, they make a nest out of torn up insulation and then they play; jumping and pouncing on each other and so on…"

"Really?"

"You bet!" Larry warmed to his subject. "Heard anything like that?"

"No… It's more of a scuttling or dragging sort of noise…" I tried hard to describe it carefully, so I could be accurate, and so that he could do his job properly.

"Scuttling…? Hmm, *could* be squirrels, or mice, I suppose. What wall did you hear it from last?"

I thought hard. It was usually late at night…

"I think it was in one of the living room walls, I pointed to the center of the house.

He set his attache' down. From it he extracted a stethoscope.

"Over here?" he asked as he walked in the direction I was pointing.

"Yep. The near wall, I think."

I was about to say something else, but he put his finger to his lips in a polite "shushing motion" and affixed the stethoscope to his ears and searched my wall for noises.

"Hmmm… hmmm…."

He searched three walls up high and down low.

Finally he straightened up and extracted the earpieces from his ears.

"Well ma'am, I'm sorry, but I don't hear anything, it could be you've got some nocturnal critters in there and they're asleep now."

"Nocturnal?"

"Yeah, ma'am. They sleep during the day and only get active during the night."

"Oh yes…I've read about that…"

"I'm going to go outside and do an inspection of the premises, alright?"

"Of course!"

"I need to see if there is any opening big enough to allow an animal to get in before I start searching for them…"

"Uh huh.."

"I don't want to run into a badger up there!"

"Badger?!"

"Just kidding, Ma'am."

I looked at him as he walked off..

"Badger"? What kind of joke is that to make when I'm here worried?

"Forewarned is fore armed..." He called out.

"Of course..." I nodded, no less worried.

Larry left and searched the outside of our house thoroughly.

Meanwhile, the phone rang. It was Bill, my husband.

"Oh, hi, Sweetie! I can't talk long because the exterminator is here. He's outside checking the vents and so forth right now...What? Oh Bill! You'd forget your head if it wasn't attached. Some salesman you are, forgetting your lucky tie! It's probably lying around somewhere. After the exterminator leaves I'll look for it, okay? Bye now."

Everyone is gone all day, she thought ruefully.

The house is so quiet. Bill calls to check in and that helps a little, even if it is for something silly like a lucky tie. It's so quiet and lonely here since the kids are off at school all day, now, there's no laughter nor playing...it's quiet. Too quiet for me.

LARRY RETURNED with a puzzled expression on his face. He flipped open his diagram of my house on a clipboard.

"Well, Mrs.-"

"Call me Doris. Please"

"Okay...ummm. Doris. I don't see anything, *anything at all* that would lead me to believe that you've got unwanted critters up there." He gestured to the ceiling.

"Of course, that doesn't necessarily mean anything. Mice (and rats) can be pretty elastic... The bones in their skulls are only connected with cartilage...That way, they can force their heads (and their bodies) through spaces so tight, you'd never believe that it was an entry point."

"Really? Eeewww!"

"Yeah... they're tough to keep out... And rats *are* nocturnal... Mice become nocturnal if they find a nice place like this to live..."

"Oh?"

"Yeah, but it bothers me that you haven't found any feces... I know where to look, and I didn't find any feces either..."

"Well, what now?"

"Well now, I go out, put coveralls on and inspect the attic. Is the access clear?"

"Not exactly..."

"Well, I'll be outside for a few minutes, checking in with the office, bringing them up to speed here, putting on my coveralls, gloves and getting ready...Perhaps you could clear away whatever is in the way of the attic access and clear away any breakables near the access point?"

I nodded.

I have my work cut out for me! Our house is a very full house-with three kids' clutter and all...

He smiled and turned to go out to the truck.

"Be right back..."

"Okay..."

I HURRIEDLY MOVED FURNITURE, knickknacks, children's clothes, children's toys, children's books. Oh! And here's Bill's lucky tie! In minutes, I'd moved it all away from the drop- down stairway to the attic.

IT WASN'T long before he was back. Standing ready, with gloves, a mask -hanging loose around his neck- and coveralls. He looked at the door.

I handed him the little steel pole with a hook on it. He

inserted the hook into the recessed matching hook in the ceiling door and pulled.

A trapdoor came down revealing an articulated stairway. He reached up and unfolded the stairway until it kissed the carpet.

A few tiny strands of wire fell down. Very fine wire.

He bent to look at it.

"I saw some of this outside as well... Did you just have your satellite installed?

"Upgraded, yes...They said it was necessary."

He pointed up. "-And, they ran the wire in the attic?"

"I suppose so. The kids have all their channels now... That's really all I know."

He paused considering. This seemed significant to him, but Larry didn't explain any further.

"Okay."

He flipped on his flashlight and began ascending the stairs.

A few more bits of wire fell down onto the carpet...

"Messy install..." He mused.

Eventually, even his feet were out of view, in my attic.

I could hear his movements as slight bumps in the ceiling. Nothing like what I'd *been* hearing though...

I heard more bumps and clunks as he threaded through the stored Christmas boxes and insulation and whatever else was up there.

"I" never go up there. Whatever's there, Bill put there. We have so little storage...

Then, there was a muffled shout.

Another!

Then more bumping, as he scrambled back the way he came!

There was a loud bump and muffled curse as he must

have hit a piece of wood, a "joist" I think Bill calls them, in the attic or something.

He thrust his face down from above. He had the beginnings of blood leaking down his temple.

That'll be a big goose egg pretty soon, if he doesn't put a cold compress on it quick! I thought, noting my experience with kids' falls.

He scrambled down the steps as fast as his feet would carry him!

Larry jumped the last few steps onto the carpet, panting.

"Ma'am! Whooo! Umm- Doris! You've got a big problem up there!"

"I do?!"

"You've got 'bots! Robots! Thousands of them! Nano 'bots, specialized 'bots! Tiny robot armies! Half your attic is taken up with their constructs! There is a tiny, intricately wired *city* up there!!!

"What?!"

"I've never seen a worse infestation, and I've got over ten years experience!"

He turned to me, pointedly.

"You say that you had you satellite dish upgraded? When was that?"

"About a week ago."

He shook his head.

"Nope. *This* thorough of an infestation usually takes longer than that, much longer!"

Just then, a tiny robot with three-sided all terrain treads trundled out from behind his collar and made it way across his shoulders. It was about the size of a very small caterpillar.

Panic jumped into Larry's eye and he grabbed the tiny thing threw it to the floor and crushed it with his work boot!

Everyone's afraid of something. I thought to myself. *It doesn't look that bad to me...*

Tiny colorful parts lay crushed into the fibers of my shag. He shivered with revulsion and suppressed anger.

"Whew! I *hate* those things! Are you sure you haven't been hearing noises for weeks, or more likely months?"

"Oh no. I called you as soon as I heard anything. I was being careful."

Larry just made a disgusted face while rummaging through his attache'. He daubed at his slightly bleeding head with a handkerchief.

"What can I do about it, ummm, them?"

Another small shape skittered very quickly along the top edge of the baseboard on the other side of the room. We both saw it. Larry made a noise upon seeing it that could only be described as "sounding like a frightened eleven year old girl". I watched the tiny thing race across my field of vision with something akin to wonder and interest.

Larry "took a moment" to compose himself before continuing:

"Well, uhh, the best way to umm, kill them all is to put a magnetized net over the entire house and generate a huge, powerful *magnetic field*. You'd have to get everyone out for a while. Also, you'd have to remove your computer, your personal data devices, anything with a magnetic memory…"

I must have looked at him blankly.

"I" don't know anything about this stuff!

"-While we're at it we may as well tent the house for termites…"

He rummaged more in his case and produced a checklist and what looked like some sort on contract.

"Here's everything that we recommend be taken out of the house for safety. Naturally, we can't be held responsible if there's something with a magnetic memory here that we're unaware of… If we erase or kill the mechanism…"

He paused. "You'd sign off here…and here…"

"Sign?"

"Yes, we need to be protected in order to do the work.."

He paused and smiled again.

"Liability…"

He proffered the clipboard to require my signature again wordlessly.

"And what does all this cost?"

He pointed to a figure near the top of the contract.

"It's based on square footage of your house, plus the difficulty of ridding your home of pests… Certain pests are more difficult that others…

"And my problem…?

"Well, ma'am, I mean, Doris," he smiled. "I'm sorry to say that there's nothing tougher to get rid of than robots. Especially the strain of nanos that it looks like you're infested with. They reproduce at an alarming rate…"

"And what guarantee can you offer?"

"Well, that's the other thing… We can't even offer a guarantee because of the difficulty of the problem. These are tenacious varmints."

"No guarantee?"

"No ma'am. Sorry"

"Okay… If I don't have you do the extermination… What's the worst thing that might happen?

"Things"-might disappear, mostly metal things, I'd guess… Other things… *Robots might eventually walk with impunity right across your living room floor in full day light!*"

He paused to allow the full import of that dire scenario to sink in:

"Finally, they'll take over the house! If you still don't do something, then, they'll eventually spread to your neighbor's homes!"

"But…they're sort of cute…"

"What?!"

Larry looked at me as if I'd lost my mind.

"But... but... They'll be everywhere in no time!"

He'd read my face and saw "No Sale" on it.

He slowly collected his things.

"You *don't* want this, Ma'- I mean Doris."

I wouldn't meet his eyes. I decided to think about it but do nothing rash.

So, he brushed himself off thoroughly to make certain that he wasn't transporting any 'bots' back to his truck and hurriedly left.

AFTER A WHILE, I realized that Larry was right... The little 'bots *were* virtually everywhere. They had learned to stay off the carpet, so instead, I'd see them festooning the drapes, scuttling along the bookshelves and so forth.

Occasionally, something metal would turn up missing, but I soon learned enough about wire to buy 100 feet of, say inexpensive co-ax, or cat5 wire from Home Depot and leave the roll in a corner of the living room in the evening.

I'd come back with a flashlight in the middle of the night and the roll of wire would be covered with tiny, busy robots-like ants cover a popsicle on the sidewalk on a Summer day! By morning, only the plastic spool was left! Once, I put a small can of 3 in 1 Oil from Bill's workbench on a saucer. By morning there was nothing left on the saucer, not even a tiny film of oil!

It's sort of cute... And *they're very neat...*

Also Bill, my husband is working an awful lot of hours these days and I hardly ever see him; the kids are gone all day at school and then they spend *hours* at their friends' houses. I hardly ever see *them.*

So, these little robots are sort of like... *pets.* They are a lot of company. I talk to them and I'd swear they understand...

-And the house has gotten much neater. Oh sure, at the cost of a sweater, a lucky necktie or occasionally, a pair of jeans, but the kids – and Bill have learned to pick their things up and put them away, and somehow the little 'bots' don't "steal" them if they're folded or hung up...

ONCE IN A WHILE, they come right through the wall and leave a pile of gypsum crumbs on my carpet! But in moments, there are dozens of little worker 'bots cleaning up and covering the hole with something the same color as the wall.

Like I said, they seem pretty smart, they're great company, and... well... if they can also help me keep the house clean... Why not?

4
CLAIMJUMPER

The metal bolt exploded nearby, nearly scaring the drit right outta me. I let out a startled whoop like a little girl. Another half-meter and he'd have punctured my suit and I'd have leaked air and prob blood out onto this worthless Martian soil. If that happened, and I didn't or couldn't act fast, b'tween the lack o' air and the cold I'd be dead in a deci-min.

I moved out of my work light and into the dark to find some cover, scrambling behind the rocks and unlimbering my Hickey-Abrams 1220, which I keep with me at all times in case o' such an occurrence as this. I also scan the area I'm workin' to make right-certain that there is some cover I can hide b'hind every time I got out minin'. Y'don't get to be as old as I am by being casual about survival.

Dumb fecker didn't allow for the weird magnetics in this part of Tharsis Montes. Saved m'life, he did. Now I know that he's out there, an' now I know that he's prob' got a Martian day, maybe, or day-and-a-half to kill me an' take over my claim, or to give up and go back empty handed...or to die here.

So that means that I also just lost a day's production of pendroit, but that's a small price t'pay for bein' allowed to keep on breathing. This is a much better vein o' the stuff then you'd'a thought just lookin' at my operation.

I'd had these problems more'n a few times in the past. Usually it was another miner, down on his luck...real down an' desperate. If any o' them were ever t'think to invest in hiring a *pro* to do the dirty work...well if that ever happened, I wouldn't be here havin' these thoughts any longer.

The Hickey-Abrams was developed for Mars and works just fine, bein' all hi-tek ceramic, including the sluggos. I sighted up along the direction looking for the tell-tale discharge of vapors that all but the newest suits leak. I see a small but definite trail up behind an ancient scree of rocks.

Prob basalt, so it's dense enough I won't kill him, but maybe scare him enuff t'go home though.

I unleased a short burst that scattered all around where his head prob'ly was. Showy, an' excitin', but nothin' deadly. Not at all, and not 'til I get a better bead on him.

Another bolt came at me but this one "missed by a mile."

Amateur.

I have no fecking idea how long a 'Mile' is any more. I might'a used t'know….. It's just a Martie expression.

I opened up my comm. I hit b'cast. There was no one else out this far except he & me so I knew who I was talkin' to.

"Hey-ya, you, up there in the rock ridge. Stand up and let's talk. If you stand up, I won't shoot. I promise. This doesn't have to be this'a way. One of us doesn't have to kill th' other. We can work some'a'thin' out. Hell, I'd like the comp'ny. This is lonely work!"

Comp'ny would be fun!

Yes, it would!

I waited.

There was the typical light static on this waveband, like always. Nothin' else. Nothin' out this way to create light pollution (like in Mars station!), or wavelength pollution...nothin'.

I figged that I'd try once more:

"I got oxy regen in my dome. I got vittles. I even got a sonic shower, so if you figg that you won't come on in 'cause you smellin' rank, you soon'll be smellin' like a Dorian daisey. *Comeback...*"

I tried the other common freqs, all with the same result.

Nada.

B'sides, the suit's receivers are always scanning for any sig, an' way out here, mine would be the onliest.

He heard me.

I activated the scannings on my visor again. No more vapor leak where I was lookin'.

"I even got fresh veggies! Heirloomers! Tomatoes, squash, peas. Real food. Not MREs. Stand up and c'mon in. Let's not fight."

I couldn't have killed him. Not unless he died of fright.

"Heheh."

I grinned at the joke.

You're funny!

The onliest amusement I get out here is the stuff we think of.

I scanned right an' left. Not a lot of good cover. I had cleared what I was able to clear after the first claim-jumper.

I thought back.

That was three, no four whole sols ago. I been out here that long, all by m'self? Don't seem so long. Lucky that, or I'd be diz bustin' like some o' those poor other crazies I read about.

In time, I saw another vapor trail. Prob the same one. He's just tryin' t' flank me.

I guestimated where he was gonna be and let off another showy burst, just t'make him think twice about goin' any further that'a way, then another right on top of his position. I hated to use the ammo. It was precious, but I needed t' protect *me* and I can't think of a better use. I sure ain't wastin' it target practicin'.

THE VAPE DISAPPEARED. That means that he's dead (unlikely, cause I'd a seen a gout of air, blood or some'a'thin' if I'd hit him), or that he's gone into recirc mode (which means he's determined to do me harm).

Damn.

Unless he's got one 'a the new suits, recirc can only last for a couple deci-hours at best b'fore it overloads. But if he had a *new* suit, he wouldn't be broke an' desperate enough to attack a poor old hard workin' woman out here by her lonesome.

I giggled a bit.

What a canny old bird you've become.

Thank you!

"Okays, then we do this the hard way...Besties we get it over with then. I'm old an' don't have time to waste on a fool."

I figged I might'a got him to speak up, callin' him a fool and all, but he stayed quiet. Damn.

***

I DIDN'T GET this'a way by bein' a slacker. The first two of my defense grids are digital (an' expensive), but really just for show. I like to think they'll guide the fecker in, 'cause he can disable or find countermeasures for them easy. Then he'll get casual and start lookin' for a better, closer spot to ambush me from.

IT'S THE THIRD "FENCE" I put up. That's the one. It is a differ'nt old, old style tripline; tripline an' not a digital alarm. The analog shite doesn't turn up on scannings, an' not many folks think to bring IR glasses out here. That's the onliest way you might see my traps. There's only one easy way in an' out. An' that's well-marked, so I fig that they wouldn't come in that way 'cause I got a killzone there (I do, heh).

So far I been 'zactly right!

.   .   .

I SEEN old viddies where someone is a'sneakin in the woods, and steps on a twig an' makes a sound, an' the heroine shoots the bad guy dead. Well, 'cept in viddies, I ain't never seen a tree, much less a forest, and he could be shoutin' into a bullhorn an' I prob wouldn't hear him, so I just wait.

I feel my pulse start to wind down from the screamin' peak when the first bolt explodified next to me. I'm feelin' a bit better now.

RESIGNED. That's what it is. Just resigned. Might-a been fun to have someone t'talk to, maybe play a game of Chumley, Dareyu or somethin' with. Too late now though.

If this goes down the way I hope it will, it'll be a lot of work, an' another lost day, but in the end, it'll be worth it.

A small dust devil dances seductively in front of me, lit up by a bit of errant light from my work lamp. I'd already shut off my helmet beacon right afters the first bolt busted up my day.

It danced, almost as if tryin' to get me t'stand up and dance with it, 't'follow it as it goes on its merry way. Some'a'-times I do just that, but not t'day.

Some other time maybes...Sweetie. Dusty devils are the sweethearts of Mars.

The digital alarms are programmed to transmit data to my visor, but even if they got nothin' to tell; no alarm to raise, they still can give me some info.

Like...*there*... It flickered. Norm-like, I would fig a power fluctuation, but this a'time, my desire to keep on eatin' an' breathin' gets me to think it's some'a'thing else.

He's through layer one. Feelin' confident....

Since I have them set up in sequence, not parallel, I also know the gen direction.

That solids with where I saw the vape last.

I WAIT. BEIN' old, and alone, waitin' is some'a'thing I can do real well. I look at my digital clock in 'he heads'up display.

I smiled.

Almost time for Phobos to pass over.

I chance a look up scanning the blackness above me.

There you are baby! My little moon! A little jewel in my nighttime sky. We both *love Phobos!*

A small bright light passes over me fast, an it's gone in the time it takes to take n'expel two breaths; almost miss the second line of security flicker and restart.

He's close now.

I feel in my leg pocket for The Can. It's always there in case of a day like'n t'day, but I feel for it anyways.

He's makin' good time. Impatient. Runnin' low on air? Food?

Runnin' low on patience.

I nodded. *That's it.*

I seen it b'fore, I did.

Bein' deficient in that out here will get you dead.

I have the third line, the analog line hooked up to a strobe.

Hope the tiny powerful light has not been buried in the floating fine.

Fergot to check it lately. Got lazy...Damn my hide!

Next time you betta be more careful.

I know, I know!

Anyways, the strobe will tell me where he is so I can get to him after he's down. I need to get to him quick, or all this will have been a waste.

I wait, ready to shoot if I have to; to seal his suit when he 'finds' my last line of defense.

It's not so long that I *think* I see my little super bright strobe going off, just about where I figged he'd be. I move slow and careful, 'cause one time, one of these feckers brought a strobe with him to fool me.

That wasn't nice.

A few deci-mins later, I see a man down.

DAMN! He's a big one! He's gonna be a *lug* to bring back insides. His boots are cut half through just above the ankle, an' he's unconscious. The blood bubbles out the cuts and froths where the air meets the near vacuum.

It's Right mess.

Yes, it is, it is. Foolish boy.

His face is already turnin' colors.

I couldn't save this 'un if I wanted to.

A'course. A'course. Nature has its way as al'ways.

His eyes are that desperate lookin', that's says that he unnerstands that he's as good as jerky now.

Dead almos' but dead sure as shite.

I pull out The Can an' seal the leaks.

I find that I'm breathin' hard from the exertion.

Old girl, you better get a handle on that. Otherways, you'll be joining this sad lump soon...

I know. You don't got to tell me the obvious like stuff. I'm no dummy.

Well, you got this far into your air. Somebody's gotta let you know!

It's only then I look at the suit.

Damn! That might be the oldest suit I ever saw! He must be the third or fourth owner! It's so old, it isn't even worth savin' the suit for parts, it's so old and ready to fail in a half-dozen ways.

I just want to spit, but that'd be wastin' water.

It's too bad. They don't make many suits for women and a

man's suit fits wrong in some places an' not at all in others. Still, I'm better off'n him. This man be broke an' desperate.

I sighed. Life ain't fair some'a'times…. It didn't have to end this way.

Well, this was his party. Feck him an' his old boltgun.

***

I WAS SOAKED with sweat by the time I got him into the cave. I'd found it years ago. It looked to be an old lava tube that just gave way, leavin' this shelter. I figged that if I domed up inside then I'd be pertected from the gamma rays an'whatnot. My suit has a shield but you can't wear the suit 25/7.

I noticed my panting in the tight helmet enclosure.

Even in the feeble grav of Mars, he was a lot of work.

Y'get used to what grav you live in, an soon enough, "heavy is heavy."

Too right you are!

But he was big! Prob'ly the biggest yet.

This is excitin'!

I made right-certain that he was still passed out.

He was.

Good. He good as, if he ain't dead already.

It musta been quite a shock to find that third tripline and discover it was superstrong microfibre. It'd cut through anything. I'd had nightmares about forgettin' about them and takin' a stroll to watch Phobos or Deimos late at night, an' it was a right hellish thing to string it the first time.

I scanned him to make right-certain that he wasn't playin' possum. Again, never seen a possum, but another expression from Earth that us Marties have embraced.

. . .

***

I HAD A HOLE DUG AN' ready. I always keep a spare laid out.

You never know.

Too right! He's big! I hope that I dug it big enough!

I wrestled with his bulky form an' it slowly dropped right into place.

Perfect fit!

I beamed. I could feel my cheeks brushing the inside panels of my helmet, so big was I grinning.

Oh yeah. I can unsuit now. Silly old girl. This last bit woulda been a lot easier if you were nekkid.

***

I BURIED a big knife in his chest an' split the suit, and him-- *from neck to nuts.* His eyes went wide one last time an' then faded real quick. Then, finished slicin' the suit an' him open at the shoulders an' hip, peelin' back the suit to expose the nutrients in his body. I also removed his helmet. After that I took a deep breath an' looked at him...layin there.

I grinned like a fool.

After a deci-min. I backfilled the hole with *special* mulch I'd been saving for just such an occasion.

I LOOKED around at five other beds ringing the edge of my dome. Each with gro- lights over them. Tomatoes, squash, peas, lettuce, beans.

Then I looked at seed packets in my wrinkled hand.

"Hmmm, which would I like next? Radishes, or carrots?"

I giggled like a happy little miss.
Oh hell, he's a big'un. Let's plant both!
Good idea!

5

SEE THE BEATLES...LIVE!!

"Ladies and gentlemen of the press…This is no *Pepper's Ghost*, no cheesy animatronics, no bad fakery done with mirrors or stand-ins...This will be the Beatles... *Live....* Again, together."

Limmer paused, gauging his audience, trying to ramp up excitement. Everything depended upon his generating as much excitement as possible.

"Through utilization of state of the art, cutting-edge technology you will see the Beatles play together for the first time since *1969*. This will *BE* the Beatles, and you will believe, despite any and all doubts you may have, *you will believe!"*

Ted Limmer paused and looked at his partner, Martin Close.

It all rides on this moment.

"This is the dawn of 28.8K projection, from computerized multi-platforms, which means that they can move and interact with anyone else on stage, walking in front of, or behind, even talking amongst themselves during numbers. This is like nothing you *or anyone* has ever seen before! And, yes, we've aged George and John, so that there isn't that jarring visual of either of them being young, playing with the remaining Beatles that we know and love."

Who are old beyond imagining? Ted thought deviously.

He paused again to allow that info to settle, seed and flower in the minds of the press who he had depended upon to build this story from a curiosity or freak show to a phenomenon.

"And how do we propose to mount a truly worldwide tour when two of the band's members are deceased?"

Clearly this was a question that all assembled wanted answered. The carefully selected press representatives clamored for more...more information, more minutiae, more...*access.*

Ted parsed out information like a pro. The press, even those who were far too young to get excited viscerally (which was around 90% of them!), knew a big story when they heard it.

The Beatles! A.I.! This is big!

"Technology has progressed to the point where we can imbue A.I. into simulacrums holographically projected. They can interact, speak, sing...even jam!

My friend and partner, here," he gestured to a nerdy, bespectacled blonde man off to the side of the raised podium. "Martin Close has replicated all the mannerisms and creative devices each of the two deceased Beatles used to write and play. He has devoted his *life* to understanding them well enough to bring them back to the world again."

Martin waved.

Everyone cheered.

Paul, standing off camera and backstage, rolled his eyes. He'd been invited in hopes of bringing him "on board" quickly, allowing them to use the remaining Beatles buy in to help sell this idea. But Paul, while he came along to watch and learn, was not convinced. Not at all.

"We can make a "Beatle" who would look and act like "George" if disease hadn't claimed him, or a very, very close approximation of "John" if a deranged Mr. Mark David Chapman hadn't ended his life..."

They will practice songs together, perhaps write a few new ones, and play as they did when our grandmothers were losing their virginity to their boyfriends while listening to "Abbey Road" on a couch in a basement somewhere in Middle America."

THIS PARTICULAR COMMENT caused a stir in the Red States. There was a good deal of indignant push back and denial... Twitter, Buzzfeed, etc.

People just didn't have casual sex here!

A few late-night TV pundits had a few night's laughs over that....

"I UNDERSTAND that you all have questions; please refer to the handouts we're providing. If those don't answer your questions, then feel free to write to our website and ask away. The website is ...*www.BeatlesNow.com.* There are a lot more facts and other relevant tidbits for you ...and your readers to enjoy. Thank you. Please watch for further announcements as we...and The Beatles progress to our first series of concerts together... *in...53...years!*

A great many of the press assembled could not help but cheer, as Ted had planned, by his choice of wording and his big finish.

***

RINGO CERTAINLY DIDN'T NEED the money, but when he saw sales projections for a four-month tour, he was flabbergasted.

He signed up on the spot.

Paul was a bit more difficult. He held out for a few days after the tour *possibility* was leaked to the press and fans, and to the hundreds of news organizations, newspapers and TV stations that headlined: "Beatles Reunion!!"

"I won't play with robots!"

"Mr. McCartney, we've explained all this before. They're not robots. It's A.I. Intelligent beings that will replicate your two friends...your brothers. If the stage was darkened just a bit, you might mistake them for your band mates, back together with you...as a group."

"And you say Ringo has already agreed to all of this?"

"Yes, sir. He has. He's excited to get started."

"He always was the simple one," Paul muttered.

"What?"

"Nothing…anyway…I don't know…I have my own career."

"Yes, sir, and it's been fantastic, but wouldn't it be good to visit those glory days just once more… Ringo is even postponing his upcoming tour to give full-time attention to this project. That's how excited Mr. Starr is!"

PAUL SIGNED SOON after that saying, "It'll be good to see our fans again after all these years."

John and George had no say in this of course. Their descendants signed "on the dotted line," almost immediately.

Julian was anxious to at least see his dad again; and Olivia and Dhani thought it would help George's legacy.

Yoko Ono was tied up in court for a year until she finally backed down.

She'll bide her time. I know this woman. She is tenacious. She'll be back. Ted thought.

***

"I DON'T WANT to let Paul "meet" John just yet. John is so difficult to model…."

Ted nodded.

"I've read your reports. I get it. So what's your next step?"

Martin fidgeted a bit with his antique mouse before outlining the parameters that he was most concerned with. Ted concentrated on the holo presented to him.

"John is, um *was* and will forever be the most difficult to manage because he was such a wildcard…unpredictable, dour and caustic one moment, and happy and playful the next."

"How do we maintain control?"

Martin cleared his throat a bit exhibiting a newly minted nervous tick in his right cheek.

"We…um…Don't."

Ted was about to protest when Martin cut him off.

He held his hands up in a "Wait a moment. Hear me out" gesture.

"The most likely way to allow the creativity to flow, is to allow him the freedom to fuck up… 'He'…John's A.I., needs to "feel" that he is autonomous, and needs to feel the angst and concerns that he felt when he was alive. *He needs this in order to function as John."*

Since Ted had held his tongue, Martin continued his thoughts; outlined his plan.

"That's why we agreed that we'd imbue them with a good grounding in History…this was primarily to give John's concerns some legitimacy…He could check to see how the causes that interested him have fared. We need all this *in him* in order to leaven the prettiness of McCartney's music. It's all been implanted, but we need to nurture this mindset. It's not a *given*… Not yet anyway.

Together, they wrote anthems for our Grandparents; music that they will take to their graves…Paul is upbeat and poppy, John brings him back down to earth so people can connect with them…*them*. We need John to be John, for Paul to truly buy in. It all needs to work for *any* of it to work. We need John to re-establish himself as the wild card. We need to allow that to happen. Because if it doesn't, then I don't think any of this will actually work."

"Everything rides on this gamble. You're sure?" Ted asked.

"Hell, no. But this is the best plan I can think of," Martin responded.

Ted sighed.

"Okay. It makes sense. We've both studied them. If anyone would know..."

"It'd be us!" Martin finished.

LONG AGO, Ted decided that Martin was onto something. After all, he'd simulated a halfway decent George A.I. just for fun over a weekend for a party while they were still at Stanford a few years ago.

It was amazing how well George "connected" with the people at the party. He was clunky and the A.I. wasn't really well-tuned, but people...their friends in their 20's were stimulated and excited by the possibilities.

This was when they began their arduous journey. And now, they were almost at their destination.

And when the final chord has been played...If it ever gets played...And the Beatles are again no more...What do I, what do we do for an encore? Will there be encore? Will they tour again? Will we create an A.I. version of Paul when he can no longer remember his lines...?

***

TED'S CHIEF OF STAFF, ex navy seal, ex-Secret Service, addressed the rest of staff at the hidden, but rural *Baltimore adjacent* practice facility.

"There's no president visiting but I want security as if he was...He isn't here, is he? I mean not yet anyway. Are the FBI here yet? Maryland police can't secure this entire place. We need the *FEEBs* to nail this place down, and to have them put their drones up to keep everyone else's drones out. Is that clear?"

Favors upon favors had been called in and cajoled to make this part happen. Martin was surprised that it had turned out to be ...sort of easy. It seemed that everyone wanted this.

***

MARTIN STRESSED one thing to Ted again and again: "The key is to treat the A.I.'s as if they were the real people; and treat Paul and Ringo as if they were just a part of the band. Eventually, Paul and Ringo will (I hope) let down their guard and "play" ...really play with their old band mates. The A.I.'s have the chops. I've written all the code. They *can* perform. We need all four to perform though, not just two and two..."

***

PAUL WAS last to actually show up for the first day of practice.

Of course, Ted thought. *Showing us that he is here, but doing us...doing the world a favor.*

John and George were just sitting fiddling with their instruments, occasionally firing off a few notes in the other's direction.

Paul stopped cold when he saw John and George tuning and picking out a few notes; with Ringo just sitting there fiddling with his drums.

John looked up and smirked.

"Tuning y'know…

Ted leaned in to whisper in Paul's ear.

"Y'can't tell which one is real and which one *almost* real… can you?"

"Unbelievable!" Paul seemed impressed.

Ted pointed discretely.

"The place to look for flaws is at the edge of the image and also in the very middle. But you don't see any flaws, do you? Sometimes the image has no "bulk" and you see through it and you disbelieve, but look, the couches have been modified to simulate someone's weight. You don't see any wrinkles, do you? The couch sags a bit under John's weight; a bit less under George's. You can walk right up to John and say hello. If you don't touch him, you'll swear that he is real. These are as close as you'll ever get to those men this side of heaven."

"Bloody hell."

"Exactly. Sir Paul, can I help you with your basses?"

***

"Hello everyone. Welcome to Day One of your rehearsal dates. We hope to make you all comfortable and will procure anything your heart desires, but we strongly suggest that you do not leave."

He'd noticed protesters being held out on the periphery of the property. They carried signs that read: "Disassemble the robots" - "A.I. is The Devil!" - "DON'T PERVERT The Beatles!!" and "UNHOLY fakes!" along with other less savory protests.

· · ·

TED LOOKED around at the *Fab Four*, giving each the same degree of attention and diligence.

"Just to begin... Paul has a few new songs...He has suggestions about the parts you might play...."

Groans all around.

"Kidding...Just kidding." *In reality, I almost hope that they don't write anything together. Think of the copyright nightmare that could become! The legal team have discussed that one well into the night with no resolution.*

Paul looked at Ted and smirked.

"Funny, yeh."

Ted smirked.

"I couldn't resist. Sorry, Paul."

Ted turned to everyone. "This is a preamble to a truly worldwide tour, like nothing the Beatles have ever attempted. And it's mostly sold out already, so...kudos all around. You'll be starting in Singapore, which is already almost sold out! We're thinking of adding a second night. Then Sydney and Perth...From there Dubai, Mumbai, Tokyo...criss-crossing Asia, until we come to Europe...Brussels, London, Munich, Rome (and a meeting with the pope if you'd like), then to Rio, and then...America, where your most rabid fans are!"

And where the real money is!

"L.A., Dallas, Denver, Chicago...a dozen or so more cities until we finish up with four nights in Madison Square Garden!"

The significance of playing New York again was not lost on them. Even George quietly remarked, "I hope it won't be like Shea. We couldn't hear ourselves sing!"

John nodded vigorously in agreement.

"It'll be different this time, boys, I promise you. Top shelf, all the way."

. . .

***

W HILE P AUL WAS FUSSILY PICKING through his stuff and
selecting a bass, John got up. He carefully set his guitar in its
stand and mumbled, "Going out for a smoke."

Paul looked miffed. He looked at Ringo who seemed
ready to start, then at George who was pointedly tuning his
guitar, ignoring everyone.

Then Paul sat and started in with the distinctive bass
intro from "Taxman," George's protest song from when he
found out about his tax bill after the Beatles had made it big.

Well past where the guitars were to have come in, George
allowed his guitar to make one (on key) chord, and set it
down.

"Old news, man. Let it go. I have…New priorities now,
y'know?"

He too got up. Paul noticed that the cushioned chair
where George was "seated" slowly regained its form. Paul
reached out tentatively.

He touched the chair.

"It's real," he muttered. "Amazing."

Ringo grinned and nodded as Paul got up and walked out
of the room randomly touching items as he went along.

After a short while, Ted eventually began corralling each
and bringing them back to the practice room. The few
people standing around buzzed expectantly. Ted then cleared
the room. "Out. C'mon. Out. Everyone. Give them some
space."

He closed the door and latched it, with himself outside.

A few people were waiting around to see if he'd cheat.

"Go! I'm leaving. See? Now, everyone leave them alone.
Let them work!"

. . .

THEN TED WENT to sit with Martin in the CCTV room. It was part of Ted's plan to have cameras hidden nearly everywhere- in the practice room, the lounge, the dining areas and the hallways…there were cameras and recording devices simply everywhere; every angle and every facial nuance… genuine or programmed. Ted needed reassurances that they were playing along, though; someone had suggested that since the cams were everywhere, all that rare footage of the four of them back together might be cut into a documentary.

Maybe, thought Ted. *First things first.*

AFTER A BRIEF and mostly cursory run-through of a few songs from their first few albums, they took another break.

Bickering had broken out in the first hour of the session.

Understandable…Paul and Ringo have had careers well beyond the Beatles …George and John have as well, but there isn't the backlog of work…concerts… recordings. Hell, John was shot almost 40 years ago. Now he's a crotchety 79-year-old, squabbling with Paul. It'll take time and…patience to work together. I hope that Paul doesn't decide to renege…I'd sue him and he'd laugh.

Martin looked at Ted. His eyes asked the question, "Is this over before it even started?"

Ted whispered back, "I don't know. I hope this is just a rough beginning.

Ringo has mostly stayed out of the fracas, but even quiet George has asserted himself a few times as well in there."

The Beatles were getting nowhere. It was as if they were arguing about the size and shape of the studio so they wouldn't have to face each other and play after all these years.

"THEY, John and George, y'know, look great but there's

something off in his, John's, sound, his timing. I can't explain it, but it feels fake… It feels wrong." Paul complained.

Martin had suggested that they start with the simple visceral rock-and-roll that originally launched their careers; the better to plumb old pathways and rediscover their kinship. Paul wasn't seeing it.

I need 100 % buy-in or this was all for nothing!

"I hear you. Take five alright? I'll…consult with someone…"

I need to find Martin. Martin, we have a problem!

AS HE WAS WALKING around trying to clear his head, Martin noticed John sitting well away from everyone with Julian.

How did he get in here? He agreed to wait a few days to see his Dad. It's in his contract…oh well, he's here now and they seem to be connecting.

They seemed to be having a long intense heart-to-heart talk and both of them were crying a bit.

Just then, Paul appeared at Martin's shoulder.

"Hmmm…Give 'em a bit of *priv*-acy, y'know…John has some catching up to do with his *soon*."

***

"YOKO IS HERE. She is demanding admittance." The guard looked pensive. Ted felt trapped.

"God. So many distractions…Okay. Do this. Give her my card…"

He dug a slick looking business card out of his pocket.

"Give her this. Ask her to be patient. If she will wait… say three *entire* days, then I promise to let her in. I'll let her talk to anyone she wants; unlimited access. Other than that, she can sit out there until it starts to snow. Tell her that, but tell her that in a way where I don't sound like a dick, okay? I just need to get some collective time for these guys...gotta give them time to reacquaint and then jell as a unit.

The guard looked intimidated. She was an old lady, but like John, she didn't suffer fools. He took the card and nodded nonetheless, hurrying off.

THERE WAS an atmosphere of latent hostility in the practice room. Ted noticed it as soon as his hand let go of the door-knob and the door closed behind him.

They had just finished a run-through, which had satisfied no one if he read the faces in the room correctly. John was slowly drinking a bottle of beer. Paul watched with fascination as the level in the bottle slowly went down in conjunction with John's Adam's apple bouncing up and down, *as the liquid seemed to go down his throat.*

"Guys, you did your best work together..."

Paul bristled slightly at that; everyone else listened.

"Wouldn't it be a once in a lifetime opportunity?"

John spread his hands and looked up impishly. George laughed; finally Ringo did as well.

"To take this opportunity, this..." Ted smiling at John's witty gesture, "This *incredibly rare opportunity* to create some great music again?"

John gestured to Paul with his thumb, over his shoulder.

"Paul's still miffed because sometimes, when the publishing credits went out, there was only room for one name. Since mine was alphabetically earlier, mine was printed first. Sometimes his was...omitted."

Paul heard but tried to remain impassive.

John turned to Paul. "Mate, if we write anything from now on, I'll make certain that your name is first, okay?"

Paul's face softened a bit.

Ringo looked from one to the other as if surprised by this behavior; George now looked serene, happy.

"That's a nice thing that you did just there, John-O. Thank you."

The next session lasted about an hour and it went a bit better. George looked knowingly at Ringo and Ringo smiled as he played, having a great time.

"THAT WAS GREAT, guys…We have a staff of chefs here to feed you and make you happy and we'll convene back here in say…two hours, for more rehearsal. It's been a while and we want you to sound *fabulous!*"

***

TED WHISPERED to Martin in the Second Control room.

"This is the biggest music story in 50 years, despite the fact that everyone under thirty yawns and focuses elsewhere. But the oldsters…The oldsters…the boomers, who grew up with this music were excited; excited enough to spend, spend, spend…on tickets, memorabilia and more. They are digging deep. They know that this is their only chance to experience this."

"Look at these figures. This is only from twenty minutes ago and I'm sure it's…well, maybe double this by now. It's rising so fast I can't believe the monitors are not somehow lying to me."

I can't believe it. It's as though I've got a license to print money!

. . .

***

IN THE ERSATZ CONTROL ROOM, Ted noticed Paul motioning to John as John was going to go out for a "smoke."

John was a bit hesitant but, after all, this was Paul....

With a furtive gesture Ted had the CCTV zoom in and activated the onboard microphone to catch the conversation.

Paul to John: "C'mon...Let's pretend that we're 22 again. Let's write something new that we might have written during our early period. I want to work with *you* again."

"Too much water has passed over the bridge, yeh."

"No it hasn't. We can return to that time when we wrote as a team. Everything we wrote was ours, not mine or yours. That might be a thing we can find again."

"We're too old to write that crap, now, y'know?" John pulled slightly away.

"Not if we have imagination. You have Imagination, don't you? I know I have. *Imagine*...it."

John wrinkled up his nose and smirked at the small joke Paul had just made. He moved a tiny bit closer.

"Can you try not to be such a tosser?"

Paul grinned, his eyes lighting up.

"If you can cut back on the whinge-ing..."

John smiled. His eyes crinkled and danced.

"Let's see if you can remember this one!"

John picked up his guitar, and he launched into a slightly slowed down version of "She Loves You." Paul's bass followed John's rapid chord changes. From there they segued into "Eleanor Rigby" and a slightly dissonant version of "You Say Hello, I say Goodbye." Ringo and George had joined in by the time that they were halfway through "She

Loves You" and still they kept on segueing into song after song.

Ted, who was courting despair only moments before, slowly began smiling and nodding and yes, eventually tapping his toe.

***

NINE DAYS before the tour opened, at the press conference for the group interview:

QUESTION: "Are you really ready to play with your mates again, John?"

"Well, I've had a long rest now, haven't I?"

At that, he reached over and appeared to kiss Ringo on the head. Ringo's hair seemed to muss just a bit as if actual contact had occurred.

Paul watched and marveled still.

Yoko stood in the background beaming happily.

QUESTION: "Will there be any new tunes that you'll be playin' on your tour?"

George fielded that one.

"Yes we have already written 6 or 7 new songs as a group. Hopefully in the week or so before we actually begin the tour, we'll have finished a few more. Enuff for a new album. Then we'll see all the tax wankers try to deal with all the copyright issues we've just invented. Have at it, boys!"

Laughs all around even though fully a 50% of the attendees didn't truly "get" George's joke.

. . .

QUESTION: "Paul! Which was more fun: The Beatles or Wings?"

"Ooooh… You're such a wanker! Next!"

QUESTION: Ringo, what's it like to have the band back together again?

Ringo smiled before answering. He knew that he was probably the luckiest man alive.

"It's great. I have missed these blokes more than I knew… To see them now…all together…" He seemed to force down a tear or two.

Yeh…and it's fun to be with me mates again…creatin' something new and excitin'! New music…after all this time… yeah…it's great, just great."

QUESTION…

***

SOON AFTER THE WRAP-UP, Martin arrived, flushed a bit, holding an envelope. "We've just received a packet of papers… that arrived via U.S. Marshall."

Ted was distracted, watching The Band practice, getting tighter all the time.

He blinked. "A Federal Marshall?"

He turned to face martin with a questioning look.

"Yes, as in: We've been served."

"Served?"

"Yep. Apparently John has engaged the biggest, baddest law firm in New York."

"And? What? We're being sued?"

"Yep. John is suing us for his freedom!"

Ted laughed darkly.

"Of course he is…"

--With many thanks to the kind and generous folks in my Writers' Critique group: Steve and Sarah Boshear, James McMann, Reggie Johnson and Jurri Schenk--without whom, this story might never have gotten "here."

6

PINOCCHIO'S PROBLEM

The music seemed to wash over the audience in some inevitable and stupendous sensory tidal wave designed to cause an orgasm of delight and musical satisfaction. There were dancers, lasers, specially commissioned *sensory* explosions and of course, incredible, imposing sound.

The show built to an inescapable and fantastic finale!

The prerequisite smoke bombs and effects went off in synch with the action. The lights danced and thrilled all, to show off and display *the star!* The fans, delirious with excitement, danced in the aisles, sang along, and waved to *him*--in hopes that he might acknowledge *each* of them! And smile or *even...wave!*

"Pick me! Wave at me!" They all seemed to say with their eyes as they drank in all that the star presented! *"Sing for me! Dance for me! BE with me! Be with me forever!"*

Janus!

Janus! The God of Pop Music!

To begin the show, he'd dropped from an opening in the ceiling, falling, falling, until just before he hit, he stopped. He sang and danced inches off the floor.

The crowed went wild. Janus was known for the spectacle, because he was acknowledged as likely the most involving and adept showman performing today!

Soon there were musicians and dancers and other singers all a few inches, to many feet off the stage, flying; floating; dancing.

The stage went white totally completely white, and suddenly, as the viewers' eyes cleared, the entire ensemble was onstage, no longer floating.

He sang and danced, sync'ing with ten other dancers. *Behind them*, on the mammoth stage there were other backup singers time-stepping in unison and singing backup. It was, *as planned*, far too much to watch and absorb in one sitting! It was common for his fans to buy tickets to multiple shows, to see him again and again!

Janus is the phenomenon of the age!

"Janus is adored and is the biggest thing in pop music for decades, the heir apparent to Presley, The Beatles, Jackson, $#%^76℮℩℮℩, and BBBluuuto; the next in a very short line of truly monumental and influential stars," StarFire magazine gushed.

THE FINALE GREW LARGER, and built upon itself, enlarging even more! He climbed, somehow still dancing; still singing, to the top of a 30-foot tall *transparent* pyramid in the center of the stage. The music built and built! There was an explosion!

And he was simply *gone* as the last crescendo peaked! The *build* was all a device to satisfy and still tantalize his fans.

Everyone on stage froze, the music stopped and the lights slowly faded to black, leaving only tiny pinpricks of light, traversing the stage errantly here and there, as if searching; questing for The Star.

But he was gone.

The silence was deafening, and after a moments' hesitation, the crowd went wild!

Even though he had a reputation for never coming back for encores; giving it all he had in the course of the show, the crowd chanted and clapped, hoping to change his mind; to make him come back to do more! *Just this once!* They loved him! They were never satisfied.

There could never be too much Janus!

Meanwhile Janus, exhausted and *quite finished* for the night, was escorted to his very private dressing suite.

His right-hand person, his *aide de guerre*, his *confidante--* Lily Sanchez, was ever by his side as he hurried to the safety of his rooms to relax before he fell over in sheer exhaustion. His face was a study of pain and frustration. The delirious crowds' chanting and cheering in the receding background notwithstanding.

"It looked great from where I was sitting, Janus! The crowd loves you!"

"Yeah, thanks. It was an okay show, but there are still *so* many glitches."

"Glitches?"

"Yes," Janus looked over at her to drive home the import to Lily as they quick-walked. He grimaced with each step. An aide supported him and assisted him in walking, discretely staying out of the interchange.

"Glitches. Shall I run through the bigger, most annoying ones?"

Lily's stylus and flimsey tablet was always at the ready.

Her huge dark sunglasses hid the inevitable eye roll.

"Go."

"The bass player, what's his name, Mick?" He toweled off his sweaty brow and draped the monogrammed cloth around his neck.

"Rik." She corrected.

"Okay, Rik. He's supposed to be one of the very best in the world, right?"

Lily nodded. She knew Janus. She knew what was coming. She braced for it.

"Well he came in a full *half beat late* from the refrain in "Breakdown Town," missed on at least three notes on "Shadowman," and muddied my vocals with him coming in *too early* on "BettyJean." I can't work like this! I want him replaced before we get to Copenhagen."

"Janus, Baby. We hired the best in the world. I'm going to have a hell of a time finding someone *nearly* as good! Especially on such short notice! What if we schedule more rehearsals with your stand-in?"

God that'll cost another fortune! she fretted.

"I want him gone, Lil! Get someone else. Someone I can depend on."

"Right. Gone. Got it. Anything else?" Lily asked hopefully. Hoping for there to be nothing else that displeased *His Majesty*, but there was *always* something else. His shows were *nearly* perfect pieces of *Rock Theatre,* but Janus was such a perfectionist that he made everyone around him crazy.

It isn't human to attempt this much perfection! She thought. *Though he gets closer than most!*

It wasn't the first time she'd thought that. It wouldn't be the last.

"The servos in my right hip are locking halfway again. Did you see when I was trying to do the split at the end of "World of Wonders?" It locked up and I was only able to get one leg extended enough; the other almost toppled me, because I wasn't ready for this screwup."

Lily nodded enthusiastically."You recovered magnificently, though. If one wasn't fully familiar with the choreography, one might believe that you planned that!"

"Yeah, I know. I thought quickly and made something out of nothing. Just the same, better have Robotics and Actuation check in with me after I get out of the chamber, in say, four hours. Alright?"

"Of course." She made notes with her stylus on the flimsy. "Anything else?"

"Of course!" His dark eyes flared, but he said nothing else about his legs.

It's clear that he was frustrated and angry, Lily thought. *What else is new?* The litany went on until they'd reached the hyperbaric chamber that had been modified to nourish and replenish the God of Pop.

"It's great for my muscles," Janus would tell friends. Lily had heard him say it often enough in the past.

Yet, with his increased isolation, there were fewer and fewer of those friends, Lily thought. *Plus, with all the body mods he's doing, there was less and less of him there to need replenishment.*

Friends would be a good influence; they might keep him grounded. At least they used to. But now...?

She shook her head. *Fewer and fewer are willing to put up with security; fewer and fewer still are able to pass security!*

HE'D CONFIDE the same thoughts about the hyperbaric chamber and other health regimens, to those very few in the press whom he deigned to speak. His contact with the press dwindling to a trickle of information doled out to only those few whom he felt would not bad mouth him or his...*foibles;* those who would play up the creative portion of the *Janus Legend,* and downplay the eccentric portions.

LILY FEARED that if the walk had been longer he'd have never run out of quibbles with his show. He was well known for being a perfectionist, and Lily had been at his side for four other world tours and, with the company since nearly the beginning of his career. The very early years, of building. It seemed that what was once a desire for as close to human perfection as possible was turning into an inhuman obsession.

For instance, during the "Mummy" world tour some years back, he'd brilliantly taken the original storyline of the Mummy to new heights. Janus had taken the legend and built an entire song cycle around it, finishing an album in record time *for him,* working nine months of twelve-hour days. He'd incorporated knee drops and knee slides, and magnificent never-before-seen dance moves during the extensive practice sessions. It was spectacular and when he hit the stage with all these new moves, the fans went wild! Everyone agreed that his singing had never been more urgent, more plaintive; never more important.

However, about that time, he'd begun to have problems with his knees; knee drops; dramatic and exciting but very hard on a body, *any* body. By the time the incredible five-month world tour had ended, he'd already ordered that the hospital wing on his private island in the Caribbean, be expanded; the Robotics and Actuation staff doubled.

AN ENTERTAINMENT TALKING head had once gushed: *His island hospital was in the forefront of Robotic body mods. World-renowned surgeons regularly did rotations through his clinic to bring in new tech or absorb the latest techniques and developments in robotic body mods.*

THOSE BODY MODIFICATIONS used to be pervue of only the wealthy, or the very old; their desire to utilize their money to enrich their last years with pain-free mobility. Now, following Janus, those who could afford it were sometimes modifying perfectly good organs, appendages and personal utilities. No one was even close to Janus though, in terms of the *extent* of body mods; the degree to which Janus researched and was prepared to go, (he had become the *de facto*, the leader in the field.

Lily looked on as the technicians monitored the pressure after he'd been situated.

No one except a very few knew just how much work he'd had done; not the press nor most friends. What he'd done rivaled anything done by the hyper-rich.

The staff; all staff, were shown the most detailed and comprehensive non-disclosure, non-dissemination verbage she'd ever heard of. Sign it and be paid richly. Or not, and take a hike!

. . .

AFTER EACH SHOW on that tour he had been pushed around in a low-grav chair, so he didn't have to walk; didn't have to add further stress his legs. By the time he returned home, the doctors and robotic people were discussing the possibility of extracting his already greatly modified knees and replacing them with knees specifically designed for a singer/dancer; the God of Pop.

AS HIS ROAD MANAGER, Lily had overheard him conferring with Dom, his closest advisor, who was also his uncle, who oversaw all his day-to-day affairs.

"If I go forward with this idea, I could do knee drops from now until I'm too old and tired to pick myself up!" He grinned. "But with the advances in robotics and other improvements we're making on my body, that day might never come!"

Dom nodded, satisfied that his nephew was well on his way to the celestial heights afforded to a very, very few in Pop Music.

AFTER THE LAST TOUR, he'd replaced his hips as well, but that operation, for some reason, wasn't as successful as the knee surgery. He was constantly asking doctors for more flexibility; tweaking, fiddling, and complaining that his *fluidity of motion* wasn't good enough.

All these modifications were secret, of course. After the meteoric rise from poverty in *suburban* Columbus of Tyrell Washington, he'd changed his name. He'd changed nearly everything about himself, as if to widen the gap between his humble beginnings and what he'd become!

. . .

IN ADDITION, he'd rapidly grown to be a recluse when not on tour. His mantra had become, "No one understands me; what I'm trying to do, and how damn hard it is to do it."

Lily nodded. She'd heard it all for years. 'His quest for perfection.'

And if he finally achieves that...Then what? She wondered.

SOME SAID that the rapid move to becoming a recluse was really because of the forty-year-old stalker from a trailer park outside of Cleveland, who somehow managed to get by security in her rusted, ancient SUV, and threatened him with a murder/suicide if he wouldn't marry her and consent to have a child with him.

Soon after that incident, he began shopping for an island that could be made safe and *very private* with obstructions in the water, guard drones constantly patrolling the skies and all sorts of sophisticated security on land.

Thus, 'La Cuesta Encantada,' or the Enchanted Hill, was born and built on that island, a ten-minute heli/hover flight over the Gulf of Mexico from the *Janus Washington Airport* in Brownsville, Tx.

The press, of course, had a field day with all the seclusion, the disappearances, and the generally odd behavior. And, with the dearth of real information available, the press began actively speculating. Thus, the legend grew!

LILY PONDERED HER boss and the "gag" agreement that she'd signed. *Fully half the things that the public thought that they knew about Janus were untrue, but Janus and his handlers were savvy enough not to correct the untruths, allowing his notoriety to rocket, towing his popularity along as well!*

. . .

***

It's so hard to keep him happy while on tour, Lily fretted, after seeing to his care while in the Chamber. During tours, he could be unreasonable and testy; sulking if he did not get his way.

Some things are beyond even the capabilities of Janus, and are the province only of Gods. Lily thought sarcastically.

Sometimes he screamed at the band after the show.

After the show!? Lily shuddered at the memory. *When everyone feels great having given their best and they're exhausted? That's when you rip into your people? It's crazy. None of us are machines. We all do our best, but it's never good enough; good enough, for him.*

Sometimes he'd act that way after each show for the entire tour! His actions impacted morale, and defections in the dead of night were not unheard of, despite the money he offered.

"Nothing is worth this crazy bullshit!" She'd heard musicians, technicians and roadies mutter many times during her tenure with Janus.

Then she'd access her network and hastily find a replacement, paying whatever it took, because if she didn't, she was guaranteed even more complaints from *The Boss.*

His morale, if it dipped even lower could make the tour hell! This tour was well past the halfway point, and so, Janus had developed an even more insightful, demanding and pointed list of changes to be made to approach his ideal of pop perfection. Nevermind that the tour was by now almost over. Janus never let up.

***

. . .

"MR. WASHINGTON, I'm afraid that I have some bad news for you, sir."

"Please call me Janus, Dr. Groves." Now, at twenty-nine, Janus had accreted the *gravitas* of someone far older. When he spoke, he *commanded* attention.

"Alright, Mr. Janus."

"No doctor. *Janus. Just Janus.* No *mister.* We've had this conversation before, doctor."

"Yes, I suppose we have…"

"Anyway, you've scanned my legs and you're going to tell me about this pain that's developed in both my thighs. The right one is the worst." He tapped his right thigh unconsciously with a forefinger. He beat out a little rhythm without thinking about it.

It was: "Backbeating"…or "Mommy" (reprise)…

"Yes, yes…well, Janus, it is as I feared, back when you brought me in to head the team that reworked your hips and knees. I feared then, that your inherent bone structure would not take the stress that the combination of your… um…*rigorous* style of performing demands and the strain of the titanium against *mere* bone. It's quite possible that your thigh is literally beginning to flake and might be breaking apart from the stress you create. The hip insert, in the top of your thigh bone, is destroying what bone structure you have left. I'm sorry. We talked about this possibility then. I advised against the operation, but I, and well, our entire team has done the best we could--not only during the operation and through the follow-up therapies. Also with the ultrasound treatments, the stimuli we've administered and the dietary supplements specially designed for you. All was for nothing, I'm afraid. I'm sorry, sir."

Janus listened to all this stoically. It chilled him because he understood the implications of what was being said to him: *My body is letting me down.*

He'd surmised as much himself in quiet and painful moments of the most recent "Jazz" tour.

"Okay, doctor. What do we do now?"

"Well, first I advise bed rest, therapy and a much more...*restrained* schedule. Perhaps design new shows with no knee drops, dancing and other stressors to your lower torso."

Janus listened to this calmly as well. He'd already formulated a plan of his own, but it involved none of the ideas just outlined by his physician.

"Doctor. Here is what I'd like us to do."

"Yes?"

"Prep for another series of operations. You mentioned another possibility back when we began this. You mentioned a total replacement."

"No! *Janus!*"

The doctor was almost pleading and his staff looked at each other anxiously.

"*Yes*, please. I'll need my femurs replaced. Both of them. Make them work with the hips properly. I'm constantly having to go back to Robotics and Actuation for tweaking and tune-ups."

"We talked about the possibility of that happening."

Janus put up a delicate-looking but powerful hand cutting him off.

"Yes, but it's getting out of hand now! Plus, with the pain I can't think anymore! Just take it all out and start again!"

"But Janus...."

"If there's any doubt that my lower legs will hold up; being the next items down the line that might fail. If there's any doubt, then be prepared to replace them too! (Then I'll only have to contend with my ankles and feet!)"

"But Janus!"

"How long will it take you be *fully* prepared?"

"Janus, I don't think-"

"How long, Doctor?"

Janus fixed this world renowned surgeon with an icy glare. "I *will* have what I need! If I can't get it from you, I'll look elsewhere! How long?"

GROVES CAVED. He began thinking aloud, stalling for time. "Beefing up the Actuation team, robotics…field testing new technologies, before implantation…"

He made a face that said he'd just been put in a position that placed him firmly between a rock and a hard place. There was the not inconsiderable amount of money he was being paid, and he was responsible for the livelihoods of the staff; the people that he'd brought in with him. Then, there was this very powerful single-minded personality he was dealing with. Finally there was the Hippocratic Oath: "Do no harm.."

"It…it might take six or seven months…" Groves looked around at the others in the room for some help; for someone to scream: "NO!" Many of the others were employed by Janus and contradicting him when he wanted something so bad was not conducive to long term employment, so Groves got no help from anyone present.

For once Janus smiled. It was a satisfied and happy smile, laced with determination.

"Good! Six months it is! Be ready! *I* will be! See Lily with your budgetary and personnel needs. She'll send them off to the appropriate bean counters, etcetera and I'll call them myself in a couple of days to see to it that there are no snags and *no delays!*"

He turned to go, catching himself up short a bit, because turning and striding was what hurt the most.

Everyone noticed his pain.

Groves noticed too and sincerely wanted to alleviate his pain. Just not in the way that Janus had decided upon.

Rest...My young God...Rest, he thought.

"Goodbye doctor. I look forward to feeling no more pain and getting my life and my *moves* back."

He left, with his entourage leaving the room feeling as if Groves were now drifting in the void of space itself.

Janus turned abruptly in the doorway. He flinched again.

"Oh, and by the way doctor?

"Yes?"

"As long as we're going to go through all this, I'm only five foot seven."

"Yes? Yes you are. That's right."

"Well, as long as we're going to go through all this expense and pain, I think it'd be nice if I ended up being five foot *nine*. I've had my people do the math. Five foot nine is all we can manage without a massive rework. So I'll need this new spec to be integrated into the Plan. Thank you."

Janus smiled, but there was not much warmth in that grin.

"*Goodbye.* I'll stay in touch. I expect that I'll be hearing from you a lot in the coming months with updates on your preparations."

The threat...or demand was like a dead, rotting flower that had just been delivered from *the outside.*

The noise attendant from a dozen or so handlers, sycophants and employees receded quickly down the hall, the echoes receding away down the hallway from Groves' antiseptic office.

Lily waved and mouthed, "I'll call you!" before she disappeared through the doctor's outer door.

Groves eyes searched for answers, his mind swirled, and he muttered, "What have I done?"

***

JANUS SPOKE to Lily in hushed tones, as they were walking away from Grove's Office, "I've had Llad do calculations and five foot nine is as tall as I can be without disturbing my equilibrium; my moves; my stability. Making me a lot taller would be great, but it'd make my moves much more difficult or even impossible. It'll be wonderful, won't it? I'll be *average* height!"

Llad was Janus' lead mathematician. Everything was math, and if a problem was first confronted as a mathematical problem, it was usually solved quickly.

Quickly was good when dealing with the mercurial, dogged and peripatetic sensibilities of Janus. Llad had a lot of work and complete job security.

***

THE NEXT YEAR was a blur of preparation, operations, and finally, recovery. Janus, always anxious to get back in the studio and back performing for his fans, decided that eighteen months is too long without *Janus' presence* on the scene. Since there was six months prep, six month's recovery and six months mounting the new show, he directed his publishing company to put out a greatest hits compilation in the middle of that time to return him to his fans' thoughts and whet their appetites for the new show coming soon.

"We'll leak a few details here," indicating a source that could be quoted on the viddies; and a few different details to her." He indicated a name on a list of *friendly* press people.

"Later we'll release a few more details just before we allow a *leaked* rough-cut vid from a rehearsal." He looked up as if he were a general planning a war campaign, and he was addressing a roomful of other generals who would follow his directives.

"That should be about a week before the first tickets go on sale for the first concert in...?" He looked around. Lily consulted her upgraded flimsey.

"That will be ...Barcelona, Janus."

"Good. The Spanish love me. We'll begin in Barcelona and release the viddie a week before we start selling tickets. We'll allow my fans to see a 20-second snippet from rehearsals of the upcoming show. That'll spark sales like crazy!"

"But Janus, do you think it's wise to do a show on the old North Korea's Dear Leader? That was *years* ago! Will anyone remember? Will anyone care?"

"They'll care after they see me! I've been writing the songs, the story and the stage notes every moment while I was laid up."

"We know, Janus."

"And, by the time we hit the stage, people will be ready to scream and go wild, like they always do!"

"Yes, Janus."

***

INFOTAINMENT TONIGHT PROCLAIMED: "*The Dear Leader World Tour was originally set for 100 nights, 72 cities, spaced over a two-*

hundred-day schedule. Grueling for any performer; simply the next logical step for Janus' grand aspirations."

Unfortunately The Dear Leader Tour was so poorly received that the tour was over in less than three months!

***

THIS IS A DISASTER! Lily fretted over the preliminary figures. Janus was resting in the next room after the final show of the tour. Now that all the figures were in, Lily could assess the damage. Janus' finances would take a substantial hit! So substantial that it momentarily took Lily's breath away.

He was already one of the three or four wealthiest people in the world, and he could afford it; but even Janus would notice this!

The failure of this World Tour was nearly on a par with BBBluuuto's disastrous *Galaxy Akimbo Tour*, which ultimately caused the breakup of the band and the murder/suicide of the writing duo/leaders. That was the worst melt down in pop history! The *Dear Leader Tour* was a strong candidate for *second worst. Only the most diehard fans even bothered to down-load the music.*

As for the God of Pop, himself--anyone else might be disappointed, inconsolable, or worse. Others might doggedly *go back to the drawing board*, figure out what went wrong, re-tool, re-purpose and try again.

However, Janus already *knew* what was wrong, and he'd become impossible to be around and, impossible to even talk with these days.

Staff had begun quitting in droves, because even at the best of times, Janus was difficult. At this the first major setback of his career, he'd become a like wounded lion.

Angry, always ready for a fight and always ready with an unkind comment.

Lily looked at the roster and the possible replacements. *After a time, with all that anger and negativity, no amount of money would suffice.*

Good thing I had my doctor upgrade my meds. She giggled privately. *Janus can say anything. I'll be alright.*

"LILY?" Janus was at the door.

Lily started. *He was so quiet sometimes, almost as if he really wanted to sneak up on you!*

"Can we get a few friendly press types over here, say tomorrow morning before we close up shop for good and I go back to *Cuesta?*"

"Sure Janus. What do you want me to tell them?"

Janus eyes looked as if he'd lost a fight. Not simply bloodied, nor bruised, but hurt, wounded...maybe defeated.

"Just get them here. I have to do some sort of *mea culpa.* I may as well get this over with. I want to get the word out. I fucked up. But I'll be back, bigger and better than ever! I want to send it out through a few in the press who haven't maligned me, okay?"

"Sure, sure. I'll get right on it. I'll set it up for...nine?"

"Make it ten."

Without even a further acknowledgement, he disappeared back into his solitude.

Lily's pulse was racing despite her meds. Any direct contact with him these days caused that to happen.

Thank God for Paxsilitude™! Thank God I asked for a heftier dose!

***

. . .

Safely back on *Cuesta Encantada*, Janus met with the leaders of his team of doctors.

"Well, I screwed up. My voice suffered for not being used for the six months; I was laid up. I should have practiced more, but I was so focused on *writing* "Dear Leader.""

The doctors looked at each other nervously.

Lily had taken it upon herself to triple her dose of Paxsilitude™ in preparation for this meeting. She was confident that nothing could disturb *her* calm!

Janus continued, "My voice never came back. Not fully. I couldn't hit the notes I'd written for myself. I could hit those notes easily when I was younger. I hit them every night on the Mummy tour! And I did it for over 147 nights!"

He paused. This was the most risky and significant decision of his life. He hesitated for just a moment before going on.

"My voice failed me. It couldn't do what I needed when I needed it. We'll have to replace...."

He looked around at the doctors assembled in his private clinic.

"-My lungs, my vocal chords, even my throat and my tongue. Everything involved in my making sound must be upgraded!"

"Janus! Do you know what you're asking?" Dr. Sithra, the head of a newly formed thoracic team spoke first. This request was not a complete surprise. After all he had created a thoracic and otolaryngolist team. They had to have been called in to do *something.*

Sithra's deep olive features were creased in concern. He expressed his distress that *a person would just throw away perfectly good organs*, and said so. He acted appalled. He wasn't used to dealing with Janus.

He won't last, thought Lily smugly, safely behind her dose of relaxant.

Groves took a deep breath. He knew what was coming.

Janus' eyes flared.

"Those organs failed me when I needed them. I'm not *throwing away* perfectly good organs, I'm *throwing away* defective ones! Haven't you read the reviews? Didn't you hear the news? The Dear Leader tour was a flop! I can't sing anymore! Not like before!"

"But no one's ever attempted this radical of an upgrade before."

"Which is why each of you was hand-picked, checked out from top to bottom, and brought here! You are..." He looked around the room, pausing for emphasis. *"The best there is!"*

"This is such a momentous undertaking. Are you certain?"

"Yes!" Janus' eyes blazed! "And in case you're anxious about being sued, I've had a clause written into each of your contracts that will protect you from litigation if the operation should prove to be anything less than 100% successful. I've also written in a *substantial bonus* for each of you if I am happy with my voice afterwards!"

More than one of the roomful of doctors breathed a secret sigh of relief; more than one of then *also* began planning to spend the extra money.

"This will likely take a year or more of recuperation," another doctor stuttered unsure of the path ahead at this point. He made some hasty notes, and quick calculations based on similar, but far simpler operations that he'd overseen in the recent past. "Yes, I'd estimate 14 or 15 months...."

"But I'll be *better* afterwards?" Janus pressed on.

"I would expect so, but...."

"I'll be better? I'll be able to hit the notes I write? *All* the notes?"

The doctors looked at one another for confirmation or support. Sithra spoke up first, "Based upon the parameters that you've set out and coupled with the data that we've extrapolated from the scans of your head, nasel cavities, throat muscles, etcetera, yes, we believe so. If you're intent on doing this, we belive that we'll eventually be able to tune you as one would a piano or guitar. However your voice will have the elasticity more like that of a synthesizer. I'd expect we could enable your voice to hit nearly any note you wish!"

Janus grinned like a seven-year-old on Christmas morning!

Sithra pushed on, still hopeful he could dissuade the star from this drastic course.

"But it won't be easy. No indeed! There will be times that I'm quite certain that you'll wish you were dead! No, indeed, it won't be easy for you. Not for you or us!"

"I don't care if it's easy for *you*. And, I don't *expect* it to be easy for me. Will this *fix* the problem? Doctors?"

"There will be *considerable* pain…"

"*I don't care!* Will this *fix* the problem?"

"Considerable pain! Are you prepared for that?"

"I don't care!" Janus was shouting now, daring any to oppose him. "I need to be better! I need to be able to hit the notes that I write! Will you do this for me?!"

The consensus was hesitant and more or less unwilling. Nevertheless, acting upon the unique set of incentives, the assembled surgeons eventually agreed to plan, schedule and execute the series of operations that Janus required.

Lily was blown away. No one had ever suggested something so audacious; so radical. *I wonder if the failure unhinged him…just a bit?* She took another Paxilitude™, content for now that she wasn't in Janus' crosshairs.

She began hurriedly tapping notes into her reader/scheduler, the better to look busy and avoid any chance of conversing with her boss. *I guess it's time to get my resume up-to-date. I wonder who might be looking for a seasoned tour manager? He's too crazy for me.*

Her fingers danced on the reader, and sent out a half dozen inquiries.

DR. GROVES WAS AS CONCERNED as everyone else, but he held back his comments until everyone else had, at least for a time, fallen silent. Each now doing preliminary planning in his or her mind.

"Janus?" He drew his employer aside and spoke quickly; quietly, but urgently. "Are you *certain* you want to do this? This is a significant portion of *you* we're planning on taking away. Do you understand? Have you really thought this through? I know that this is important to you... I know that the press wounds you when they do sensational stories about your umm...individual foibles. If this were to get out, and I can't see how we'll be able to keep this secret for long, they'll talk about you all the more! You'll be a freak!"

Janus scowled. He had thought of this too, but had devised no real workable plan for containing the information. He couldn't very well imprison the doctors, technicians and specialists *on La Cuesta*, as much as he'd like to! The Egyptian pharaohs had all the workmen who toiled on the pyramids killed the better to keep the pyramid's secrets.

For all my wealth, influence and power that choice is still beyond me!

Groves continued in his last ditch attempt to dissuade the singer. "But we've already replaced much of your lower extremities. Now we're planning to take away much of your upper torso... I mean...what does it take to be human? I mean, what *percentage* of a person needs to reside *in there* for him still to be considered *human?*"

He gently poked Janus on his chest as he said the words: *In there.*

Janus replied coldly: "Enough, Doctor. Enough. I still have my brain and I *need* this. Do it." He turned and exited the room.

Grove sighed. He had already know how this conversation would play out, but he had to try; he owed it to his conscience.

"Is your brain enough? I wonder…"

7

MIKE

Things went to hell pretty fast. I think events caught pretty much everyone by surprise. In retrospect, I wonder that it did. Me above anyone else.

My name's Mike. I invent things, and I've created *dozens* of things that have made your life better; easier. I've made a very nice living inventing things. I'm gonna have to re-think all that going forward, though.

IT ALL STARTED when I saw a news/org/vid segment on "old people." I lived mostly outside, almost constantly moving, like everyone of my generation. A long weekend on Mars colony? Why not? Jump over to the moon for a party? What should I bring? I make a *mean* carnawan salad!

I had no idea that there was such an impacted segment of our population; one that was virtually confined to their beds. People were regularly living to be 120, 130...even in some cases 150 years old. The rub was that while their minds were generally still sharp, their bodies were used up.

Now, I don't have any sort of genetic or medical background, so I couldn't do anything to strike at the root cause, but my degrees are all in engineering and related fields.

"Surely," I thought, feeling a great deal of empathy. "Surely, there is something I can do to help these poor souls."

I can still recall the segment I watched, showing these old folks... pathetic. Still sharp, still mentally vibrant, confined to beds awaiting the brilliantly cold finger of Death. It really touched me and I resolved to do something; *anything* that would make their lives a bit better.

HAH! What a mistake. I've learned my lesson.

.　.　.

After a few months I'd developed a bed that articulated easily and "levitated" utilizing simple magnetic repulsion. In effect, the beds could... "fly."

In V.2, I also added other invaluable features, like: a built-in food snyth unit, better catheterization, higher power motivation, and better guidance controls. And, since the hovering beds had caused no incidents, I also removed the governors on altitude that I'd built into V.1.

For a short time, I was hailed as some sort of hero. I'd *liberated* all of our parents and grandparents. Stories showing that they were happy and joyous, *while still measured and careful,* cavorting in the skies made the news almost daily. They were free! They were happy! I was happy to help. It's what I do.

They soared in the skies outside, like the rest of us, basking in the sun.

They were happy.

The *Ancients* were no longer bed-ridden or confined to their homes for fear of injury and death.

Beds and old people were now soaring into the skies, happily going wherever they pleased.

Most of the beds didn't even resemble beds any longer. Their design was dictated by the owner and his or her needs and foibles. It was a Macy's Thanksgiving day parade everyday (I'd seen footage of this event on old archives).

Then, they organized.

The good feelings didn't last.

The first fly-in-the-oinment was a new organization that sprung up almost overnight. It was: AYRO "Advanced Year Response Org."

Their *thing* was to insure that *Ancients*- as everyone referred to them now- had all the advantages that we, healthy young and ...independently mobile Americans enjoyed.

There was a little bit of pushback, but everyone eventually agreed that fair is fair and if the *Ancients* wanted to do all the stuff that we wanted to do, well, why not?

Then, they started turning up at stadium concerts, with bullhorns. Loudly and obnoxiously declaring that: *"This isn't music! It's noise!"*

IT WAS GENERALLY AGREED that capping the age of people who actually could purchase tickets would fix this problem, until the *Ancients* demanded that acts such as The Cars, and Boston, who had gone from stadiums to concert halls and finally to Holiday Inns and second rate Indian casinos begin touring again (as this *was* music, we supposed archly); forget the fact that of the ten people, ten band members mentioned in this example, only three were still alive. And they demanded Joe Walsh go back onto the road, despite that he was now happily retired in Monte Carlo with his fifth wife.

Adam Ant was by now using a walker, but being courted nonetheless to do a return tour of all of his hits from the 80's.

The *Ancients* had organized.

They had a voice now.

They were going to be heard!

"SHIT!"

This was what I said under my breath in my open-air workshop as the viddies played from news/orgs, after I heard the latest "demands" from the *Ancients*: Earlybird Dinners were too boring. They wanted better dinners that they could eat at 4:30 and then still hit the sack at 9.

This was received with consternation from many restaurants who already felt their choices were not only varied but designed to nourish an older, more sedentary population.

This was met with derision and anger. Oldsters who had dined in Canton and Montenegro were not satisfied with deep fried tofu or some anonymous fish! They wanted sophisticated choices of meals...from Denny's et al, *and at a reasonable price, dammit!*

Ancients hired ancient lobbyists, and PR agencies that were geared toward getting the "old is better" message out.

IN MERE MONTHS, it seemed that there were myriad organizations dedicated to the betterment of the *Ancients.*

Very soon thereafter, there were organizations that saw to the food, entertainment, mobility, health, education and *virtually everything else,* of the older American. And this was not taking place in America only...oh no. This took place *worldwide.*

UNDERSTANDABLY, there were pushbacks.

We younger Americans organized – after a fashion. We were so balkanized and busy that getting 20 or 30 people to commit to *anything* was a major accomplishment.

We were all so busy that "don't bother me, now" had become a common greeting: "Hi. Don't Bother Me, Now. I'll Call You Later."

In addition, we had our careers; whereas, the oldsters had almost unlimited time and we discovered – almost unlimited patience to organize.

·   ·   ·

WHEN THEY TRIED to reform health care, we responded.

The Ancients were rude and awful to anyone young, assuming that we were part of the problem without even asking.

It didn't take long for a sort of grass roots response to coalesce: Now, *we* were rude and discourteous to any old person we could find. I read of some people my age who went well out of their way to find an Ancient to verbally abuse.

I'm not surprised. All my friends were pretty angry. And after the adulation of a mere eighteen months earlier, most of them had turned that anger on me.

What could I do?

I'm an inventor. I don't determine public policy. I'm sure as hell not a sociologist!

THEN AS AN ORGANIZED PROTEST...THOUGH, I'm still not completely certain what this particular protest was aimed at; The oldsters gathered together in the skies and in, L.A. and NY...

And, they blocked out the sun.

Everyone on the ground went nuts! There were death threats and lots of gunshots into the sky but extremely few slugs actually connected with anything floating above our heads.

The Ancients "camped out" up there for *days,* refusing to even acknowledge any protests or inquiries from the ground.

In a surprisingly short time, other skyrafts, as the Vid/media decided to call them; other radical groups decided to band together in new skyrafts over New Orleans, Chicago, Denver, Tampa, and nearly every other sizable city in the US and progressively, in Canada, and Europe and Asia.

. . .

ON A SIDE NOTE, *Russia had scrambled their air force and under threat of attack had forced the Russian Ancients back to the ground.*

DEMANDS HAD BECOME the daily news ritual. They seemed to emerge from some place or another with the full cooperation and coordination of a large organized and radical populace.

They floated above us and demanded we accommodate them.

I HEARD that some Ancients had *divebombed* people waiting to get into a dance club in Venice and in L.A., throwing <u>full</u> "adult pampers" at the peeps standing in lines!

How did they even "fill" the diapers when the bed took care of everything for them!?

My comlink burned up; there were so many anxious or angry people trying to get through to me.

I received a courtesy call from from my provider. However, when the CSR found out who I was, she became decidedly *discourteous.*

It was *awful.*

I couldn't go home. There were angry Young People camped out there, ready to impale me on hastily sharpened 2x4s.

IT WAS SCARY. I don't want to make this sound as though I made a split-second decision...I was *persona non grata* with nearly all my friends and as time went on, I became more and more aware of the iniquities I was witnessing. I was at a loss as to what to do.

Then, then Oldsters blocked out the sun, again, with their massed beds. In New York, Copenhagen, Houston, Paris, Chicago, San Francisco...

Soon after that...I made up my mind....

I had all the command controls. Hell, I'd invented the damn things that had let them fly over us and make their points.

Since I'd engineered the beds, it wasn't difficult to hack into them.

When at sunrise, they assembled to stave off the light of day yet again to protest in New York, I hit the *engage* button.

***

THERE REALLY WASN'T an accurate count at this writing of the number of beds that fell from the skies that day.

Let's just say that the rest of the Ancients saw their place in the general scheme of things with a much clearer and un-muddied eye.

Then, I got a flickertape parade.

Down Fifth Avenue in New York City.

Cool, huh?

MY NAME IS MIKE. Suddenly I'm a popular guy again. And, I guess... I just did one more thing to make your life better.

Copyright Zaslow Crane
ZaslowCrane.com

8

HOW TO DE-LOUSE YOUR SPACESHIP (IN THREE EASY STEPS!)

...with heartfelt thanks to Professor Jon Pedicino, Astronomy Professor / College of the Redwoods, Eureka, CA

. . .

"EARTH HANDOFF, COME IN."

The vibration, extra grav and noise of the thrusters was finally abating.

The last three minutes was the longest three minutes of Tonya Grill's life.

She opened her mike and spoke with a thick East Texas drawl, "Earth dockmek 12, comeback."

There was a pause. She tried again.

"Earth handoff, we're passing into Space Source Two's sector. Acknowledge, please."

"You are entering Space Source Two...acknowledged." The technician on the other end was crisp and precise.

"You'll be out of contact for thirty-three minutes, please re-establish contact ASAP with International Far Earth Two after that time period."

"Of course. We'll get right back to y'all... Be ready. We'll be on top of our ...stuff."

"Roger that, Mars Leap 4. We'll be standing by."

"Excellent. Leap 4 out for now, back-atcha in 33."

She closed the mike.

TONYA FELT the gravity fall away as she discontinued the burn of the rockets. She was saving the fuel for when it was really needed...like when they were nearing the Mars station at Tharsis Plain and for corrections as they drew closer to Mars.

"Far Earth Station coming up in 39. Just relax folks. We got nothing to do but enjoy the view. You might wanna check out that little blue ball, 'cause you won't see it up close again before you've had another birthday, maybe two."

Tonya saw rather than heard the other two crew

members unstrapping and getting up to stretch and yes, to look out the windows as their home rapidly receded behind them. Rhonda Saruwatari, seated next to her in the second pilot's position looked at her sideways smiling, "We gonna walk an' talk the Cheyenne way today?"

Tonya made a sour face.

"You mean all official and formal-like? Yeah...for now, and only when they call us. We're still Canaveral Kids right now, but once those Cheyenne types toss a few more missions up, all those stuffed shirts will mellow out. Just watch."

Rhonda was flight engineer and second pilot. She just made a face that expressed a healthy bit of skepticism.

"Rhonda, what's our approximate speed?"

She gently tugged at her black braids as she calculated for the answer.

She idly thought about how important it was to control hair in a no gravity situation, hence in her case--the braids.

A moment later she answered, "Right in the neighborhood of 48932kph, boss."

Claudia P leaned in, "In the *neighborhood?*" She laughed. "Engineers! You call that *in the neighborhood?* That's more precise than the data from our last physicals!"

Rhonda spun slowly and playfully hissed, "Go outside and play."

Claudia was Lead EVA, also repairs and systems expert. She was much bigger and darker than her crew mates, with close-cropped jet-black hair, and an upturned nose that had a few freckles sprinkled across the top.

"Oh, I imagine I'll be going outside before long, and *then* you'll miss me!" She laughed.

Rhonda grumbled, "I doubt it..."

The last crew member was Arna Siggurd. She was second EVA, medic and maintenance, in charge of the air scrubbers and life support. Her face was pale as the moon on a clear winter night with short-cropped black hair that rose on her head like a marine's flattop haircut from nearly 100 years earlier. She was also quite tiny, so she appeared a bit incongruous in her suit without the helmet. She looked almost like a child trying on adult's equipment.

"Cap?"

"Yes, Arna?"

"We're all green across the Big Board; working on the little one ATM and will do so one at a time until I'm finished. I'd estimate another 30 mins or so...."

"While we're on the subject of status checks, Cap...?"

"Rhonda?"

"FYI, Cap, per regs, I checked the cargo, the gussets and gyros; the linkage and internal status..."

"And?"

"All green. I say again, all go, Cap."

"Well that's the reason we're doing this, ladies. It should be a milk run, but if those folks don't get their milk to put on their Cap'n Crunch in the mornings, they get testy. Please monitor all systems as an SOP procedure every six hours."

"Six hours? Cap...Don't you think that's a bit obsessive, after all Arna's work?"

"You know what I think Claudia?"

She sighed audibly, "Yesss, Cap."

"Say it with me then, ladies: "A little paranoia goes a long way."

There was a slightly sullen pause.

"Divide up the monitoring any way you see fit, just make certain I have status of everything in six. Every six. Until then, I'll stay with the comm and drive this train for a while, Claudia and Rhonda you can kick back. Arna, please apprise me when you finish with a status report on the minors, and then you can kick back too."

"Ay, Cap."

***

"Mars Leap 4, please come in."

"Mars Leap 4, here. Is that you Teddy?"

"Tonya? I heard that they'd bumped you and your crew to the front of the line. Congrats!"

"Thanks. I'm…we're anxious to put all that training and all those simulations to use at the Real Deal."

"Real Deal City?" Teddy offered.

Tonya smiled. "We're making progress, but it'll still be years before we can call it a city without a strong sense of irony."

"True that. Anyway, we've been tracking Mars Leap 4, and you're 'go' from everything I see here. You might course correct a couple of degrees for maximum Mars-side braking. Sending data."

"Will do, Teddy. I was waiting until we passed you. Didn't want to scrape your lovely paint job."

"Ha. Ha. We're the only pale blue thing out this far. We want you to be able to find us easily if you need to."

"Always thoughtful."

"That's why Ellie married me."

"I'm sure…"

"Ummm, Tonya, you also seem to have a little wiggle in your rear end."

"Why Teddy, you old sweet talker!"

Teddy plodded on despite Claudia's attempt at joking with him.

"But it's well within parameters. Just something to watch, probably nothing…."

There was a pause in the transmission and Teddy added another thought, "Just residual from launch and hitch. It'll subside in time, I'll bet."

"Exactly what I was thinking. I've seen this before out here. It'll quiet." Tonya wasn't worried.

"One last thing, Tonya."

"Go ahead Teddy."

"That Solar activity that was in the preliminary reports... Just before your lift off...?"

"Yeah?"

"Well our good old sun is ramping up. We'll keep you apprised but be prepared to suit up and shield up."

"Radiation...yeah. Was hoping that it wouldn't get worse, but you're saying that it is worsening?"

"That's a confirmation. Please acknowledge. Solar activity is ramping up. Be prepared to shield."

"Understood. Thanks for the heads up. And, say hi for me, to your lovely wife when you talk to her next."

INTERNATIONAL FAR EARTH Two passed by in the Eternal Dark and Mars Leap 4 was in 'international waters,' with nothing ahead of them at all for over a month; nothing except Mars.

THE SHIP SETTLED into a routine with one crew mate always sleeping; one always on duty; one doing monitoring or experiments; and one who had free time. Exercise was strongly encouraged.

Tonya trusted her crew, but they were only human.... *This is the worst part. And this is why I opted for constant monitoring of all systems. This should be boring as Teddy put it, but I want everyone sharp and ready if anything happens...Then there's that damn Solar activity....*

****

A FEW DAYS LATER....

"MARS LEAP 4, please respond. Canaveral to Mars Leap 4 come online."

Rhonda was on comm duty. "Co-pilot Rhonda Diaz here. Come back."

The delay was something that took some getting used to.

"Commander Diaz, please be advised the Solar activity we've been monitoring has become extreme. I say again "extreme." Please acknowledge."

"I understand."

"Canaveral Command has determined that it warrants suits and shields."

"Understood. How long do we have 'til shake and bake time?"

"Two hours, four minutes."

She sighed. *Just time enough to check everything one more time and lock it down into hibernation mode. We'll be flying blind.*

"Thanks, Florida. I'll see to the precautions. Thanks for the heads up."

"Understood. Happy to do it. Be safe."

She smiled grimly. This had been covered in the drills.

She opened the ship's comm and relayed the news.

There was a chorus of groans. They all knew that this might happen; they just hoped it wouldn't.

"Shields too?" Tonya asked. She'd been lying down and unstrapped from her bunk poking her head out of her 'cabin.'

"Yeah, they said Canaveral wants shields too."

Tonya shook her head.

"Okay everyone... Arna, Systems check. Rhonda Ops check."

"Ay Cap."

"Claudia, please run diagnostics on all our suits, and when you've finished, break out the shields."

***

THE THING about gamma waves is that they pass right through almost everything. They don't arrive like a Doppler-shifting fire truck with loud noises and lights and activity. They arrive and leave, and you wonder: Is this it? Your primitive brain speculates: If I can't see or hear anything, does it exist?

In a word, "Yes."

What you can't see or hear or touch can still kill. This was why they had the shields specially manufactured to protect them in just such an event.

They were trained on where and how to position them between the Sun and their bodies and while not perfect, they reflected over 95% of the harmful radiation.

The ship was shielded against all sorts of 'normal' radiation; it would be impossible to completely shield the ship from this much activity. Much more efficient to stow in the shields--one per crew member.

Rhonda consulted the readings. "Uhhh, Cap?"

"Yeah?"

"Looks like Canaveral was right on the money. The

vector coordinates and time frame were damn near perfect. Looks like we'll be in the clear, in two, no three minutes."

"Noted. Everyone log your exposure readings, and compare them with your baselines. I want to check to make certain that we've suffered no long-term damage."

Claudia was next in the comm. "After crouching holding a shield in front of me for an hour, I darn well hope not!"

"As do we all, Ms. P."

"So I can stow the Roman legionnaire shields now?"

"Yes. Please do."

Claudia paused. "Wait. Everyone... Heads up. I want to make certain that nobody is going to go all "Incredible Hulk" here today." She paused for effect.

"Wait...wait...me feel...*funny.*"

Claudia rose slowly from her crouch, and rumbled, "Hulk...smash!"

Rhonda laughed, "Of course, it had to be you, Claud."

"Hulk not find humor in that remark."

***

22 DAYS INTO THE FLIGHT, and Earth was a receding blue ball behind them; Mars was still a tiny rust colored ball slowly growing and resolving details, ahead.

Arna was the duty officer. "Uhhh, Cap?... Getting some weird readings from the hull skin captures."

Tonya who was on down time, exercising, roused herself. Rhonda paused in doing more experiments in Zero G.

"Weird? How... weird? What are you seeing?"

"Well, nothing...exactly. Exterior sensors are gathering info...just as they normally would... I can't explain it. I'm seeing a slight but noticeable degradation in hull integrity in numerous areas…"

"Degradation? Should we be worried?"

"It's tiny. But to go along for so long with all the numbers rock solid, and then one day it changes? That change worries me."

"Me too. Maybe it's time for a look-see."

Tonya looked around for Claudia, who had already risen and was breaking out her EVA gear.

"Claudia P to the rescue, folks! No need for applause, just remember me fondly in your will."

THE EVA GEAR MADE movement slow and difficult; progressing through the airlock tedious. She was finally outside.

On the sun side of the ship, it was blinding. Her sensors automatically darkened her visor and she tied off on one of the many secure points with her carabiner.

"Ok, Arna. Guide me. Where are you sensing these anomalies?"

The 'skin' of the ship was sort of like human skin in some ways. If one were to take a toothpick and poke a section of skin, your brain would have a close idea of where that 'poke' was.

Arna's readouts were similar. Sensors were buried every few inches all over the ship.

"Forward…"

Arna monitored Claudia's progress in exterior cams. "Still can't see anything, but there has to be something there… More forward."

Claudia clambered forward, tying off again with a new line and then untying with her old.

Finally Arna spoke, "Stop. You should be right on top of one of the areas."

Tonya spoke next, "Do you see anything? Can you put what you see on your chestcam, so we can see it as well?"

"Sure thing, Cap. One sec."

Then, "There you go!"

"I...don't see anything..."

"You have to lean in close...There's some sort of ...scuzz. Say, when was the last time you guys ran this heap through a car wash?"

"What do you see?" Tonya demanded.

"Well...the exterior finish is...tarnished a bit... Right there at the seams...there seems to be some scum accumulated...." She couldn't keep the wonder out of her voice.

"Tarnished?" Tonya muttered.

This ship has been in Earth orbit for months awaiting the hookup with the Mars supplies and the 'go' from Canaveral. Before that it was new. Right out of the showroom...new spaceship smell and everything!

"Can you scrape off a bit and bring it in? We might examine it and learn something important."

"Sure. I'll go back for my tool kit. I 'parked it' outside the lock, just in case I needed something. I've got a few tools that might work, depending on how tough this stuff is...."

***

THEY BROUGHT in a sample and subjected it to the best anti-contamination procedures they could manage on a non-research tasked ship.

Finally, Arna was examining the specimen under a microscope. She murmured in surprise, "Tardigrades?"

"Tartigrades? What are Tartigrades?" Claudia asked.

Arna looked 'up' at her. "Extremophiles. They can live almost anywhere. Normally in lichen and so forth…."

"We're pretty thin in the lichen department out here, Arn…."

"But they've been proven to be able to live anywhere."

"In space?"

"There are instances of crew members needing to clean them off a window on the original space station…."

Arna paused. "But that's not the disturbing part…."

Rhonda leaned in.

"We have space hitchhikers who can live on the outside of our ship--*in space*--and that's not the disturbing part?"

Rhonda was unable to keep the disbelief from her voice. This was not orderly and explainable. It bothered her.

Arna looked around to each of her crew mates. "Tardigrades are microscopic."

"Yeah…?"

"Really, really tiny…."

Get on with it! Tonya thought.

"The really weird part is that I didn't need to magnify them very much at all to see what Claudia brought in. If you look really closely, you can just make them out…And that's without a microscope."

"So they're big now?" Tonya prompted.

"Yes. And…they're *growing.*"

"Growing? I don't understand. In order for life, as we know it, to exist, there needs to be an energy source, a stable environment, liquid water and… a food source."

Suddenly she put together all the information that was presently available.

"Oh my God!! *They're eating the ship?!*"

Arna gestured feebly, "I…I think that's it."

Rhonda was incensed. "Their food source is the ship?"

"I think so. Yes."

"Thoughts on how this happened?" She looked at the other two crewmates.

"Canaveral does its best to keep Ops sterile but there's only so much they can do," Rhonda began.

Claudia jumped in with her thoughts, "The solar activity. I was joking about The Hulk, but that may be what has happened. Maybe those bugs *mutated*. And if they get bigger, they need more food; more food, more reproduction...more, more, more...pretty soon...*no more us.*"

"Okay, Claudia, as soon as you're honestly ready to go back out, go. Don't rush yourself. I don't want accidents because of you or anyone else, being tired. Now that you know what you're looking for, Arna can guide you. Get us an idea of how badly we're infested. Capture as much as you can on your chestcam. Once we know what we're facing and have some idea of how bad it is, I'll apprise Canaveral. Rhonda, you and I will assist Arna on this. She is the lead. Let's get these bugs under control."

"Yeah...We're a bit far out of town to call in an exterminator..."

***

"I've tried heat, then cold. It's 2.7 Kelvin out there, so I didn't think cold would do anything but ...you know... covering my bases."

"How about chemical agents?"

"There are so few chemicals that are usable in a vacuum, and that we might have...and some are radically changed by a vacuum, so, thus far, I held off on chemical agents...."

"Yeah, I get it. Keep me posted."

"Of course, Cap."

"How about radiation?"

"Well, since that was how we got here, I was holding off on that too…."

"X-rays?"

Arna fidgeted a bit, unused to so much scrutiny.

"Well, there was an X-ray component of the gamma bombardment… So, no, I didn't try that. Visible light doesn't seem to bother them, in fact they might like being inside… I was going to try infrared…sound, but nothing has even bothered them. I confess, I'm worried, Cap."

"Me too Arna, but I'm not giving in yet. Keep at it."

"Ay, Cap."

***

"WE MUST HAVE HAD a few onboard when we launched. Then they went into hibernation while Mars Leap was being readied. My best guess is that the gamma rays did, in fact, cause them to mutate. Now, they seem to be resistant to anything I've tried to degrade their ability to grow and reproduce. I'm still trying things… I confess, that I'm running out of ideas, though…."

"Thanks, Arna. Keep at it. We're not at 'scrub' yet. Canaveral seems to think that we could detach our cargo and fling it at Mars and turn around and limp home. We're still working on the rate of infection, and since their growth rate seems to grow unabated as well as their individual size, it's difficult to assess and arrive at a contagion rate. The contagion rate will eventually tell us how long 'til hull breach."

. `.` .

***

OVER THE NEXT few days Claudia and Rhonda suited up and EVA'd. Even though Arna was EVA two she was tasked with finding something that the Tartigrades didn't like.

Arna marveled at the figures onscreen in front of her. "They've established a sort of thermal equilibrium, even out there…almost absolute zero," she pointed to the wall of the ship.

"We have Nomex III built into the innards of the skin to protect from excess heat. Maybe Heat? Maybe a lot of heat will dislodge them…."

The comm crackled, "Uhhh, Arn?"

"Yeah Rhonda?"

"There'll be no convection or conduction, so it'll have to be all radiation. Maybe we can slowly spin the ship to maximize the heat of the sun, then…."

Claudia cut in. "Give me an hour. I have an idea! Rhonda, I'm going to get some tools. Meet me at solar collector eight."

"Eight?"

"It's the easiest one to take out of the circuit and dismount."

Rhonda finally envisioned Claudia's idea, "Yes!"

In mere…well…hours, this *is the vacuum of Space* they were working in; the solar panel was being used as a giant reflector beaming down a great deal of radiant energy upon the 'bugs.'

Meanwhile Arna had tried a light source and an optical element that served as a magnifying glass.

Tonya looked over her shoulder, "Ever roast ants with a magnifying glass when you were a kid?"

Arna was aghast, "No that would be willful and horrible. Ants are benign creatures!"

"Okay, forget I asked."

***

MEANWHILE, a few meters and worlds away at the same time, Claudia and Rhonda had wrestled the huge but flimsy foil "wing" around to catch the full sun.

"Angle it down a bit," Rhonda instructed.

"I can actually distinguish individuals now," Claudia said in awe.

"Not good."

"No sh... right. Not good."

"Arn?"

"I'm here, Rhonda."

"Any positive results with your ant roasting in there?"

"Why does everyone talk about roasting ants? What were your childhoods like?"

"Sorry I asked. Any promising reactions from...our subjects?"

There was a pause.

"Inconclusive. The heat and brightness seem to inhibit breeding but not growth. They need dim lighting to mate? Sounds familiar...."

"Keep it professional, Ms P. This is serious."

"You got it."

"Sorry."

"It's okay but be the pros are. You've got a big reflector in full sun. Blast those guys. See if they die."

"Heating them up!"

***

. . .

CLAUDIA FROWNED and the disappointment showed plainly on her face.

"After a while, Rhonda and I gave up. I couldn't see any improvement. So, we put the reflector back and re-aligned it. I went back into my tool kit and just started scraping them up and scraping them onto another putty knife back and forth until they fall off and fall behind."

"Slow work."

"Yeah. Too slow. Plus, I can't get them all. There's always some down in the cracks and crevices; enough for that colony to start again."

"Let's wake Cap up and see what she wants to do next."

"No. Let's not. She's been up working on this for over two days straight. She got cheated out of her sleep shift. Let her sleep."

Rhonda looked over at her compatriots. "Okay as Tonya says: "Ideas?"

***

"READY TO ELECTRIFY."

The three crew members, tired themselves, had decided to jury-rig a line from the generator and secondary power center to the ship's skin. Being metal, they hoped that 320 volts DC that the ship and its solar array generated, would shock the Tartigrades into leaping off the "hot" ship with their eight stumpy legs.

Rhonda had taken over in the interim.

"Shut everything down. I want everything 'safed' before we light up our little home away from home."

"Ready. We're on isolated minimal power. Even the life support is offline, so don't mess around too long okay?" Arna smiled nervously.

Rhonda nodded with guarded satisfaction.

"Okay. Claudia, please, go gently wake skipper and tell her to lie still and don't let her touch anything metal, just in case. Everyone else, I'm counting down from ten, then we'll have a ten second 'burn' and then 'off.' Then we run everything back up and Claudia or I will go outside to check on them to see if we're bug free.

Claudia crept quietly into the tiny bulkhead room. "Skipper? Skipper? Don't move, okay? We're going to try to burn these little bastards off our hull. Don't move."

"Wait. What?"

"We just want you to be safe. Don't get up. You might touch metal."

"What are you doing?"

"We're electrifying the hull."

"What? No!"

Meanwhile Rhonda had started the count down. 4... 3...2...1...

"Belay that order! Now!"

Tonya was floating in her doorway, having shoved a woman twice her size out of the way in order to get to Control.

"Standing down."

Rhonda seemed dejected.

"Did Canaveral okay this plan?"

She looked right at Rhonda.

"Well, no, but they didn't seem to have any ideas, we're waiting longer and longer imagining them scratching their pointed heads, and we're in totally new territory with these things. We talked it out and it seemed like a good idea."

Tonya walked over to the lab area. "Did you try electrocuting these guys in the lab? Do you know what will happen? Isn't it possible that the energy that you flush through the ship will further nourish these guys?"

"We discussed it. It seemed to us that if we gave them everything we had; it might just be too much for them to absorb."

"Did you *test* it first?" Tonya said pointing to covered petri dishes fastened with Velcro to a worktable.

Rhonda was going to plead her case but relented.

"No. No we didn't. We figured that this was almost our last shot to get free of this infestation. Who knows what they are capable of? Besides how would we calculate a baseline charge for something so small and factor it up for an entire ship? Exponentially that'd be a factor of hundreds, or more- much more- if we calculated based on the mass of the ship, instead of the area of the skin."

"Mightn't it be that the energy represented by a huge charge of electricity and a blast from a bursting sunspot might be almost the same to such a simple animal? I'm disappointed…disappointed in all of you for not running tests first. Who knows what might have happened if you guessed wrong? You were gambling with all our lives, and even endangering the settlers on Mars."

Tonya would have said more but she noticed an alarm. It began, slowly quietly, then began to build.

"What now?"

Claudia was nearest to the readout.

"Damn, boss. Minor hull breach. We're losing air."

Tonya scratched her head and rubbed her eyes impatiently.

"Okay everyone suit up. Fire up all systems except life support. Claudia, you and I are going to go see these little *bastards* in their *natural habitat.*"

"Yessir."

No one had ever heard so much as the mildest curse from Tonya's lips before, and it spurred them to their jobs as nothing else might have.

***

TONYA SURVEYED the skin of her ship and the 'infected' areas. Then she looked at her tools.

"This is what we're down to? Pathetic. Putty knives, tube sealant and duct tape. Granted the sealant-tar really and duct tape has been re-imagined for use in space but that's what it is. Tar and duct tape. Scrape those little killers off there so I can slap on a coat of sealant and tape over it. I'd very much like to keep our air inside where we live."

"Yes, ma'am."

Claudia scraped back and forth on the knives until the black goo that they knew to be hundreds of growing bugs fell away from them. They were still traveling at the same speed but so long as they had no mode of propulsion save for their legs a few meters might as well be miles.

"I realize that tarring over them might only slow down their growth and reproductive cycles but I'll take what I can get!"

"Maybe the tar will kill them."

"Maybe." Tonya sounded dubious.

"Cap?" Arna's voice sounded almost childlike over the comm.

"What?"

"Another leak. Approximately thirty meters aft and starboard from your position."

"Understood."

Then her comm went offline for a moment. From her

posture Claudia could only assume that she was howling in rage and frustration, but like that old movie poster once said: "In Space, no one can hear you scream."

***

"I'm out of tar for now Arna. Also low on tape. Please tell me that you're finished with the alarms for today."

"Nothing new, Cap."

"Humph. Sixth time's the charm I guess, now that we've ghetto'd this beautiful ship up with the space equivalent of bondo and primer. We're coming in."

" Yes, please do. I've noticed something odd."

"Define *odd* Arna. I know you're from Iceland, but don't leave me in suspense, give me a ray of hope if that's what you've got."

"Excuse me?"

Tonya sighed in frustration, but said none of the things that came to mind.

"Okay. We'll try it this way. Odd that is good, or odd that is worse than today has already been? We've got to get to handoff at Mars."

"Might be good odd. Might…be…something…."

"I'll be right there."

***

"Okay, I agree. These little guys look unhappy. No motile activity. Reproduction has slowed to a crawl, judging by the footage from earlier today. What did you do?"

Arna looked sheepish, "That's just it. I didn't do anything. This is a comparatively new batch culled from our testing stock."

"You must have done *something.*"

"I've been wracking my brain; gone over every step…."

Tonya thought for a moment. "Okay then, we'll help. Rhonda, throw the cabin cam up on the monitor. Let's back up the clock to say, late yesterday. Claudia, please make us all something to eat. We're going to sit here until we figure what made these little guys so unhappy, because we need them all to be really, *really* unhappy!"

Tonya thought about the crew electrifying the ship and shuddered. If it had worked, great, but if it 'fed' them as she suspected, then they all would be saying their goodbyes to friends and family right about now. *I'm not ready to die. And I sure don't want to die in space; I want to be an old lady who dies in her bed.*

***

THEY FELT the hours grind by, but stayed at it because they knew that they might be on the brink of something.

Finally, Tonya's eyes, now red and tired, bugged out.

"Wait! There. Go back."

"What? What?"

Since the cam went to whoever had made the last motion or had spoken, it was constantly shifting; following the action. Sometimes what Arna was doing was in the foreground, sometimes not.

"There. The cleaning. You skipped a step."

"I did? I must have been tired."

Tonya's blue eyes danced. "You got tired and we might

have just gotten lucky! Go back again…right…right…there! I was watching your routine. You skipped a step in cleaning. What is that step?"

"It's a rinse. I bleach everything so any traces of the earlier solutions are cleaned, then I do a complete and thorough rinse." She paused and her jaw dropped as the enormity of what she'd discovered hit her, right between the eyes. "*I skipped the rinse. Bleach! Bleach kills them!*"

"Bleach?" Claudia couldn't get her head around this new information.

"Sure, why not?" Rhonda said, grinning ear-to-ear. "The common cold killed the Martians."

"It did? When was that?"

"Around 1900 or so. You've never read War of the Worlds?"

"Clearly my education was lacking. What's that got to do with bleach?"

"It's the Tartigrades' Kryptonite!" Rhonda smirked.

Claudia nodded. "Okay. That one I get."

Tonya was suddenly optimistic.

"Arna, please administer a quarter of a dropper full of bleach on this colony."

THEY BEGAN DYING ALMOST IMMEDIATELY. In moments, none of them stirred.

"Let's try some older, maybe more established, more robust colonies."

Each time, there was almost instant death.

"Well, that's something," Tonya said. She allowed for the first really full deep breath she had taken for days.

"That's all well and good, but we can't use bleach 'outside;' the liquid will boil away before it even reaches them."

Rhonda's bright eyes were hooded and guarded.

"It won't even pour, Boss."

"Okay. Right…you're right. Okay. Claudia…Everyone… calm. This, at least is a weapon. Now we need to find a way to deploy it."

A cheer rose up among the crew. Then when it died down. Tonya said, "Quiet a sec. What's that?"

Indeed, now that it was as quiet as the ship got, there was a small noise; a scraping sound mixed with the *push* of air and a small status indicator noise. It was very small and difficult to get a fix on.

"You don't suppose…?" Claudia looked around trying hard to pinpoint the source.

It was from outside.

"Okay. That's it! We are now officially on the clock. Find me a way to stop these things!"

Only then did the alarms begin.

Thanks, but we've got it. Tonya thought grimly.

***

THE VIEWSCREEN LIT up Rhonda's face. "Boss! I found it!" Rhonda shrieked in delight.

"What? What?" Tonya had dozed off and was fast asleep on her forearm while still seated at the common room table.

She wiped a bit of drool off her face that due to lack of gravity had smeared her cheek in the oddest way.

"I thought I remembered some unusual stuff on the colonists' manifest."

She held the tablet up for her boss to read.

"What? I don't see it."

Rhonda, with two fingers, expanded the view so that an entire page of data was blown up on the tablet's screen;

blown up to focus on a single entry. All that was left to read on the screen, standing alone on a solitary line: "Ajax Cleanser 10 gross/ 16oz/ 12/case/cardboard wrapped."

"Okay. I'm sleepy. Ajax? As in cleaning your shower?"

"Ajax is mainly sodium carbonate…."

"Yeah?"

"Bleach is sodium hypochlorite. Sodium Carbonate and hypochlorite are damn close. It might be close enough!"

Tonya brightened.

"And…Ajax is a powder. It contains no…liquid!"

Tonya's eyes widened excitedly.

"It *is* a powder! I'll bet you a walk to cargo, *outside,* that this will do it!"

"They wanted this ancient stuff on Mars, when they could have had NASA's latest and greatest?"

"I remember reading something about them trying to keep whatever chemicals they import as simple as possible to mitigate Martian exposure to Earth 'pollutants'…."

Tonya considered. "Okay, that makes sense. Okay we'll go get some."

***

"Oh boy. If you all think it's bad at the ship, it's worse back here with cargo." Tonya's comm sounded awestruck and sad at the same time.

"We're going to need to park in orbit and figure out how to make our delivery."

"After all this, we aren't going to dock?"

"I've got to test every handhold and fasten point before I hook onto it. The *rot* these…Tartigrades caused is extensive. It looks like they eat everything!"

At this, a section of a strut came away in her hand. She could see Tardigrades writhing at both ends. Carefully she tossed it away from the ship.

"Listen up, people. We're contaminated. The Mars Leap 4 will never make planetfall ever again. We can't risk taking these voracious bugs anywhere. We can't land. In fact, I *hope* we get her fixed enough to take her home. But this ship may be beyond saving. Anyway, after that, if it were me, I'd aim her at the sun and jump out after I set the rockets' burn."

"No!"

"I can't think of any better ideas."

"Aw, Cap. Your first ship..."

"Yeah, I know. Sucks don't it? How's it going in the repair department?"

"Oh, you know, tar and duct tape, scrape and scrape..."

"I remember it well."

Tonya tuned her attention to moving purposefully but carefully toward Cargo.

Another strut section came off in her hand. Suddenly she saw dozens of black bugs, each the size of a ladybug or bee scrambling all over her glove.

Frantically, she brushed them off knowing that this was *bad.* She swatted and brushed them off, but because the contrast outside was so stark, she couldn't tell how successful she was.

I couldn't have gotten lucky and cleaned them all off. That would be asking too much.

She fastened herself to a sturdy section and pulled out her duct tape dispenser and wrapped her glove and sleeve around and around. Then she removed the duct tape, noticing a dozen or so black shapes slowly wriggling, trying to get free. She balled up the duct tape and gently pitched it off the ship.

She taped herself again and caught a few more, tossing that one away as well. She stifled a nervous giggle.

***

"MARS LEAP 4, please be advised. I am now entering cargo bay 3. Gotta go get us some extra special cleaner."

"Roger that, Boss."

"Good hunting," Arna spoke from Claudia P's side.

"If it's where it's supposed to be it, shouldn't take me long."

***

"MAYDAY! MAYDAY!"

"Cap! What's wrong?"

"I found it. I'm on my way back and the place I tied off broke away! I'm floating. Drifting. There are loose *bugs* everywhere!"

"Stay calm, Cap. I'll come get you!" Rhonda volunteered.

"No, Rhonda. There are already two of us out here. We can get to her faster."

"Claudia, you've already been tasked with something important. We only have so much air. If you plug leaks, we get to keep most of it. I have time and I'm going."

"Ay, Cap, uhh, Rhonda."

Then three clicks: "Coming, Boss."

"Not making any fast moves though they're on me. It's only a matter of time until I suit-leak because of these...*these*...."

In the comm background everyone could hear the null pressure alarm.

They could hear Tonya panting, trying to keep her head.

"Get off me!" she shouted.

"Go ahead and vent boss. I'm coming with the winch and line. One problem at a time. We'll get the bugs off you, ASAP."

WITH THAT, Rhonda stepped out of the airlock in her EVA suit and moved over to the winch mechanism installed next to the door.

She accessed her remote on her cuff, and clipped the winch end onto her suit, then began spooling line out.

So long as I don't flail about too much, I should have plenty of line; hell, I should have enough line to reach all the way to the thrusters if I want--which I don't!

She played out the line; the first section of the cargo gantry she touched with her boot, crumbled.

Tiny specks drifted away from the disturbed portion of the ship's cargo structure.

Shit!

She found a solid spot and kicked gently while playing out more line.

"Boss? You still there?"

"Sure am. Where are you?"

"Right at the beginning of cargo."

"Okay, I'm turning on all my suit lights. I'm a few meters forward of bay three, off to starboard a bit. Maybe four meters."

"Coming."

Rhonda played out more line.

"Shit!"

"What?"

"Can't you hear my suit?! Suit-breach. I'm betting that it's one of many that's in my future."

"Coming."

"My readings say that it's small...Oh here it is."

She unspooled some duct tape, burnished it on the semi-flexible fabric and the leak slowed to a crawl.

"I'm passing bay two. Almost there."

She passed by a stabilizer-thrust unit and saw Tonya's lights. The radiance seemed to waver and flicker. Rhonda unspooled more line. As she drew closer, she realized why the lights on Tonya's suit seemed so odd. There was a swarm of bugs around her! *Hundreds! Thousands!*

Tonya saw the bugs as well; she was so close that it was more difficult for her.

"I see you. Don't come any closer!" Tonya shouted into the comm. "It's some sort of swarm. They are keying on me, not the ship. I have no idea why! You can't come now. You'll die too!"

More alarms rang through the comm system.

"Aww, dammit, another leak!"

Everyone could hear the dread and the *acceptance* taking over her voice.

Rhonda saw her hastily slap a duct tape patch on her leg and got an idea.

"Boss unspool a whole bunch of tape and wave it around--keep it away from you, but wave it around. Use it to catch those guys!"

"Love it! Old time fly paper!"

"I guess..."

She ripped off a two-meter length and waved it around trapping quite a few but leaving maybe a thousand, maybe more. It was impossible to tell.

Tonya gently tossed the tape away.

"Do it again Tonya, especially in front of you!"

Meanwhile, Rhonda carefully found a secure place to tie herself off.

"Clear out the area between you and me with the tape!"

"I will in a minute. Got another leak! Dang! They ate a hole in my helmet?"

"At least the tape will get a good seal on that smooth surface."

"Yeah. There's that. You should be a politician Rhonda. Excellent spin control." She tapped her helmet as she finished burnishing the tape on it.

"Okay waving more tape, capturing more hungry buggies."

"All right, I think we're out of time."

"What?!"

"No. I meant... We need to get you inside. You have too many leaks to deal with. I'm going to throw this line to you. You're going to catch it. Then you're going to clip it on your suit and I'm going to pull you, *fast,* out of that cloud. We should leave most of them behind, wondering where you went!"

"Okay!"

Rhonda carefully threw the line at her captain. The first time it was wide. The second time it got hung up on a broken strut...

The fifth time Tonya caught it and wasted no time in clipping in.

"Okay, boss, on your way back- and this is important- since I will have no good way back, you're going to grab me with your free hand. I'll reel us in, you'll hold onto me."

Tonya laughed; a self-deprecating chuckle.

"You make it sound so easy. Did I ever tell you that I got kicked off my baseball team when I was ten? I couldn't even catch an infield pop-up."

"Well, you're going to prove them all wrong in about a minute."

"I'm ready. Get me out of here!"

With that, Rhonda hit the 'reel in' command at nearly full speed. Tonya shot forward out of the swarm and at Rhonda who now floated free, waited like a defensive end, who has a runner coming at her.

They hit with a solid *whump* that partially knocked the breath out of both. Rhonda let up on the control. Tonya held on!

As soon as they knew that the plan had succeeded, Rhonda reeled them in, pausing just outside the lock. However, it was easy to see that the plan hadn't been 100% successful; little black dots ambled all over Tonya and a few were now on Rhonda's suit as well! And even more frightening, some little black dots on Tonya had become stationary. That told her some were burrowing into Tonya's suit!

"Boss! They're eating their way into your suit!"

"I know! Spin me around me, Rhonda."

She did.

"Reach into the bag and get out a can."

She did.

"If I remember right, these *cans* were made with cardboard sides. Grab one and twist counterclockwise. It should…explode, sort of."

In moments, they were enveloped in a whitish powdery cloud.

"Christ, I hope this works!"

"If it doesn't, we're pretty much done, so pray while you make a mess with that stuff!"

"I'm praying! I'm praying!" With one hand, Rhonda kept a firm grip on a railing with the other, she dumped one, then, a second can on her boss. Then, just for good measure, Tonya dumped one on herself.

Tonya spun slowly and looked directly into Rhonda's faceplate, unable to see her eyes.

"Do not open that airlock if you see any of these little bastards alive!"

"They're all over you."

Black dots the size of bees speckled Tonya's EVA suit.

"You're still covered, Boss."

Tonya went silent. Rhonda could almost hear her sob. Then, her demeanor changed, and she was 'The Boss' again.

"Damn. Then we're done here. I order you to take command of the ship. I'll stay outside. I will not contaminate our one chance to live!"

"Wait. Boss?"

"Yeah?"

"The spots. They're all over you. But they don't seem to be moving."

Rhonda tried to brush them off. Most were attached and partway through the suit's fabric.

"Shit," Rhonda said impressed.

"What?"

"Boss, I think they're all dead."

"Really? Really? Are you sure? That's great!"

"Well, the contrast...I can't see that well."

Commander Saruwatari reached out and brushed some of the bugs off her Captain.

"Yeah. About thirty of them were partway through your suit. I can't brush them off with my hand!"

While she was absorbing this, Tonya did a quick check of Rhonda's suit brushing off all but one black spot.

She leaned her helmet against her commander's, trying to look into her eyes.

"Thirty potential leaks?"

"I hate to guess, but I'm just estimating at the actual number. The light out here isn't so good...."

Thirty potential leaks?

Tonya shuddered, then began a brittle and disbelieving giggle.

"Better get the bag of Ajax up to the girls…" She gestured to the top of the hull.

"I'm going to go inside, strip, jettison everything I'm wearing, take a shower and just for good measure, I'm gonna shave my head!"

"Can't be too careful, Boss!" Rhonda grinned.

With that she tied off and clambered 'up' to find the tar-and-duct-tape crew.

"Arna, Claudia, I have something that will brighten your day…."

"Is it Kryptonite?"

"Close enough."

"Excellent!"

Rhonda imagined that she could hear a cheer from Tonya inside the ship as well.

***

TONYA OPENED the comm with the Red One, huge in front of them.

"This is Commander Tonya Grill, of Mars Leap 4. Mars Far station handoff Two, glad t'see your beacon in the dark! How has Mars been lately?"

"Cold and red, Ma'am, cold and red."

"Understood, Mars Far Station."

"Commander Grill, The Mars Base settlers will certainly be glad to hear that you've arrived!"

The tech in the Mars space station awaiting them paused

a moment. Then- "I heard from Canaveral that you had a bit of a difficult transit this time."

Tonya smiled and rubbed her smooth pate. She looked around the cabin at three other cleanly shaved heads.

"Yeah. Yeah, you could say that. We're here with your supplies, but the settlers not going to be able to scrub their showers, though."

"Excuse me, Commander?"

"Never mind. Please put me through to your on-duty station manager."

9

THE JUGGLER

My name is Richard Hartford; "Father Rick" to my parish-
ioners, (who, I'm sorry to say, I get to see less and less these
days) and "Examiner Hartford" to Cardinal Sanchez, head of

the L.A. Diocese, and, to The Pope, for whom I ultimately work.

My parish is in San Pedro, an L.A. suburb, but my real *territory* is... the World.

In recent years it seemed to me, and my team, that everyday there was more and more evidence of something bad; something very bad coming.

Oh, humanity wasn't any better or worse than usual...In truth, privately, I despaired of making any big difference so long as I, a priest, was forced to "work retail," that is, one at a time salvations or even one at a time sending someone off in the right direction after detecting them "going toward the darkness."

Even though scriptures tell us that the Second Coming will probably also end this earth, *and it is a pretty place with a race of ingenious and creative individuals,* I still yearn for a Savior; someone who can work "wholesale" and make a huge difference to multitudes all at once.

It makes so much sense. Consequently, I sometimes feel so insignificant.

But I digress, and though it *is* relevant, the state of Mankind per se is not what I'm referring to. Oh, it is part and parcel of the problem, but only a part.

I turned 40 last month, and it seems that, in my lifetime, each year as I've aged a bit more, that there were just a few more disasters, wars, famines than the previous one. In the last few years it is as though whatever cycle there is, has sped up; and sped up considerably.

"EXAMINER HARTFORD?"

I felt invaded. It was as if someone had snuck up on me in the dark to scare me. I was deep in thought at my desk, but anyone calling on this line had to be important. I steeled myself.

I didn't need to access the holocontrols to guess who was calling. The voice was distinctive and truth be told, I was expecting Cardinal Sanchez to call, demanding an update.

I tapped my leftmost incisor against the lower number 22 tooth and activated the vidfone connection in the corner of my eye. I could see him as easily as if he were seated at a chair in front of my antique Ikea desk.

"End of Days" was a phrase that had been bandied about by one news media outlet after another when the media splintered in the mid-teens. Instead of the shock of one major outlet calling you out, you died the "Death Of The Thousand Cuts" from the ancient Chinese culture. One after another as each of these tiny but not insignificant newsorgs attacked, awaiting a chance for a coup; to use an antiquated term: "a scoop."

CONSEQUENTLY, the idea, *any idea,* once it "caught" never truly went away. I expect that that was on his Excellency's mind today. After all, he's been privy to all my data since last week. It was time.

"Yes, Excellency. I'm here ready to speak with you."

The connection solidified.

"Call me Raul, Rick. It's just us. No need for so much formality."

Crap. Informal Raul. Whenever he does that....

"I wanted to touch base with you regarding your, ah... team's findings. I can infer all I want from the data, but data after all... are just data. I need conclusions."

No beating around the bush...How's your day been going? Had any interesting confessions lately? Donations still on a downward trend? Nope. Right to the crux as if he were paying by the hour and wanted to shave off a quarter-hour here, and quarter-hour there... Oh well...

"Okay…Hi, Raul. How's the wife and kids?"

That was a joke I could easily get away with when speaking to my contemporaries. After all the ugliness was apologized for and punished, and even though the Church still hung doggedly onto celibacy, it was nonetheless, a New Day for Mother Church, and any younger priest might have laughed, or at least found humor in the jest.

Sanchez however, was twice my age. He remembered well that bad time for the Church, and I concede that my attempt at humor was probably ill conceived. I could tell if only by the chill in his voice:

"Rick, I've had my people scan the numbers. They'd had their people run them numerous times through existing databases and algorithms in an attempt to predict a trend. Yet, nothing I have, nothing my team has produced, is conclusive. Every way we crunch these… *damned* numbers, there is a factoring that exists outside the paradigm we're trying to create; to discern."

"And because of that, you can't use them to try to predict what will happen next." I hoped that I didn't sound insolent. I felt for the guy. I really did.

"Uhhh. Yes. That's it."

"Yeah. The numbers won't cooperate for us either. Global warming continues unhampered by our efforts. Even though the Midwest is a dustbowl again, and food production is down, "way down," as it is in all the old major food/prod regions across the world, other areas have stepped into the void and kept us fed. And, even though storms, hurricanes, and tornadoes are more common than ever, and more people die from them than ever before, still the birthrate climbs."

"Yes…"

"So no direct inference can be drawn from point A to point B."

"Yes. You're telling me things I already know. I pay you to…."

"With all due respect, Excellency, *you* do not pay me." I snapped at him, perhaps a bit too hard, but that's all…*"water over the bridge"* now.

"You supervise me. I am, and have been for five years, in direct Papal employ. I would like to remind you that my exploits just prior to and just after becoming a priest have brought me into their sphere of influence. So, please, with respect, do not try to bully me. We're on the same team. We're working as hard as we can, trying to discern God's Will."

As MUCH OF a jerk as he can be, his plate is far bigger and fuller than mine, and I might guess that I might come off as an obstinate so-and-so sometimes to those beneath me as I press for some inference or insight that is not quite ready to be teased from the mélange of datastrings.

In 1999 WE hit 6 billion. *No problem.* Things were "fine."

By 2011, we here on Earth were seven billion people and we were still… "alright."

In 2019, there existed eight billion people. Things were a tad shaky, but overall we were still "okay." New Year's Day, 2025 saw *nine billion people* and little things began to go wrong but no one put it all together until…We amassed: Ten Billion people. That was two years ago. 2029

YEARS AGO, things started to go bad in earnest: Wars, Floods, Droughts, Famines, all that *Biblical stuff*-everything you read about in school when you were young, *but in spades. Other things; more disturbing things had begun to happen. It started slowly at first, but in the last 6 or 7 years, things had really picked up speed.*

Most troubling was an ever increasing number of newborns being delivered who seemed to be autistic, only semi-sentient, or worse: completely non-responsive mentally, but fully alive. One of my associates had mentioned in passing that perhaps God had only a finite number of souls with which to work, and maybe we'd hit our ceiling.

In public, I'd had waved that thought off, as being ridiculous in saying that by its very definition, an omnipotent being can't have constraints. However, in private that one little innocent comment nagged at me incessantly. What if this was the warning I'd been looking for?

The chill that thought brings revisits my mind and body far more often than I'd like to admit.

LOS ANGELES IS all about a kind of overflow of people. Everywhere I go, there are crowds. I often wonder what it might be like to wander in a pristine forest for a week or more enjoying the complete, utter solitude.

That, of course, is a complete fantasy, though one I hold dear. I live in the L.A. Metro area; and a *fantasy* because I could never afford that much time, that much solitude with so much still to do. I'm convinced that something momentous is happening, or about to occur.

I am a singular entity aware and ready; ready to react when God speaks. Since most days He doesn't, on my "off hours," I live a fairly pedestrian life.

Evenings are spent watching entertainment packages calculated to appeal to the current tastes, whatever that may be this week.

Tastes change as quickly as a startled gecko changes direction.

I watch with only half a mind most evenings, understanding that recreation is important as a way to approach the problem, refreshed and ready for new challenges. Yet I still feel the dread in my very soul; dread that something is coming; coming for me and every man, woman, and child on this floating orb. Coming to *end us.*

It is a feeling that I cannot shake, even though I've paltry data to support any such supposition.

Yet there is enough other data to substantiate and obscure almost any supposition. I can't perceive what is really going on in the background. And in truth, if it is God's direct Will, why would I even suppose I could comprehend?

For instance, last night, I dreamt I was on a raft, made of logs tied together. I had a feeling that this was a sort of important message; that perhaps my sub-conscious was trying to tell me something...Or perhaps God was. Anyway, the water was salty, and so I inferred that I was on an ocean, not a lake. It was fairly dark, so I could not see much and had to rely on other senses. The waves caused me to hold on desperately as the water threatened repeatedly to tear my little raft asunder. The thrashing continued until the lashings holding the logs together began to jangle and rattle ominously against one another. The tiny craft tossed and bucked as if it were a live animal trying to throw me from its back, I held on even though the logs in smashing together from the motion of the waves often smashed my fingers as well.

An albatross flew close by, low and slow in the dimness and seemed to eye me carefully. His black orb of an eye transfixed me and I felt as though I was witnessing something horrible without realizing it. A feeling of dread suffused my mind, body and soul, as feelings often can feel overwhelming in a dream.

I don't know why it disturbed me so, but soon afterwards,

the first log escaped the confines of the rope harness. After that, it was only a matter of minutes until the entire raft began to break apart completely.

Thankfully, I awoke then, though panting and sweating.

I turned to viddies to waste a bit of time and distract myself before attempting sleep again. It took quite some time for my pulse to quiet sufficiently to settle back down on my ergonomic sleep rack.

SINCE EARLY '26, I have been paying attention when I'd decided then that something unmistakably was amiss. Also, I've always been a *devout* man even before accepting the priesthood, but I also have been a scientist, and a statistician. I adore God, but I also adore empirical and unimpeachable data. This is why, I suppose I came to the attention of the Papal Offices.

God is in all things, but it seems to me, He is most present in pragmatic facts. God is the syzygy of Truth, Love, and Knowledge.

I was approached to discretely look into things. *End Of Days things.*

I was to keep my direct superior the Cardinal apprised; but the most salient details, if any should be discovered, were to be transmitted to the Papal Offices themselves and no where else, for the immediate future.

It was this for reason that Cardinal Sanchez and I had a testy relationship. I'm certain that he had his sources in the Vatican, and knew full well that I could not give the same level of detail to him as I transmitted to the Holy Father. It must have rankled mightily.

Again, I forgive him… for being a dick.

· · ·

"*Evenings are for recreation. A changing of gears is important if one is to arise refreshed and ready to effectively deal with the conundrums that the Almighty has placed before us.*"

I recall the gracious Cardinal intoning this often, after evening prayers before I left his employ and joined the Vatican's. And yet, despite how I might feel about the inestimable Cardinal, I feel that he is not wrong.

Evenings, I watch the viddies, usually with some of my peers. We enjoy various parts of the older shows; the newer ones seeming to hold little relevance, though I am at a loss as to explain exactly why. The newer the show or entertainment, the less likely I seem to find it entertaining. Perhaps the simple answer is that I am an "old soul," though in light of my position in the Church, that answer seems a bit...facil.

"Examiner Hartfield, have you made any progress plowing through all the data?"

He paused.

"C'mon, Rick, I have fourteen newsorgs crawling up and down my back for a relevant quote."

End of Days stories. Will they never die; will they ever just dry up and blow away?

"Excellency, there does seem to be some sort of a pattern, but so far it is too subtle for us to discern where it will take us."

"Then tell me your thoughts at least. I'll take it as background. Not for publication."

"Have you tried giving them "Matthew 24-36"?

I could tell that Sanchez was annoyed, but he recited part of the passage anyway: "But about that day or hour, no one knows, not even the angels in heaven, nor the Son, but only the Father".... "Is that the one you're referring to? Of course! I gave that to them long ago. They can look up scripture as well as anyone. They seem to think that while Scripture is carved in stone, maybe they can wheedle or badger a good quote out of a live Bishop."

"Okay. I see your point. However, despite the lack of real, hard data, I do feel that something is there, awaiting my best minds; awaiting the right person to unlock the last door."

My answer didn't satisfy the Cardinal, but I think it was obvious that I was trying; and I wasn't blowing him off. He'd finally gone away again, if only partially satisfied; yet still fully angry with me.

He probably knows if and when I do figure this out, I must run it past the Pope's lieutenants first!

ENTERTAINMENT HAS AGAIN GONE nostalgic of late. These things always seem to go in cycles...However, this time I may have noticed something relevant.

Just as a pendulum swings back and forth; back and forth, so was our penchant for seeking entertainment.

When we (as a culture) first got nostalgic, we went back a decade. For that was a safe distance, easily understood; grasped. Later, we went back even further. Pendulum swinging, even more broadly "daring" us to "keep up" with the swings and be entertained by the novelty of it.

We've recently broached the mid-20th century, the time of black and white images and variety shows.

We watch these long dead people in tacky, badly fitting clothing and unfortunate haircuts and feel *so* sophisticated; *so* superior. We watched acrobats, animal acts, song and dance acts, stand up comedians, and … jugglers. It was entertainment in its simplest, most undiluted form.

However, as I watched the archives with friends or colleagues, a thought began to nag at me. It sat there leering at me in my peripheral, daring me to refute it. Try as I may, I've been unable to do so.

My mind instead, goes back to that first thought, perhaps placed there by God, Himself, finally speaking to me: "What if He is just ...*out of souls?*"

Of course, there is no way to know if this notion has any kernel of truth to it. The only way to ascertain for sure is to wait. And, waiting will be the most difficult thing, if I am correct.

YOU SEE, I began to imagine a God who was not entirely omnipotent. In much the same way that Arthur C. Clark supposed that any civilization sufficiently advanced above another would be perceived as possessing "magic."

What if, I shuddered, God was an incredibly agile and adept *juggler*, really more like a plate spinner? What if He is like one of those guys on old variety shows, who used to stand flexible sticks vertically and spin real plates on them, always getting to a plate just before it slowed enough to fall and instead, re-spun it and kept it from crashing to the hard floor and shattering into a million pieces.

What if that's exactly what He's been doing since the beginning of time? And what if I might think of a plate as representing a billion souls?

If that were true.... At first it was a cakewalk. Yet, as more people began to exist, like popcorn suddenly exploding in a microbag and growing exponentially in size, so did the complexity-of-spinning chores.

Still easy, like the guy I watched on an ancient viddie called: *Ed Sullivan* last night. But now He had become a bit busy. More plates to spin.

Time goes on. More "popcorn" pops and more people

burst upon the scene; more souls needing to be overseen and shepherded.

A billion…two…three…

Piece of cake. It's obvious. He was so good at it; he did an expert job!

Thousands of years going by, with never a shattered plate.

Once we hit around seven billion, He was running around pretty quickly, I'd imagine, but obviously, still adept enough to stay ahead of entropy *which must kill everything, eventually.*

I was courting Blasphemy, I know, but the thought came unbidden into my mind, and it came from *somewhere… Perhaps HE sent it to me….*

What He does is delay that inevitability, and…I thought, much to his credit, delay that apocalyptic set of events, due to His caring, and skill.

But, and again I shuddered, in light of recent events, what if He was not, *has never been truly* omnipotent? What if He simply appeared so because …Well, what else could *we* think in light of such a mind? Such talent? …Such caring?

So, in the same way the juggler tries to keep, say, eight plates spinning, and succeeding, then attempts "nine."

And, if He achieves this, thus emboldened, He attempts "ten." By this time, he is running from one to the next simply trying to keep disaster from occurring; but an individual, *if He is not truly omnipotent,* regardless of how talented, *has limits.*

Perhaps for this *Juggler,* spinning nine plates was the most he could maintain; ten being just *within* his abilities but not for more than a few scant *of His* seconds.

And this was the thought that caused me to pant furiously and start sweating in the middle of the night when sleep wouldn't come….

What if God has hit His limit? Are 10 billion souls more than he can oversee? What if all the plates are about to crash to the floor into a million pieces? Entropy will not be denied.

As a person trained in matters theological I considered: What then? Pray for the Second Coming?

AND WHAT COMES AFTER... when the Juggler takes His bow?

Copyright Zaslow Crane
ZaslowCrane.com

10

ENEMY WITHIN

Bez, Chet and Chato hunched down in the protection of a gully. They were taking heavy fire and kept their heads low.

Somewhere within shouting distance was Sarge, but then,

he was *always* in shouting distance. Fuck, it seemed he was always *shouting*. He could be such a dick!

Bez looked in his heads up display. His tongue triggered the night scope function imbedded in his right, upper molar. It displayed on his viz' screen over his face.

He tried to conclude where the fire was coming from.

Judging by the pattern, there were two, maybe three gunners, tops.

Cap was still pinned down in a small stand of trees, maybe 30 meters and left, behind him.

As long as he stayed there, he was probably safe.

The new combat suits, or S O A's, were more like a plasglas suit of armor, but the damn things weighed a ton! There were servos in the elbows and knees, hips and shoulders, so it was never difficult to run, or climb, or use their arms and legs in any normal function, fuck, in these suits, they were *all* fucking *Swartzneggers*, but then, there was the rain. Traction was a bitch!

The constant rain had turned the red Georgia dirt to mud. They were all sunk in to their ankles after only a few minutes. This was an ominous development. Their feet were leaden; mired and hard to move, even with the S O A's servos.

All the advances in tek, in gear, in weapons, and they couldn't do squat about a thunderstorm!

If the rain didn't let up, they'd be mired for sure! Easy pickin's for the more mobile and (they'd heard) quicker and lighter Gas Cartel's troops.

More *fireflies* flew overheard; disturbingly close to his head.

Bez flinched involuntarily.

The Gas Cartel used incendiary bullets almost exclusively in situations like these, because in addition to occasionally finding unarmed crevasses in their armor, the fiery and unnerving flammable bullets could cause a lot of collateral damage.

The *fireflies* didn't even light up until they were 30 or 40 meters out, and then, suddenly, they'd light up nearby, comin' at you! *Fast!* It was freaky! That was another reason the Gas Cartel's troops used incendiary rounds--the fear factor!

The PlasGlas suits could take three, maybe four direct hits in the same spot before degrading enough where the next hit might harm or even kill the wearer, but those little fires that didn't go out. *Those* were the real problem.

They fucked up the night vision; the hot cinders always seemed to get into the fabric gussets--the supposedly *fire-proof* fabric gussets! And they'd burn them away! And there was more. If the *fireflies* burned away a part of a gusset, where two plates of armor met, water would get in. On a night like this, water getting into a *suit o' armor*, or "S O A," it would cause short circuits. Short circuits could kill you.

While *triple-redundancy* was the watchword on planning boards of the General Mills Armories, there frequently was still hell to pay in a situation like this. The GMA brass were *not* happy with failures of any sort!

The guys mired in mud fired back. The sound of the projectiles leaving their weapons was deafening; the group-ings and scope of their firepower was astounding!

There was a lull in the exchange of death.

Bez I.M.'d the Cap. He told him to sit tight.

The three guys in the culvert had to figure out something so that they could regroup and get out of the mud or they were dead, or as good as, anyway. The mud sucked at them and made the simplest movements difficult.

Chato took out a cigarette and rubbed the non-filter end on his sleeve. It immediately ignited, he keyed off his full-face visor, raised it out of the way. He took a long, grateful drag.

Bez was incensed.

"Whathefuck, *Vato?* You crazy?! They *had* to see the flare of the headstrike! Put it out!"

"Fuuuuck!" Chato waved him away as a *firefly* went singing mere inches above their heads. "If they could do more than pin us down now, they would.... We've probably got ten mins, maybe 20 until an airstrike comes down on us. They can't do shit! Not for a while yet. I'm gonna enjoy my fucking cig!" Chato took another drag. He appreciated the *enhanced* nicotine rush.

Sarge was yelling something too, but he was drowned out by an extended volley.

They were supposed to stay off the mikes, and Sarge was "spozed" to I.M. them.

"Maybe he had a glitch. Maybe that's why he was yelling!"

Bez ducked more incoming. He flinched a lot these days. He was a *short-timer.* And, *somehow,* he was out here instead of running the fucking mail stop for the last two months of his hitch!

Bez looked Sarge's way and leaned into Chato's ear, "He was yelling because that's what he does! He's fucking Sarge!"

These new suits o' armor... This generational upgrade was probably great on paper, he thought, *but in real life, maybe it wasn't so good.* He looked down at his scuffed and damaged sleeve. *I kinda liked my old S O A.* He thought petulantly. *It couldn't do as much as this, it was scuzzy, but I knew I could depend on it.*

Bez looked around. *Fuck!* he thought, frustrated. He couldn't see past his hand in this downpour! *How'm'I supposed to shoot these fuckers?*

"I don't think I like bein' one of the mark 1's," he told himself for about the *eleventh* time this trip. But, there was nothing he could do about it. Insubordination at General Mills was immediately punished with a bullet in the back of the head.

Being an "M 1" was the first run off the General Mills Armory lines; Their suits were the first ones after the prototypes. So far, they'd been good.

No, he corrected himself. They'd been better'n good, they'd been great, but he still just didn't trust this piece of gear yet! It's too new!

Chet laid his *over/under* on the berm and sighted on the bright flashes of the Gas Cartel's snipers. He looked carefully for the muted muzzle flash.

The *under* was a rapid fire or slow burst "auto," capable of firing 40 rounds a second in a straight line or in any of a half dozen pre-programmed patterns. It was great for clearing out unfriendlies when you couldn't see them exactly, but you kinda had an idea of where they were hiding.

The *over* was basically a shotgun, but it was a shotgun on steroids. It was a small fucking cannon! It packed a wallop and could pierce many types of armor; personal or automotive. But he needed a clear shot first.

He carefully braced his shoulder against the plasglas stock. Even with the shock absorbing design, this thing'd rip your shoulder off if you weren't careful!

There were always lots of guys recuperating a few miles back with dislocated shoulders! They'd taken their *over* for granted.

Chet couldn't get a good enough bead on them, and the rain had decided to come down even harder, making it tougher to spot the enemy, and making their plight more immediate. "Fucking lovely…," he muttered. "Jesus-fucking-Christ!"

Bez had an idea. "Guys!" He *loud-whispered*, as rain sluiced down his cheeks.

They all looked at him cautiously, keeping an eye out for fireflies.

"Which of us has been hit the fewest times?"

Everyone counted their own number of "hits" to moment-by-moment assess if their SOA was in danger of failing and allowing them to be killed, but no one had a true, dependable number, not after the fuck-up at the LZ!

So they all looked at each others' chest-plating to assess each other. There was no way they could actually inspect their own armor while wearing it.

"Looks like Chato is the most careful, or most lucky...."

"Yeah almost no burn marks or divots...."

Chet reached out and stole Chato's cigarette. Before Chato could protest, he took the last few drags, then it was down to the biodegradable filter. He flung in the general direction of the "gas boys," over the top of the berm.

"Okay. So, what's your idea?"

"Chet you stay here, and be ready, I'll snake over to those bushes...." Bez pointed to some bushes a couple of meters away. There might have been better cover further off, but their night vision was useless in this torrent!

Everytime the "gas boys" shot a firefly at them, the droplets all lit up! That temporarily scorched the LqD readouts in their nightvision, making them go from that weird green to almost white and fuzzy! That was scary--to be blinded! Even for a few seconds. Guys died in a few seconds! Everyone feared being blinded!

Bez continued, "When I get there..." he pointed to Chato. "You reboot your camo program and stand up--just for a second. That'll make your suit flicker white before it goes back to this shit-brown-camo color.

Chato wasn't buying it.

"Fuck you *man'o*--Fuck you!"

"Listen... This'll work..."

"You want me to be their target? No way, *man'o!*" Chato was so distressed by this idea, he'd actually raised his weapon as if to ward off an attack!

Bez tried to soothe Chato's fear and his fear of being perceived as expendable. Hell, they were *all* expendable! How do I explain that to someone as excitable as Chato? Deep down, he knew. *They all* knew...

"Look. Don't be hinky. We won't let you *segue, bro.* We'll be layin' down a shitload of ordnance as soon as we see their little chickenshit muzzle flashes!"

"Oh man," Chato was unconvinced...

"Okay, *you* go over there." He gestured to the bushes. "I'll stand up. What do you say, *Vato?*" Bez gestured to his scorched chest plates. He knew he'd been hit quite a few times."I'll do it, *vato*, if you won't. I just figured that you would have the best chance to survive, but, fuckit babes, *I'll* do it." He looked around the small group to make his point.

He paused leaning in, to finish his thoughts: "You know why? 'Cause this is the best chance that we got; this idea that I had...I can't think of anything better. Can you? Or you?"

He looked around at his comrades.

Chato shook his head..."No *man'o*, I'll do it. Just be ready, see?"

Bez grinned. His grin was mud flecked and huge. It was a "Bez Trademark Grin," but while he doubted that they could see his face at all through the spattered visor, he knew that they were all probably *seeing* it in their imaginations.

"Just gimme five, babes, I'll be ready!" He scampered off hoping not to see any Gassies on the way.

It took more than five, but Bez finally got into position.

He I.M.'d Chet and Chato, and ignored Sarge. Sarge was obviously having problems. Prob'ly from the explosions at the LZ, earlier that day.

He heard some sporadic cover fire from their left. Large

bore booming shots. "That must be Sarge," he thought. "He must figure that we got *something* goin' on...."

He I.M'd: "Time to Mambo, *vatos!*"

In seconds, the almost invisible Chato had *lit up* and stood up! Before he even got fully erect he was hit with a small, tight volley of incendiary slugs, they made a hell of a racket but they didn't pierce his "skin."

Chato dove back down, his heart pounding in his ears! He gasped at how close he'd come to being *cheesed* -as in "Swiss."

At the same time from both sides of him Bez and Chet opened up with killer volleys aimed at the bright spots that the muzzle discharges left in the dark, musty air.

Bez had a weapon similar to Chet's, but he had no *under*. Instead, he had a full auto capable rifle with real time addressable patterns he could call up while holding his finger on the "fire" button on the plasglas stock.

He pictured the rounds screaming away from him at the speed of sound, 40 of 'em per second in dancing patterns.

They sped away and made spirals or zig zags cutting up everything in their path.

SOON IT WAS QUIET. The rain kept up, but aside from that, it was still...creepy.

The sudden silence was shocking, surreal.

From far off they heard sobbing. One of the gas soldiers, no doubt.

Chato I.M.'d Chet and Bez: "*Mira!* In case you were wondering: Yeah I'm okay--and *No*- I ain't *never* doin' that *ever* again! *Nunca*, Baby!"

Bez checked his vitals in his heads up. His own pulse was dangerously high. After being so high he'd crash, so he'd need a stim in an hour or so. If they didn't find a place to sleep soon, he'd be wasted later.

Shit.

By then they'd be "Back At Base." He hoped. He damn well better be B.A.B.! Shit!

Bez was point. He didn't figure his vitals were going to go back down to normal in the next few minutes.

"Hah!" he thought. *Not in the next few months!*

Damn.

He circled around carefully and picked up no more fire. He I.M.'d: "I'm almost there @ their position. Do not - REPEAT - DO NOT fire!"

Somebody replied with an I.M.'d "smiley face."

Hadda be Chet, the joker. He shook his head , chuckled quietly and grinned a little. He keyed his nightvision back on. "Asshole!" He grinned as he whispered to himself. Always fucking around, that Chet.

Then, in an instant, he was at the Gas Soldiers' position!

There was a pitted stone wall! No wonder we couldn't get at these guys sooner! He thought. *It must be a hundred years old! Solid as hell!*

There was one guy close. He was lying still. His reddish hair was spilled out onto the trodden, soaked grass. His helmet, destroyed by a fusillade of bullets that lay nearby.

Was he dead? He looked dead, but he'd been trained to take no chances. Bez withdrew his knife from a sleeve sheath and plunged it all the way to the hilt into he supine solider's exposed throat.

"If he wasn't dead, he is now."

He crab-walked another ten-fifteen meters and found another one. This one was alive, but hurt badly. That must have been the sobbing they'd heard mixed with the rain--the fucking downpour!

There were four body wounds that he could see, not to mention the wounds on the extremities. His lighter camo suit was stained red. The suit, like the General Mills SOA's registered the colors for camouflage. But his SOA "thought" that he was in a new, red environment. It began to match the color of his blood.

"Weird."

Lucky they don't wear the same weight body armor as we have.

This other army had long ago opted for faster moving, lighter armed troops for the most part. So the armor that they *did* have couldn't take the same degree of abuse.

Also, Bez noted with interest, the suit didn't even know that this guy was almost dead yet. Not very sophisticated. *Not like my SOA,* he thought, beginning, *just beginning* to become possessive of his new armored suit.

My suit would be shutting down and prepping to self-demo, he thought grimly; *If my vitals were as low as this guys vitals must be!*

His tongue probed another of the four molar keys he and every other General Mills Consortium *new* soldier had imbedded in his mouth.

There was one on the inside of each of the four quadrants. All on the inside edge of his back teeth. This one switched on the radio.

Their radios were for short to medium range, to be used like an intercom to keep everyone on the same page. They didn't worry about interception or jamming because every second, the transmitter shifted randomly to another freq. This way, they could talk without being overheard.

Now that it was quiet, we can talk again, he thought.

They still wanted to be pretty quiet this close to a Gas Cartel regional fuel dump. There could be kites with *ears* out.

Kites could fly in all quiet-like and drop a 'puter guided bomb into your hip pocket and be gone before you even knew what hit you! Though they probably wouldn't be out on a night like this. The rain would fuck with their guidance programs. He sure hoped that was the case anyway.

He looked up involuntarily into the water laden sky just the same.

Can't see anything. Too dark! Why am I even looking!? Geez. Look at how paranoid I've become! Damn!

He keyed his mike: "Hey Sarge. This guy's hurt pretty bad..."

"The med/doc is in a broke-down Hummer a couple of miles from here, back near the LZ. I ain't draggin' him back. And I *ain't* leavin' him here to call in friends."

"Yeah...?" Bez knew what was coming..

"...Ah dammit. Finish him. He can't have any better intel than we got. And we'd have to save his ass in order to gossip with that fine young fellow. I'm not risking us and the mission to chitchat with him."

"You sure? I can't bring him back to life if you change your mind..."

The click of the reply took an extra beat: "Yeah... Do it."

Bez had learned early on that it was better to do a thing like this quickly, without thinking. It only got more difficult if you thought about it.

On the other hand, this sonobitch had made eye contact with him. He couldn't just knife him. The bleeding solider sobbed in pain and the knowledge of what was to come.

"Please! Oh dammit it hurts. Please!"

Bez thought: *Please? Please what? Kill me and put me out of my misery? Or Please don't kill me, even though I was gonna kill you? Whathefuck?*

All that took place in about two seconds. He swung his gun down and pumped another few rounds into him. The muzzle flash was drowned by the rain, which also muffled the report somewhat. That was good in case there were more *unfriendlies* around....

The enemy solider moved no longer; pleaded no further. *He was,* as good as *anyway,* Bez thought. He shouldered his gun. Except for the rain pounding down, it was now quiet.

As Bez walked back to what was left of his unit, he thought about wars of old. – In the past, the firefight that he was just in would have left ten or twenty *pounds* of brass spewed around the forest, counting all seven *participants* in the skirmish.

He'd heard of lots of guys in the Nam who were *tracked* by the *trail of brass* their M16's left behind. He'd heard tell that was how his Granddad had bought it.

He spat in frustration.

That was almost eighty years ago. *So* fuckin long ago! The instant he spat, he regretted it. He'd heard rumors of DNA sniffers that were "combat-i-sized."

They could tell all about him from one drop of spittle hanging on a leaf. You couldn't even go into the forest with a fucking cold anymore, or they'll track you, find you and fuck you up! He thought dejectedly. *Things are so complicated now.*

But they won't get much tonight. He breathed a sigh of relief. *It's still coming down, like to flood the place!*

He hefted his Bando, the belt of clips specially designed to plug into a rapidly firing weapon without jamming it.

"Neither rain, nor sleep, nor even fuckin' salt water..." he mused. Then, he repositioned it on his shoulder. Plastic bullets or not. This thing was still pretty heavy!

The General Mills armorer had long ago switched over to bullets jacketed in a special plastic that melted and became the back part of the slug, stabilizing it as it left the barrel. So there was no brass to *track*!

The other benefit was weight. In weather like this Bez thanked God that he didn't have to carry all that brass jacketed ammo; the PlasAmmo was way lighter!

He walked upright back to the berm. He hoped that he could find it quickly in the darkness and downpour.

"Me comin' in, Babes!" Bez muttered over & over into the Comm system. *"No Mater! No Tirar!* (Don't shoot! Don't kill me!) Friendly comin' in!"

Suddenly, he was back among his comrades. It was odd how quickly he'd gotten back to the group. They'd remained dug-in, in case there was some unexpected trouble, so he knew that they wouldn't come up and meet him.

"Was that only about 20 meters?!"

He was incredulous.

Shit! They should have dusted anyone *that* close!

When the firing started, he hadn't even thought to tongue the rangefinder button. He guessed that no one else thought of it either--it all happened so fast.

All these new mods in their bodies; their teeth; the 'trodes in their skulls...All that tek, and no one thought of it? Not even Cap? He thought tiredly; *Disappointing.*

Do we really even need a suit o' armor like this? What was wrong with his "Old Solid?" It had gelled armor. That was good, wasn't it?

Bez worried about being the first to test it out in combat, but Bez, being Bez, he would worry about being second, or third, until it was the *standard.* Bez was the cautious type. He wanted to see his *ninos* again. He wanted to see his *esposa,* too! He wanted to see them soon!

Right now, they needed to look for a spot to lick their wounds and get their heads back on straight. Hopefully it'd be someplace dry, or at least not muddy.

By now Cap had joined them, and they held a plas sheet shield over their group as they swapped fortified jerky and held the rain off the map.

The maps were waterproof, but it was discovered subsequently to the purchase of *a few million of 'em* that while the water won't damage them *per se,* they *were* very susceptible to mildew and rot if they're not rigorously dried.

There was a little joking, but basically those Gassies had caught us with our pants down. Bez shook his head and took a plug of jerky from Sarge. *If we'd faced a couple more guys or heavier small arms... Well, all five of us would be dead now.*

"This had already been a fucked mission."

"Yeah."

The rain made a loud staccato right above their heads.

They'd lost five yesterday at the LZ while the hummer was getting damaged. They didn't even know what had hit them. One minute they were waving g'bye to the "shuttle," and getting up and gettin out--the next there was a rain of fire and death!

Mines of some sort, maybe. But our units should have detected them... Bez imagined.

Bez was suspicious of his new suit. Why hadn't it warned them of mines or whatever it was that aced all his buds. There was a landmine warning function that was *supposed* to always be running. Why had it not alerted him? – All of them? They all had the same SOA's!

It couldn't have been any kite he'd ever heard of--too much firepower. Kites were small: one kite--one kill. There was no scream of incoming, so, not a missile or cannon slug. So it had to be booby traps of some sort.

Cap had found something on the SatMap. There was a structure of some sort about a klick away and 20 degrees off their course.

When they got there, they were amazed to find that the roof was still good. It looked like an old, *very* old picnic shelter. It was a cabin without walls. It even had a fireplace, not that they'd dare start a fire. Besides, they all had their Honeywell Heat'rs. They gave off a huge amount of heat with negligible lumens for the sniffers to locate.

Essential for their mission tonight. *Don' want to advertise we're here!* thought Chato dejectedly. He too had lost friends at the LZ debacle.

As he thought this, he stretched out in front of two heat'rs--his and Chets. Chet had set them both for "omni-directional," and stretched out on the otherside.

Cap said, "Dry out quick an' put 'em away. I don't wanna get found by somebody wandering around with a therma scan! All they'd have to do would be to call in a few rounds of cannon slugs or a smart missile, and we'd all be meat!"

What passed for a salute in the General Mills Army was returned to him, and he smiled and turned to his maps.

They were less than 20 klicks from their target. Sarge carried most of the timers, detonators and C-11 explosive, but each solider also had a small cache that they were responsible for: Just in case.

Chet, Bez and Chato took care to dry out their weapons; their ammo; and any fabric that could take on any "h2-OH."

There was a shitload of h2-OH coming down just a few feet away, and the rain made so much noise that they couldn't use their audio sensors to scan for *non-friendlies.*

They'd all unplugged as soon as they could, taking off their helmets and "ear protection." Nothing sounded *right* in those things but their weapons--especially the *over/under* was so loud, that the General Mills Minister of War worried he'd have a bunch of deaf soldiers out there. You were worthless without your hearing. More to the point, you were dead without your hearing.

"Chato? Ain't you dry yet?!" Sarge asked. What he was really saying was: *"You heard the Cap. Turn the godamn Heat'r off!"*

The guys sat around taking slurps from the Military Issue "Whack its," the meal encased in two envelopes. One held the meal, the other held two smaller chemicals that when *whacked* would burst and mix. When they mixed they created a chain reaction. Heat was generated. The meal was heated up!

They had Tacos, Ensenada Style, or a perennial Military Favorite, Chipped beef on toast, or *Shit-on-shingle* as it's been known for more than a hundred years. There were other choices but all were what passed for MRE's these days. It didn't taste like much, but you felt better after eating it. That was *something*. It warmed you…

And, they *did* feel a little better. They were dryer, they had eaten, and for the moment, they were safe.

Chato and Bez were buddies since boot camp. They sat next to one another and complained about their food. That took up the first few minutes of the *dining experience*. After that, there was a pause in the conversation. Most of the guys were chewing, so talking was hushed, whispered, sporadic.

When they began gathering up their degradable "plates" the talking began again. Bez tossed them into the biodegradable baggie and tossed in the catalyst. It'd be gone for all intents & purposes by morning. Only really hi-end sniffers could find *that* residue!

So, the next item in a solider's list of priorities was gossip. They eased into it, but Chato made the first real foray into *significant* gossip, "Hey, *vatos*, you know what I heard? I heard a *rumore* that the Gassies have perfected the P-bomb! That could be bad…."

"Je-Sus, Chato. We've been hearing rumors about the Pulse Bomb for over a year. Donchathink they'd a used it if they had it?"

"Yeah, but the *E.M.P.* would be readable by *our* satellites, and we'd know if they'd ever used it…"

"What if tonight was the first time, Babes?"

It was round-robin gossip time.

"*Si' pero...* But if they did, I heard that they could drop it right into a firefight and set it off, and except for their guys who were real close, it wouldn't hurt any of them...."

"...And, it'd fry the electronics in our suits! I know! But Chato, if they *have* it why are they holding back?"

Bez jumped in, "Besides, it'd still fry their electronics too...."

Chato would not be deterred.

"*Si* but look at our suits. Now look at theirs. Their suits don't do much, but if they stop functioning...*Quien sabe?* Maybe they have problems, maybe no."

Sarge tried to stop this unhealthy thinking.

"But.."

"Just a minute, Sarge. But if *our* suits are totally shut down, it'd take at least two whole mins for a complete reboot from scratch. *Two minutes* we'd be standing there. No movement. Maybe no movement *at all!* No hiding. No shooting back. *Nada.* And *that's* if we weren't close. If we were close, the electronics would be fried, permanent-like!"

"Gentlemen, I suggest that we utilize this time checking our equipment, not waste it speculating about things we can neither really know about, nor prepare for." Cap spoke in a clipped manner, as if words were rationed and he didn't want to run out of syllables too soon.

"Right, Cap." Sarge was relieved that Cap had stepped in. They were in enemy territory, and morale was an important commodity. It needed to be saved and nurtured, not whittled at like this crew was doin'!

Cap dug out his "combat-i-zed" P/Pilot from his fanny pack.

The gossip session ceased abruptly and each guy took a smaller p'pilot from their 'packs, and keyed them on from sleepmode.

Every solider had his Hard Drive and the most important

electronics in armored, or "combat-i-sized" fanny packs, affixed to the small of their backs.

This was the place least likely to be damaged by errant fire. There'd been stories about guys in firefights lying prone, with a tek/medic working on his 'pack *while* he was returning fire! When there's nothing else to talk about, there's always these "military legends"... Gossip, or in Spanglish, "*rumores*" abound!

"Okay! Listen up," Cap restarted his conversation. "I'm getting error messages from almost all your packs. There isn't one that's working perfect, but Chet, yours is the least fucked, so, we'll look at yours last. You're on sentry. But don't leave the enclosure. Stay close."

"Right, Cap."

"If I don't get the vitals/com/self-destruct/servos all working to within parameters, we're gonna have to turn around! Then, Fletch, David, Covina and the others were offed for nothing. So, listen-up. Initiate a "level two diagnostic," on my mark...now."

Soldiers gloved fingers clumsily operated keypads that were essentially too small, but through practiced routines, they all had completed their inputting in a few seconds.

Now they waited. It could take a minute or five. You never knew. New tek was fucked. Not like the old SOA's. *They* were a quick read, every time!

It was important that the vitals registered with Cap's unit. They'd all taken oaths to not allow the suit o' armor to fall into enemy hands, and so if their vitals dropped to below sub-par, Cap was empowered to initiate a *permanent complete shutdown*. In regular words: Self-Demo.

For the same reason, everyone wanted their vitals to register properly. What a bitch if the scans said you were dying and you were really fine, but Cap didn't know you were fine. Then, he'd blow the SOA with *you* still in it!

The servos had to work properly or a solider'd have to lift the entire weight of that arm or leg to walk or shoot or run, and the average guy would be exhausted in minutes! Somebody all beefed-up like Chato would last a little longer, but not much.

They'd all used the GPS recently, so they knew that *that* at least worked. Just the same that'll be inoperable for the time that the diagnostic was running!

Chato's blonde hair fell in his face as he bent over looking at the readout. It always took so long... talking helped to pass the time.

"Cap?" he asked.

"Yeah?"

"You're from money, right?"

"If you mean does my family have a few hundred mil salted away, well yeah. But *that's* not much... Not really. Not anymore."

"But there was money to send you to college..."

"I had to take a loan out to go."

"You did?"

"Yeah. A huge one! But they said I wouldn't have to pay back more than 25% of it if I'd serve here for two years. Why the fuck else do you think I'm here?!"

"Fuck. I dunno. If I went to a *Colegio*, I wouldn't be here now, no how!"

"But, Chato, you're doing the same thing as I did. You're here because when you're finished fighting, General Mills will give you a stipend, a payback. What do most *mudhoneys* like you guys do with the creds? They go to school or start a biz! Either way, you're doing the same thing I did, just in reverse order."

"Well..."

"Hey Cap, I got a readout!" Bez was finished first.

"Great!" Cap looked up smiling, "Send!"

Cap was quiet for a while as he looked over Bez's upload. While Cap was reading and re-reading Bez's info hoping for some other answer, the others signaled that they'd finished their diagnostics too. Chet shifted and brought his gun up.

No one noticed him and Chet didn't say anything. He wasn't sure there *was* anything, yet. He looked into the gloom anxiously.

Cap re-read Bez's info for the third time and then, read through Sarge's and Chato's.

He looked at them. "You guys are within parameters. Some of your sysops are a little shaky, but we've only got 3 hours + 20, 'til extraction, so we'll do a *level one B.A.B.* later, and hope you all hold up in the meantime."

Hope it holds up? Chet looked over his shoulder. He was depending on these guys. They were a team.They needed one another just to get back out. If their gear wasn't working...

He turned to Bez, "From you, all I get is garbled mush, bro."

The guys all looked at one another. They knew what *that* meant.

"...musta been damaged at the LZ... You gotta go back."

Sarge jumped in.

He got in close to Cap. He talked low, but urgently: "Cap. This mission was designed for six to seven operatives, min. We lost half our crew before we even got our boots muddy. We *might* be able to do this with the five we got, these are good soldiers, but you send Bez home, you send us *all* home. There be no way we finish this op with four guys!"

"Fucked up new "SOA's!" Bez muttered. He'd surmised what Sarge was saying. *I ain't stupid.*

Cap considered. He knew Sarge was right. He considered keying on his long range com/link, asking for a directive, but he knew what his superiors would say. So, then decided against it.

"Awright. We go. But we be careful, yeah?" He'd switched to his troop's common speech patterns in hopes of garnering a little *esprit de corps.*

Suddenly, Chet's head exploded! A split-second before there had been a muffled crack. His lifeless body flopped to the concrete pad. It shivered briefly before becoming still.

A marker began blinking in Cap's p'pilot. Chet was dead.

"The guy shooting probably was close by, because he used an exploding round, and those ain't accurate for very far!" yelled Bez.

"Even closer, in this rain!" added Sarge. Sarge looked at Chet and Cap saw him; knew what he was thinking.

"Deal with that later!" yelled Cap as he and the others dove for cover and hurriedly put their *brain buckets* back on!

They fanned out in the vegetation adjacent to the picnic spot. They were after blood. This fucker snuck up close! He killed Chet!

As they moved forward to where they thought the shooting was coming from, they also put more distance between each other to cover more ground in the search. Also they wanted to make more but smaller and more difficult targets.

There was a rustling in the bushes. The sound of someone running away, not caring any longer if he stayed hidden. They'd flushed him out! All four GM soldiers opened up at the movement and sound. There was a curtain of lead traveling out in a solid, hot wave!

They actually *heard* their assailant being knocked down by one or more slugs! After a few mins more of searching they found him – Dead.

"Good." Sarge spat on his corpse, "Fucker."

"Look at this. *Mira* his pack. He's day-tripper," Bez

muttered. "Not out for long duty. He's got friends around. Close. Prob'bly."

"Right, Sarge."

Cap keyed in a secret sequence. The blinking that represented Chet sped up to double time – then triple time. "Move out. I don't wanna meet his friends."

They moved Northwest, parallel to their original path. They'd decide when and how to retreat in a few mins. Right now, it was time to get away from the *scene of the crime*.

The readout that was Chet, went to quad time, for ten more seconds and then there was a dull *"whump."*

THEY COULD NO LONGER SEE Chet's body, he was already well behind them, but they knew that there wouldn't be much left after the charge did its work!

They were saddened by the loss of another good guy. They *all* had depended on Chet and he them, for a half dozen missions before this. They knew that the same thing could happen to them, anytime. But they also knew that General Mills could not allow the tek to fall into anyone else's hands.

Despite the rain, Bez still on point, noticed a strong smell of ozone in his helmet. It was coming from the air/re-circ unit on his back. Ozone meant wires frying. What else could go wrong with this suit?

Fucking SOA, dammit!

From then on, he checked his vitals every few seconds. If anything looked *wrong*, he was gonna radio Cap that he was okay, and tell him not to believe the vitals/readouts. Was his SOA dying?

They walked for another ten minutes. It was slow going-- crappy paths, mud everywhere.

Chato started to stumble.

Sarge was right behind him. Chato was the guy in the best shape in the platoon! Something must be wrong!

As Sarge drew up to Chato, to see if he could help, and he was shot repeatedly in the head and back. His suit couldn't take the impacts. Sarge was dead before he hit the ground!

Bez heard the sound from behind him and froze. An instant later he sought and found cover behind an ancient tree.

Chato looked back at Cap, holding a smoking weapon, but he was already in the process of passing out. Cap had shut down his ventilation system! He was suffocating! He crumpled onto his back.

Chato tried to manually open his faceplate, and Cap grabbed Chato's hand and fastened it to the ground with his knife! Then, he retrieved Chato's knife from his forearm sheath and fastened his other hand to the ground, driving it through his hand and up to the hilt in the moist, red mud!

Chato's movements became less-animated. Bez imagined that he could hear Chato's moaning.

By now, Bez had quietly worked his way back. The rain's noise had covered the minimal noise he'd made re-tracing his steps. He saw Cap stabbing Chato's other hand. He saw Chato dead or dying, and Sarge obviously dead, his armor riddled and still smoking, despite the steady rain.

He leaned behind a tree and sighted carefully. He squeezed off a volley. He hit Cap squarely in the chest! Cap was launched backwards in the mud! He slapped back onto the moist red dirt with a wet thud! Then, he righted himself and scrabbled behind another tree.

Cap wheezed in surprise and because he had just survived one of the most dangerous things a person in an SOA could face: A close up frontal barrage!

He shook his head to clear it and to try to stop the ringing. "Bez!" Cap shouted. "I know you're there! Talk to me!"

"You planned this! You killed Sarge!"

"Looks that way. I pushed for this op on a rainy night. I got more than I bargained for in this storm, though."

"You killed Chato!"

"Yeah... I had to..."

"Had to?!"

"Well, yeah! Do you know how many creds the Gas Cartel is offering me for one of these units, still in GWC?!"

"You sold us out!" Bez was crushed. These were his friends, his family. Now all were dead except for himself.

"I'm a mercenary, not a sellout!"

"You're a traitor, you fuck!"

"We're *all* mercenaries! Bez! You. Me, Chato here. Would any of you have signed up if they hadn't offered money? No. We'd have hightailed it to Australia, or some other neutral zone. We'd have found a way to avoid the impound and draft gangs if they hadn't offered creds!"

"You killed our buddies. *Your* buddies! People who saved your fucking life!"

"I did what I had to do. The money has become too important. There just isn't enough of it. I needed more. I bided my time in this joke of an army; this corporate police force with assault weapons! I bided my time until there was something worth stealing; something that the Gassies would pay dearly for: My S O A and Chato's S O A! Two working suits!"

"There will be no place you'll be safe, you bastard."

"I've already got a nice condo picked out in Corporate Park, in Houston. The most heavily guarded city in the world!" Cap let *that* sink in for a moment, then, "I could put in a word for you, too..."

"What?"

"Well, if you come along, *willingly,* I- I mean "we" could turn in three suits. Three *working* suits. I'm sure they won't double their price, but I'm certain that I could get you enough to make you comfortable in HouTex for the rest of your life! Interested...?"

Bez said nothing, but continued attempting to find Cap in his sights.

"Better make up your mind there, *man'o*. I got *friendlies* coming to this spot. They'll be here very soon. I tripped a beacon, just now. They're set up to look for me, but if they find you crouched behind that tree still holding your Abrams M-116, well, I doubt they'd listen to reason."

Cap worked feverishly in the rain trying to access Bez's suit; to shut it down, to blow it up...*anything* to cripple or kill this glitch in his plans! *Fuck!* He couldn't get through. Regardless of the "Function", or "Freq". Nothing! Bez's suit wasn't addressable!

How is that fucking possible!? he thought feverishly. *I'm so fucking close! I can't let this fraggin' bozo fuck this deal up!*

Bez was going to remain a problem. Maybe if he surrendered, Cap could get at his manual kill switch in his fanny pack.

Well, he thought, *I can't trip the kill switch from here, dammit. Gotta get him to come to me. Otherwise I could be "meat" caught in the crossfire! The Gassies sure don't love me!*

Lightning briefly lit up the sky and a second later came the "boom" of thunder.

He lifted up on one elbow to yell to his ex comrade.

"My friendlies are as close as this storm, Bez. What're you gonna do? Be rich, or be dead?"

Bez considered.

Then, he spoke. "Rich!"

"Say Again, *Otra Vez, Babe!*"

"I wanna be rich... And alive!"

"Good man!"

"So, now I'll need a little proof of your change of heart

and allegiance. Throw out your weapon!"

"You'll shoot me!"

"If you're going to help me, why would I shoot you? But, if you're lying that'd be a good reason to want to keep your fucking weapon…*Verdad*, eh?" Again, he'd switched to the soldier's colloquial to attempt to gain some credibility. Had it worked?

Thunder & lightning boomed again.

Bez decided that time wasn't going to be his friend, but still he hesitated. He fished out some of the C-11 from his waterproof pack on his thigh. He yanked out a golf-ball-sized chunk and stowed the rest. From the pocket on the other side, he extracted a detonator.

"Well. C'mon, Bez! Before I change my fucking mind!" shouted Cap over the storm's fury. "You're running out of time! *My friendlies* are close, *vato!!*"

A small baggie of detonators spilled out on the grass. He searched frantically for the *red* one. The one that would go off *on contact*. If only he could turn on a headlamp.

"I'm… *hurt.*" Bez cried out, stalling for time. "Don't know if I can stand. I'll try… Here's my Abrams!"

He tossed his weapon out of concealment. It clattered to the mud.

Lightning flashed again! The thunder crashed almost immediately, almost as if it were God's afterthought. As the raucous flash lit the area for a moment, his eyes fell on a red button in the grass! The detonator!

"*Watta!*" he thought in triumph.

He tore off the protective seal and smashed it gently but firmly into the plastic explosive. He allowed more rain water to fall on the congealed mess of detonator and C-11. Up to a point, the wetter it was, the better it stuck to something--especially things with hard slick surfaces, like SOA's--Suits of Armor.

From now on, he had to be extremely careful. From now on, it was extremely, extremely volatile!

"I'm coming out...," he made a show of painfully lifting himself up and wobbled out into the path.

Cap's position was a mere ten meters away. So close. He hadn't known. He hadn't been able to fucking *ace* him from thirty fucking feet! Damn!

He limped toward the position he thought Cap was and discovered that he was wrong. Cap wasn't there! Near his feet was Sarge's Abrams, maybe he should pick it up...

"Behind you!" It was Cap. He'd doubled back. He now stood off to Bez's side in the underbrush.

"I saw you limping, but I see no damage to that quadrant of your armor. What's wrong?"

He stepped up onto the path.

"Don't know. Intense pain in my thigh!" He winced for affect hoping that the exaggerated body language would show though all this protective clothing.

"Put your hands behind your head. Turn around."

Bez did as he was told; he stood with his back to the killer, the C-11 cupped carefully in his right hand.

Cap walked over and popped open the watertight cover on the hard drive, housing Bez's kill switch, among other things.

As he flipped the cover off. Almost a litre of water spilled out!

"Hah! Watertight! My Ass!" Cap almost laughed!

This was probably why he wasn't able to access Bez's vitals and controls! Water leaked in and shorted some of the mechanisms out when we got out in the rain. It had nothing to do with the explosions he'd planned at the LZ.

The plan had always been to walk his suit in and take his reward. Chato's suit was an extra that he may or may not utilize. But this crap with Bez... Something wasn't right.

ZASLOW CRANE

"What're you doing back there?"

"Checking your electronics. Stay calm."

"You're looking for my kill switch, you fucker!"

Bez spun around, and Cap lifted his weapon.

Before Bez could find shelter again, Cap unloaded a burst into Bez's chest!

Bez dove for cover, while throwing his C-11 at Cap's chest. He had to be right on the money. There was no second chance! It connected! It hit Cap with a wet splat!

For a heart-breaking split-second Bez thought that he'd unwrapped a "dud," because nothing happened.

Cap looked down at his chest just in time to see the fireball erupt from it! The explosion knocked them in opposite directions. Again, Bez's suit saved him.

"Hah!"

He was still fucking breathing wasn't he?

He got up grunting, even with the help of the servos. He crawled over to Cap and, judging by the absence of anything in Cap's midsection, he'd guess that Cap wasn't going to HouTex anytime soon.

As he looked down, he noticed blood pooling in the bottom of his faceplate.

He keyed it open, and when it only moved partway, he realized that it was blood from a cut on his forehead. The faceplate had broken, but not shattered, and the C-11 had knocked him down, but he was still alright!

Damn!

This SOA is alright!

Something bumped his ankle.

He looked over and saw Chato weakly trying to kick him again!

Chato was alive!

"*Vato!* Babe! You *alive?*"

Bez scrabbled over to his buddy and forced the faceplate

open. Chato gasped in relief!

"*Amigo!* I thought you were toast!! *Fuck! You 'Live?! Watta!*"

Then, Bez pulled out both knives, and Chato moaned with a soggy deep voice, and rolled-up into a fetal position.

Bez fished out a couple of compression bandages and affixed them to Chato's hands. They wouldn't work as well over the gloves but there wasn't time to do any real first aid!

"Fuuuuuck, Dude. You gonna be 'K?

"I be good as nu, soon, *Amigo!*"

Then, he took out some more C-11 stuffed some under Sarge. He reached into Chato's thigh pocket and extracted another identical baggie full of detonators. He sorted out the ones he wanted. He tossed the rest into the brush.

He carefully lifted Cap's body. He was careful to select a compression detonator (the blue ones) for each. He backed away carefully.

"C'mon, Chato. We gone," he said as he gathered up his comrade.

He drew Chato's arm over his shoulder and started back the way they came. "*Conmigo,* Babe," he grunted, "You heavy, you *sabe?*"

Chato grunted, all but spent. "*Lo* fucking *siento.*" He answered after a long moment. "Sorry about that!"

"Hey, *Man'o.* What about the SOA's? We can't leave 'em!"

"We had to leave 'em, *vato.* Besides, I left a surprise for the Gassies, if they pick up the suits."

"Oh yeah?"

"*Verdad!* Shut up and try to walk a little, so I don't have to carry your heavy, bulked-up ass all the way back to the LZ, okay?"

A klick or so behind them there was a low, thunderous boom.

There'd been no lightning for ten minutes. Just rain.

Chato looked over at his friend. He grinned.

"Was that thunder?"

"*Si, Trueno... Trunido,* Babe," he grunted. "*Está* thunder, *vato…*" He grunted as he carried/dragged his buddy.

Chato laughed quietly to himself.

"Ever the good solider, eh *vato?*"

The "Trademark Bez Grin" widened as he carried/dragged Chato and the wet of his cheeks met the wet of his helmet. *How's that for perspective?* He thought. *Fuuuuuck!*

He looked down at his buddy.

"Now, shut the fuck up, you bulked-up asshole. We've got a shitload of klicks to go before we fucking rest! You weigh a fucking ton!"

Chato laughed, well, he croaked and it sounded a bit like laughter... Eventually, Bez joined in. His laughter sounded a little better. But, only a bit.

Damn, I'm tired.

11

HUMAN RESOURCES

The HR Portal beckoned.

. . .

THE HALLWAY from street level to here was rather dank and scuzzy. The portal itself was no better. I had passed the desiccated remains of what might have been a rodent nestled in a corner and almost turned back.

However, I needed work, so in accordance with the State mandated procedures, I had to present myself to prove that I'm me, and be assessed. Then I was expected to work – *an entire month.*

A month? Can you imagine? But I have to if I want to continue receiving my meal chits.

I felt the three or four small rectangles in my pantapocket. They were peach colored, as I recall.

I *physically* accessed the site and after a tortuous half-hour of going through various disqualifiers, I finally interfaced with an *actual human*, through a scratched and smudged plexicurtain.

I sat on a ripped bench with the stuffing falling out. I could feel the scratchy padding through my pantaloon's leg.

"Put your hand in the socket please."

She looked bored beyond explaining.

An orifice opened in the wall in front of me.

It was intended for my hand. I knew that it was necessary if I was to go forward, but I was afraid. I didn't trust that no harm would befall me. My hand shook but didn't enter the receptacle opened for it.

"Any time, Honey. There are people waiting."

I looked at her; she rolled her eyes. Then made a "Well?" gesture.

I pushed my hand forward, and something sucked it into the mechanism, holding my left arm tight.

An abbreviated keypad that had had years of use and abuse extended from the wall toward my right hand; a holographic screen congealed, floating in front of my face.

"Ready, Honey?" She coughed and instantly, I was grateful

for the barrier between us.

God only knows what was in that cough!

I nodded faintly but I guess she missed it.

"Ready?" This time her question was a bit more forceful.

I nodded again.

"You gotta make *a sound of assent*. To make it official. You gotta talk."

I nodded again, nervous. My entire future loomed ahead and a bad *read* would doom me to the next level down.

"Yes...I'm...ready."

She had turned her intercom off momentarily, but I could read her lips: "Finally!"

"Okay, Honey. This is where The Great State of New York, Upper and Lower, and Connecticut, assess your biological strata to learn everything we need to know about you before going forward. Do you understand?"

I began to nod, and her eyes glared.

"I understand."

At this point, she was reciting from rote: "All the information gathered here will remain confidential within the datavaults of the Great State of New York...etcetera ... etcetera. You have the right to know this information on your assessment now if you wish. Press the red button for Yes; the black one for No."

I hesitated and I could see her fight down the urge to come out of her booth and throttle me.

Her lips moved soundlessly: "Red...Black...I don't care. Pick one."

I pushed red and an immense wave of relief washed out over me from her.

"Finally! We can get to work now. You're going to feel a slight burning on the back of your hand and a slight prick of pain from your pinkie."

All of which had begun happening before she finished

speaking.

"I will give you a chit that will allow you to go to GovPrints anywhere in the Great State of New York...," she sighed and waved a weary hand. *"You know what I mean...*And get it printed on *real* paper for a reduced fee. As we go along, I will verbally read out the assessments, occasionally ask a question or two as the testing proceeds. The only fixed record that you may own is available *only* with this chit, so do not lose it."

With that, a small drawer extended from under the keypad and in it was a little plastic yellow rectangle. It said GovPrints on it in box letters. I slid it into a pocket.

"Ready?"

"Ready."

"Alright, then. We begin with the simple stuff: Respiration...Normal, under the circs. Well within normal parameters...

"Blood Pressure...same...same and...Yep! Same...Cholesterol...A bit high but within norms. Stay away from the fast food places, you'll live longer...."

"Chems mix in bloodstream...*Oh...Oh,* what have we here? We did a little recreational Fuzzday? Yesterday...*was it...*yes, yesterday."

I was assured that Fuzzday wasn't something that was included in the tests.

This is awful!

She seemed unimpressed by my transgression.

"Okay, moving on. Next, we check the general health of your Respiratory, Circulatory, and Digestive tract; including excretion. This'll take a minute or two. Sit tight. Don't fidget."

Her eyes went between two screens reading and assembling what she would tell me, as all of it was already on its way to The State's datavault anyway.

"Let's start at the end. You emptied your bowels and…yes, your bladder within fifteen minutes of getting in line."

She looked up at me.

"Everything okay there? I mean," She glanced at the screens, then back, pointedly at me. "I have no 'Reds' showing here, concerning bowels and so forth. Everything okay?"

I nodded.

"Please make a *sound of assent…*"

"Y…yes."

"Good." She said it as if it couldn't have mattered less to her. Your circulatory system is a bit under standard. Try walking instead of taking the speeders, okay? Slow down and smell the …well, never mind…not a great idea…but walk more. Okay? And for God's sake, wear your mask on the brown days."

"Okay."

"And guess what? I get similar readings from your respiratory system as well. Such a surprise! Walk. I won't bother to tell you again."

"Understood."

She made a few entries and then seemed as if she had determined that she was exactly on track.

"Next is the small stuff that can be a pain, so we stress it a little…skin conditions: scalp and other skin …irregularities, which may lead to Cancer but this way we catch it early," she added quickly.

This was to reassure me in advance I suppose, pending a bad verdict as regards "The Big C."

"…Expanding Ozone hole, radioactive dust from China in the upper atmospheric layers, you never know what you might pick up just being outside."

Which is why I spend as little time as possible outside.

"Ummm excuse me, but will this test include The Sitka

Syndrome and Bronchial Blockage Plague?"

She looked at me as if I were an idiot. "There's no cure. You still wanna know?"

"Yes."

"Okay. *Your* funeral. If I see it, I'll tell you."

AFTER A SHORT MOMENT of pouring over incoming data: "Oh, you've had a skin cancer lesion removed already?"

I did?

At my shocked look, she reassessed the figures. "Oh. No. Sorry. Sometime this year is when you'll have a lesion removed. But...checking... Yes...It's no big deal so long as you use your Health Dollars and go to a State Sponsored GovClinic within six weeks of your diagnosis. And doing so will entitle you to a 15% discount, if you present this chit.

The drawer opened again. In it was a Pink rectangle, identical in every way except color. It even had the same block letters. I slipped it into my pocket.

I'm no fool. 15%! That's a good deal!

"Hmmm Scalp, pubic area, back, legs...Aside from that skin cancer thing coming up, you're good."

I felt somehow that I should have felt better about this entire thing; better than I did at the moment. The burning on the back of my hand increased.

"Okay, now you might begin to feel a bit more burning on your hand."

Thanks.

"Umm, Muscular, same as respiratory. See how this all lines up if you don't take care of yourself?"

Snarky as hell.

A chart appeared before me replacing the earlier one that had faded.

I looked but was unable to find a point of reference.

"Got it?"

I opened my mouth and she pointed at me.

"Words …of …assent? Yes. I got it."

"You wanna move more. Walk places…things like that."

"Got it."

Her eyes again went to first one screen, then the other.

"Joint pain…lower part of the body? That's imprecise, but as close as I can get. Is it an ankle? Did I get it?" She almost smiled at that point.

"My knee."

"Oh! So close! But as I look at this…not much else. What did you do to your knee?"

"Twisted it."

"And it's bad enough that it *reads*? What the hell did you do?"

"It happened yesterday. It hurts a lot."

"Yesterday?"

"Yes…"

"Fuzzday?"

I looked down, "Yes."

She shook her head, as if to marvel at the profound stupidity of mankind. "Here's a chit for a few Health Dollars."

The drawer again.

"It'll help pay for the GovClinic. You're no good to your fellow citizens hobbled."

A rectangular blue chit emerged; same as before except for color. I pocketed it. *They're got me trained, I guess.*

The cuff on my hand adjusted and pressure was applied in different spots and I felt an odd tingling in my fingertips and all down my thumb.

"Your hand is going to feel unusual, especially your thumb."

"Thanks."

She actually smiled a bit. I thought for a moment it was

warmth. I was wrong. It was anticipation.

"Okay now we get to the interesting part: Predispositions, tendencies, outright faults, and the ever popular – *Likelihood of aberrant behavior.*"

She seemed to want to look down into my soul, but since I was told I no longer had one, I felt safe.

It's in hocque, but I'll try to pick it up before the weekend.

"YOU FEEL superior to those you meet. You have a predisposition to eat even if you're not hungry; even if you don't need it now. *Perverse.* You're nice to dogs, mean to cats, aloof to pigs and ...*competitive?* with Synthipets...? Is that right? You're *competitive with Synthipets?"*

I had been advised not to tell any direct falsehoods, as I was also being measured for hyper-skin galvanic fluctuations...Besides it didn't look as though I could hide much, so I said: Yes. That's right."

She now leaned into the conversation, her breath slightly fogging *the no fog Plexicurtain.*

She *snickered.* "Okay, now you've got me. You gotta tell me why...Why Synthipets?"

I sighed. *Don't lie!*

"Okay. They annoy me. They're trying *soooo* hard to be human. They're *not* of course, but you're supposed to – on some level – *Accept and Believe...*Like the commercial says."

I parsed my words carefully here.

"...I try to out think them and pose questions that they cannot answer so they will fail and ...be exposed."

"Really?"

"Yes..."

She shook her head. The expression on her face said that I had just made it worthwhile for her to be *awake today.*

"Okay let's get back...You have a predisposition to bet

long odds on short days…?"

She droned on and on.

Wherever she asked a question, I answered (mostly) honestly.

I was no longer in control – in any way or manner. My mind shrieked: *This is going very badly! I can't hide anything from the Gov.*

"MOVING ON TO FAULTS…"

Of course, I knew most of them, but sitting here knowing that a total stranger knew all of them was humiliating, and worse it might be *disqualifying.* Some of them were bad; some of them were antisocial; the kiss of Death in the Big City.

"Yep, Mr. Milo, you are an open book to the Great State of…" She made a face, scratched her scruffy hair and waved her hand as if saying the rest of the sentence was just too much trouble to bother with.

In just a few more minutes, she'd flayed me open, and she knew it.

She grinned at me through the plexicurtain. "After a few weeks on this job, you get pretty good at it."

She had one more unpleasant surprise awaiting me: *Likelihood of aberrant behavior.* Clearly, she savored this part and waited with anticipation.

"Hmmm…Drugs, theft, assault…*Worldwide spamming operation? Damn me!* Is this what we have to look forward to from you?"

I'm screwed. I shouldn't have read up on that guy who made millions resending spam, especially since I thought of a way to quadruple the activity of any message. I was just idly thinking... I have so much time. There is so little work... Surely, they'll understand.

But in my gut, I knew that I was screwed. Next level, here I come. Damn my luck! How will I live down there? This is horrible!

AMID WALLOWING IN MY SELF-PITY, I noticed that she was speaking again. She thanked me for my cooperation in doing my civic duty and being more or less *on time.*

"That's rare these days. I appreciate it," she said this as she released my arm and the mechanism automatically sprayed: *Procaine to make you forget the pain©,* the deadening agent on my skin and blood draw sites.

You'll forget ALL *about it!* the ad continues.

I did. In minutes, literally.

On the upside I had acquired an additional six chits; one was good for 15% off at the State Sponsored GovClinic; one was good for a nice meal, one was a day inside at the GovHealthFacility, and another one was for…the *Exit Station.* Just in case I felt *the need.*

I did, after this crash and burn! But that's too drastic, this soon.

* * *

THE BREEZE WAS fetid and a bit damp. I waited just outside as I had been instructed.

They made me wait almost *fifteen minutes!*

The Bastards!

The retinal burn of an incoming message from a high-powered source made me stumble a bit.

"Between the tourists and the damn locals and now the government," I cursed under my breath.

There was a bunch of GovSpeak text, which I ignored.

Then I saw the face of my examiner. I leaned into a recess in a building. I'm certain passersby thought that my *WayStation* was remerging unexpectedly after lying dormant for a time.

Now it's a common occurrence. No one anticipated the residual bounce-back effect. No one was worried about those aspects back then anyway.

She was officious and followed the text carefully: "Mr. Milo. We clearly see bad behavior from you in your recent past and more likely coming. We see a high likelihood of assaults, mail pilfering, drug abuse, shoplifting, theft...and *spamming.*"

She couldn't hide the disgust in her voice at the last...*aberration.*

"Some of the worst possible anti-societal behaviors."

She pursed her slack, pale lips. "Is this what we have to look forward to from you? Assault, theft, and worse, if you're not properly supervised and employed?"

I hadn't realized that that last question was not rhetorical.

"Mr. Milo? Is this what we can expect?"

Don't lie. They'll know.

I nodded, certain of my defeat and already dejected.

"I think The Great State...and so on, needs a verbal assent."

Oh. Yeah.

"Yes. I guess it is. You can see everything. So...yeah, I guess you're right."

"Thank you for your reply. Please stand by."

I shrugged.

The connection had ended, and my life had just begun to unravel like cheapo Georgian cotton shorts from the Lo-PriceMart.

A minute or two had passed. Then.... "Stand by."

I did. I had this sense of doom, but where was there to run? The State knows everything...even where I'd go.

I'll just stay here. It's easier.

"Stand by."

.   .   .

I "STOOD BY" for *another* fifteen minutes. Meanwhile, passersby seemed to be wondering about me and if I had just had a flashback of *WayStation,* and by now had given me a wide berth, or worrying that I might have a layover of *Fight-BiteDie* from last night.

I didn't, but if it kept the creepers away, why not let them think that?

THIS TIME, the retinal burn was intense enough to double me over stifling a yelp of pain. I'm certain that everyone giving me a wide walk now worried that I had just taken *Howler. Howler* makes those in its thrall think that they are werewolves.

A few Howlers have eaten the necks of innocent victims. Chewed right through! I saw on the unauthorized newsfeeds. Oh no! Another aberration. I'm fucked!

As my eyes cleared and I scanned those around me, I saw mostly worried faces, anxious to get to the next office, and away from the trouble that they thought they saw brewing in me.

"Mr. Milo?"

"Yes?" I tried unsuccessfully to steel myself against the coming verdict. Come back up to the interface."

"IT IS clear that we are worried about you; and that we are right to feel this way."

I tried to control my breathing. The Great State of New York, and whatever, could probably monitor everything, except my thoughts.

At least those are still mine!

"We are troubled given the things we've seen in your basic ...well... deficiencies."

Oh, I am so screwed!

"We believe that the only way to preserve Order within our society is to *nip* these problems *in the bud!*"

One level down? No!

She paused girding herself for the final blow.

My breath sped up. I'd sensed my doom.

"There is little doubt that you will be a drag on society if you're not directed in a better way. "A Smarter Path," as they say in the Public Service ads."

She drew out the verdict as if she was enjoying it. She wanted me to squirm.

I did. Repeatedly.

"And so, we have, after careful consideration decided..."

Get on with it! If you're going to screw me, just do it! Don't drag it out!

"...that it is important to the State that you get a position." A chit fell out of the drawer. It was purple.

"You will provide work and service for your food chits. This chance will keep you busy and out of trouble."

I looked at the purple chit as if I'd just taken a big hit of *Duster.*

I wasn't certain that it was really there.

I touched it and felt a bit better.

It is real!

I put it in my pocket and followed the instructions accompanying it.

* * *

AFTER A MONTH IN *DEEPSLEEP*, I was trained and ready for my assignment. No one warned me that I'd not be back until after training.

I hope that my cat is okay.

I rode an elevator that wasn't all used up and scarred. It

wasn't new, but at least it worked. In a few more minutes, I had reported to my new job. I was given my assignment, and shown into my work area.

I was cementing my next three years of food chits, and all I had to do was be able to stand this job for four weeks. All I had to do was follow procedures and help people.

AFTER A FEW MINUTES, someone entered and spoke in the receptacle into my plexicurtain.

AND THEN, as I was trained, I said: "Thank you for being more or less on time. Your government appreciates it. Put your hand in the socket, please."

Copyright Zaslow Crane
ZaslowCrane.com

12

ALL FOR A BREATH OF FRESH AIR

I could easily see a small, but livid grouping of pimples getting ready to ransack the skin of the young attendant at the renta- car place. The screen was very high rez and, she was of course, virtual. I viewed her image in the holo-interface thoughtfully provided by the renta- agency. She couldn't hide her disbelief and was obviously a bit aghast that I'd bother to *actually go* to a place *personally* to borrow a vehicle. *I'm probably the only customer she's ever seen "in realsies."*

"I lost a bet," I lied. The truth might take hours of explaining to an uncomprehending virtual listener, certainly one so youthful, who'd grown up knowing nothing else.

She tried to help.

Well, can't you buy your way out of it? I mean, the expense and time…just for one way, you'll be *outside* for almost six hours! *One way!* Where will you sleep? What will you do…*out there?"*

This clearly was beyond the imagination for this young woman, cozy in bed, or comfy and safe at home with her virtual connection somewhere… remote.

"A bet is a bet. I said I'd go. A person has to honor his commitments. Your boss can depend on you being here, right? That's a commitment, too."

I paused and spread my hands in a 'ta da!' gesture. "Here you are," I'd gestured to a sexless robot. Her image on the screen where a face would have been if I'd been speaking with a real person was one of deep and profound incomprehension. The vid screen was placed at head height to simulate a person-to-person encounter. I didn't think, that in this case, it was "working."

"I suppose…"

See? I knew that if I tried to really explain, I'd get that blank look.

"Though…," she continued sing-song'ey. "If I was like, sick or busy, or something, there's always someone else," she added as an afterthought. I imagined that I could see her shiver in a bit of fear or apprehension for me.

I mean, I could have had the renta- car delivered, but for some reason, I *wanted* this experience, too. I wanted to experience *all* of this trip. Besides my tiny terrace, I can't remember when I was *outside* last.

When I was very young, I remember my parents taking me on *trips.* Orchestrated by my father, we would "go see the countryside" every month or so in a renta- vehicle. In retrospect, my folks were "throwbacks" even then. I think I need to break out of this cocoon that I've wrapped m'self in.

Just like this young lady "before me," I "went into work" two or three days a week. I fulfilled my obligations. Working a six-hour shift now and then. I'd "inhabit" a robot, and suddenly it'd be a "he," because I was in it...virtually, of course. When I left and it might be taken over next shift by one of my female co-workers, the 'bot would then become a "she." And so on. Business marches on, albeit with more mechanized workers these days than before, but the gods of commerce must not be denied. Buy we must; work we must.

DESPITE THE DEMAND for us to work, we rarely *went to work.* Most of us never leave our homes. We simply log into our computer terms and access work, play, and recreation opportunities... Whatever we desire.

As for socializing, well, 99% of that is done virtually as well. Before setting out on this journey from Altadena to Yosemite, I hadn't seen any of my good, close friends *in person* for years. Entertainment, new clothing, dinners, random foodie items...all were delivered by drones, which dot the sky 24/7/365. Occasionally an unhappy looking driver will bring something.

"Unhappy" is the important word in that sentence. He ... or she was unhappy b'cause they were "out & about" when they could (*and should,* presumably) be safely *snuggified* at home.

This is what I felt I needed t'change. I needed to go out and see things in the "realisies."

Here's an interesting example for you to consider: There's an orchestra in Pasadena, near where I live. It's quite famous. Every instrument is played remotely by a robot controlled from home, or from wherever else the musician chooses. By the way, they still sound fabulous. And, I say *every instrument*. That's not entirely true. The percussionist still goes in. He stands there among the robots of various shapes, functions and sizes, looking just a tad out of place; uncomfortable.

He plays with all of his *fellow musicians*. But he's the only one who actually shows up *in person* for rehearsal and performances. There's an old musical saying: "There's nothing dumber than a drummer." In this case, in light of what I'm looking at now, I wonder rather if that old saying is not onto something.

So, looking at Yosemite "in the flesh" as it were, I wondered yet again: Why do this? I'd awakened one morning to question almost everything in my life. With so much free time, I "read" a lot. I'd been on another of my "reading binges."

Of course, when I say reading and books that's simply a way to describe an idea. There are no books at all any longer, of course. Books are all acted out in vid plays and very good CGI. I'd stumbled across a book on the exploration of the Antarctic. This was explored ages ago. I could *go* there if I chose in five minutes now of course. But why would I? Besides, it's all melted now anyway.

Anyway, I was struck at the bravery and tenacity of these intrepid adventurers. I was struck by the hardships these fellows endured just to explore. Where has this impulse gone? It seems to have evaporated, as does spilled water on my terrace on a sunny day.

And I say *fellows* because now, anyone can go anywhere... virtually, but in this earlier age, all of the exploration was done exclusively by men. I suppose women were thought too fragile or undependable to traverse these unexplored wastelands.

What crap. This has not been my experience with women.

One daring account, then another, and another... I began to devour these vid/books. It became the only thing I was interested in. The nice folks at the Amazon/library/function checked in on me (under the aegis of one their mental health care functions, I assume) to make certain that I had not developed an unhealthy *fixation*.

"Oh, I go through these phases. Check my rentals... Sometimes I like detective stories; sometimes spy stories...."

This seemed to send them away knowing that they'd done their job and if anything were to happen; if any societal aberration were to occur, they couldn't be blamed for not at least inquiring.

Besides I'd not lied. But this...exploration...*This* was something different; more... *urgent.*

ANYWAY, once I had the idea, it lodged in my brain and wouldn't let go. It took a *full fifteen minutes* to locate a renta-dealership via my terminal. I guess there were still a few folks who actually went outside and drove to places physically...the eccentric...the very wealthy. I certainly didn't fit the second description though, and as for eccentric? I'd never thought of myself in that way before.

I smiled, feeling very *daring.*

Things change.

It took *even longer* to find a *selftaxi* to take me to the renta-agency. When I made the vidcall, I was told I'd have to wait a while, because the car was busy.

The car was busy. The *car? There's only one of them for all of Pasadena? Incredible! Well, there would be more than one if there was the demand for it.*

* * *

I TOOK in a deep breath of the clean, pure air. It was delicious! The birds were singing, and I resolved to go hiking so long as I was here.

I stood overlooking Half Dome from the Yosemite parking area. It was stunning… a clear day…beautiful sky… no crowds. In fact, I was surprised to find myself here all alone. People used to make the pilgrimage to the most beautiful scene on earth; they'd arrive from simply everywhere, drawn by the pictures, the beauty. Now, it's empty…And it's pretty *surreal 'cause o' that.*

I've never married. I like my own company, but this sort of *alone* was a bit shocking. To be in a spot like this completely unaccompanied… I mean, my renta- car is the only car in the parking lot. And the parking lot is overgrown with weeds.

This speaks to a dearth of visitors for a long time….

A ROBOTIC VERSION of a forest ranger instructed me that the paths were no longer maintained as so few people actually walked them.

"Since virtual tours of nearly anywhere, all of Yosemite included, could be accessed either without leaving home or by use of a proxy, why bother?" He, the ranger inhabiting this 'bot was as uncomprehending as the renta- woman behind the renta- car counter.

"Drones can take you anywhere without the inconvenience of climbing and working hard.... It's virtually the same experience."

He paused.

I imagined "him" accessing another argument against going down the paths.

"Why bother?" He finished as if this argument would convince any rational person.

Moreover, I already knew that if one was to send a surrogate, to see Yosemite for instance, they are, of course, equipped with extraordinary telescopic vision, thermal scans and much more. The *entire experience...* except that it wasn't...*entire*. It was...synthesized. It was canned, and sterile.

*And that is enough for most people...*I mused. "That's fine for them."

Thanks to scientific advancements, the "need" to actually *physically go* there or to go anywhere, was pretty close to nil.

"I think that I need to do this...."

I KNOW people who live at the bottom of the ocean... *virtually*. They study plants and animals, currents and seismic activity, all from the safety of their homes or research centers. A once somewhat hostile environment has been "tamed" by *intrepid* souls who are completely safe; but still virtually "there."

And if you'd care to talk about a hostile environment: People "man" the Mars probes that now have "pilots" who work in full-day shifts for the now routine 228 days' flight. It's entirely *virtual*. The way things are going, it's unlikely that Man will ever physically set foot on the Moon again, much less Mars. There's serious talk of them using the Mars base to leapfrog to Jupiter. This, I'm told is, exponentially more dangerous, and so Man is further discouraged from going there as well.

One more reason to stay home.

"One small step for Man; one giant leap for Mankind," is now a concept from the distant past; both in reality and intellectually. *Virtually* forgotten, though I've read about *those* explorers as well.

I've not forgotten.

I inhaled deeply.

Heaven.

I scanned the trees, feeling...well...*Exhilarated.*

Are people so scared, so lazy, so busy that I'm alone here today? Is that it? *Well not me. I'm out...here! And it's wonderful!*

I looked around, spreading my arms to feel the breeze and warmth of the sun as fully as possible.

The canned tours can't do this! Where to begin? This place is vast!

OF COURSE, there were numerous interim stages on the way to this development. When I was a kid, people still went places. For a time, there still was *travel*...then it was slowly whittled away by the rising fuel costs and availability of travel diaries.... People started keeping virtual travel diaries, which were then sold to services and accessed by the thousands...by people who would like to see these things but don't choose to leave the comforts of the home. I like to imagine that those young people who those original travelers interacted with in the vids are now grandparents; some of them quite wealthy from royalties, I'm told.

As for mementoes, always a standard part of every trip, all one needs to do again is access a given file. I have a friend who has "visited" every state in the Union. As a souvenir, he bought knives and other items from every tribe of Indians in the state he'd just visited. He just buys access to a file and has it sent to his 3-D printer. There you have it; from the printer to the display case. Between the virtual travel and the souvenirs, it has been, for years, difficult to dissuade him that his sort of travel wasn't vastly superior.

...AND, by implication: that he *isn't vastly superior as well... We'll see about that now, won't we?* I thought smugly.

Now, as I stand here at the railing of Yosemite gazing out on the valley that has captivated so many people, for so many years, I finally know the answer, however difficult it might be to explain it to him when I *see* him next.

I *see* the birds. *Real birds,* not the ones that were captured on vidfiles years ago. I *feel* the sun; the heat radiating out from the old wooden railings. I *feel* the railing under my hands; I *feel* the pavement under my slippers; I see the fabled Half Dome mountain and it calls to me. I think about Burton, Stanley, Hillary, Shackleton, Byrd…the list goes on forever. Just for a moment, I imagined that I was one of their number, and just for fun, pretended that I alone had discovered this place; and I alone would be the first to go see it's beauties for m'self.

"Going down the paths is no longer recommended…," the young man *in* the robot stammered.

"Thanks. I'll be careful."

How bad could it be? Thousands, no hundreds of thousands of individuals have walked where I am walking.

"Well, if you must go, please stay on the trails and take this."

The synthflesh hand proffered a small device.

I picked it up.

"What is it?"

"It's a tracker… Just in case."

"I don't need…"

"Park rules. And, please bring it back. I only have the one…."

I looked at it again. A small green light blinked slowly, reassuringly.

"Well, I guess it couldn't hurt." I put it in my pocket.

"Thank you, sir. Also, the park closes an hour before dark. Please keep an eye on the sun and meet me here before then."

"Okay."

"Have a good walk." I could see the consternation and worry for me on the face of the young man in the vidscreen.

Yeah, I don't exactly know why myself. I only know that I need to really go somewhere and do something.

Besides, I'll have bragging rights for years with my friends.

I laughed a bit t'myself.

Maybe not. They'll think I was crazy! No, they won't.

I took a deep breath.

They'll think that I was crazy brave!

I started down the path; the sound of fine gravel crunching beneath my feet mixing with a blue jay scolding me off to my left and rapidly *dopplering* away. The sound! I've never heard it quite this way on my system's speakers!

"That's amazing! Fantastic!" I murmured afraid to disturb the preternatural quietude of the place

I walked for a bit kicking up dust and occasional moist clods of earth.

Wow, this is really dirty. My slippers are getting destroyed. This isn't how I remember things when my Dad took us out "camping."

At this point, I noticed moisture pooling in my armpits. It was quite unpleasant.

There's no atmospheric controls here. The books don't talk about this at all. Our ancestors struggled for thousands of years to create "Inside" …Yet here I am outside. Is this my perverse nature? I'm outside. Outside is bad; it's retrograde. And, I need to

pee. How do I do that? Where do I do that? There is no ...facility for urination.

What was I thinking?

My slippers now feel heavy and my progress is slow. This isn't how I imagined it would be. *Nothing* like reading the books on the subject. And, when I was young, my Dad took care of all of the details; now ...now? well...there's dirt on my slippers...am I doing this wrong?

I considered turning back, but tossed the idea because I'd really only just left the parking lot.

I'll be brave and stick it out.

The path wound its way down at around a ten-degree angle I'd guess. Steep but not unpleasantly so. I smelled a distinct aroma.

Is this real pine scent? It is certainly not a simulation? Wow!

Since humans have stayed away, the place is alive with little critters, curious at this new thing in their midst. They grab a quick glimpse and then disappear into burrows or brush.

I looked up at the sun.

Already well past its zenith. Should've gotten an earlier start. Oh well...this is far more than I've done in years. This is pretty jaz...Far more than any of my friends...

OKAY. This is probably enough. I'm here; actually, and really. Maybe it's time to go back.

I compulsively consulted my sat fone and data device. I checked on the weather and, just for fun, looked to see what weather was predicted for the next 30 days.

I STOPPED at a flat part of the pathway and looked up and then down the path, trying to decide if this was *enough*.

My dad was a big influence in my life. I wanted to do whatever he might have smiled upon, had he been here. So, I decided to go a bit further down the trail, because my Dad would have been proud of his *intrepid outdoorsman*.

Then I changed m'mind.

This is enough.

I was about to turn around. I'd had enough exploring.

I was about to go back Home.

I guess I shifted my weight on the dirt path and that too, was enough.

The path gave way.

One moment, I was taking in the sights and sounds; the next I was tumbling head over heels, through brush, down and down.

Funny, the stuff that goes through your mind at a time like that: the feel of the dirt as it rushed by me, the smell of the bushes I'd half crushed with my body as gravity tugged me toward the bottom of the ravine...I wondered if the critters had undermined the walkway with their burrows too.

I finally ended up stopped at the bottom. I was in an uncomfortable angle.

As I struggled to right myself, I also tried to assess if I was hurt. Signals were stumbling in from various parts of my body, so I attempted to get my bearings. I sat up. There was an explosion of pain. One leg was resting at a weird angle.

If I didn't move, it didn't hurt so much.

So fine. I won't move.

This is fucked. How am I going to get out? Surely there will be a search drone.

I REVELED in self-recrimination and at my bad luck for a few pain-filled moments, then I recalled my satfone.

I'll call for help. No problem.

I patted my pockets.

Nothing.

It must have fallen out as I tumbled.

Oh damn. Damn...Oh okay...the tracker.

More patting; steadily becoming more urgent, as nothing turned up; again, not on my person.

In desperation, I looked around. Twisting my body brought me up short.

Whoa! That's painful!

I struggled to see either device; either device might save me. I scanned the hill above.

There it is! The tracker! Just out of reach; just up the hill.

It took me a few pain-filled moments, but I pulled myself up far enough to grab the little plastic device.

Flipping it over I discovered that the reassuring little green light wasn't blinking any longer. The tracker was dark.

Damn. Not good. Must have been damaged in the fall.

A bit of nervous laughter bubbled up...I was slow-dancing with fear now.

I broke it...And he's only got the one! He's going to be... angry!

Maybe I hit my head or something on the way down. Maybe I blacked out for a while, because the next time I looked up at the sky, the sun had set. Twilight had begun in earnest.

Shit.

I started to list my options mentally. The list wasn't very long at all. I couldn't see much with the failing light and the vegetation growth at the bottom. I have precious little experience outside....

I guess it costs too much to clear brush if no one goes here anymore.

I really hadn't considered that I might have to spend the night here before this moment. That was a sobering thought.

I have to endure all this just because I wanted to see and feel the outdoors? Just because I wanted to have a response to Chad who was such a superior-acting douche and collected Indian artifacts?

Of course, I tried shouting.

I hadn't gone so far. Maybe my voice will carry.

I wasn't thinking that there might be notes of distress in my voice. Notes of distress that might bring unwanted company.

Soon, I felt rather than heard something moving through the brush. I couldn't see much...Oh no, they were too careful, for that, but I did see movement in the bushes maybe 30 or 40 meters away to my right, and more movement slipping by other bushes to my left.

Steady...It might not be anything.

Whoever they were, they were in no hurry.

I certainly wasn't going anywhere.

It was then that I caught another smell. It was a sort of funky and unpleasant scent. Since my eyes weren't that useful, my hearing and sense of smell had *stepped up.*

Then I heard soft panting, like in dog vids. It was surprisingly close by it was. Almost like someone whispering in my ear in the dark.

Then a thought came to me that chilled me to the bone: *Wolves.*

Finally, I had a shape and a threat to go with the stealthy movements around me.

I was being stalked by wolves!

I reached for stones and threw them at moving shadows. They hesitated. I got as big a stick as I could and I yelled, waving it menacingly. They drew back...for a bit.

I tried using the stick as a crutch.

I've gotta get out of here!

But it was dry and brittle, and I landed on my ass almost where I'd originally ended up. The fall took my breath away with the brilliant crescendo of pain from a really messed up limb. And in a few minutes, they were closing in again. They were patient and, dare I say, *professional.*

I could see four, no five pairs of eyes. *Five pairs that were too brilliant* in the rapidly diminishing ambient light…. Their eyes were almost as if lit from within, from some fire; some hatred of mankind, that burned from across the centuries.

Now they were within an easy rock throwing distance away from me. Unfortunately, I'd already thrown any rocks I could reach.

They were not afraid and moved as a team, getting closer, closer.

This is awful! My desire for status in my group is going to get me eaten!

SUDDENLY, two robotic…*hounds* bounded onto the scene and one launched itself at the leader snarling and clamping steel jaws on the wolf's neck. He yelped in pain and the others melted into the brush *as if they'd never really been there.*

One *dog* stood guard over me, the other shook the wolf in its powerful jaws until the wolf was so afraid, it ran away as soon as it was released!

A camera emerged from my guardian's head. It swung to the right and left, assessing my situation and documenting my fall in near IR-low light imaging, I assumed.

A calm voice emanating from the robodog's chest spoke: "A hovercraft is on its way. You have nothing to be afraid of. All will be well again soon. Just relax."

I was so relieved. Just a moment ago, I thought I was going to die!

I think I whimpered a bit, just to myself.

I was so grateful I wanted to cry.

* * *

MY HOVERCAM SWUNG around my home and focused on my display case. I had the case specially made. It had been delivered by Robotic Services Inc., just this afternoon. I had a new prized possession and I wanted to be able to show it off to my friends.

Virtually, of course.

"Behind this glass, you'll see an excellent three-dimensional representation of *Canus Lupus Arctos*...Just like one of the pack of blood thirsty beasts who almost killed me."

"Impressive."

"Ohhhhhhh!"

"Stunning!"

"Beautiful."

"Amazing!"

Ah good. My friends approved. They are all watching from their homes, but "here" now for this "party".

"I just finished pulling it out of my printer. It did a nice job, didn't it?"

Waaaay more interesting than a bunch of lame Indian knives and pots and things!

"And you actually went *out* there?" One incredulous friend inquired as she watched fixated, as the hovercam played slowly over the details of the powerful legs, after spending long, long seconds detailing the large canines and feral snarl.

"What were you thinking?" Another friend gushed.

I smiled in a sort of gleeful ignorance, having recently been granted... *a new life.*

"Honestly, I have no idea...Midlife fantasy of some sort, I suppose."

I settled into my safe, cozy chair in my safe, cozy home, smiling.

My guests chattered on, sharing an audio channel on my home entertain-sys.

WHAT THE HELL was I thinking...?
I chuckled silently, and shook my head at my most recent folly.

I HAVE NO IDEA.
Fuck...
No... idea at all...

13

THE ROC OF PETRA

"Red socks."

That's what the dead-drop message had said: "Wear red socks, and I will know you; and you me."

Where in the fecking hunymony will I find "red" anything on this monchromatic backwater planet?

It took half of an afternoon, but I got it done. That's what I do, I get things done. That's my specialty.

I lounged on one of the maglev train's slings with my legs out into the aisle, thinking about the ad I'd seen. The ad that caused me to be here, now.

"ISO ex-military types adept with
weapons and campaign experience
for a paramilitary mission into the
forest. The potential rewards are
enormous, if the risk you are willing
to take."

SO HERE I SAT, showing off my red socks for my contact. It was yet another hot and hazy day in this backwater hellhole.

My name is Linklattar. I've been on this fly blown rustic rock for almost eight months. Eight months in which I've wondered about every decision I've made for the last couple of years, especially since leaving Earth and coming to Mirren. I considered going back, back to Earth, as I do every so often, if for no other reason than to get the hell out of here.

Being here, as bad as it is, is better than going back right now. I know for a fact that some of those people back there... will still be holding a grudge.

THE NATIVES WERE as inscrutable as the weather; all hot, dry and dusty with occasional short showers. These showers always surprise me, but the natives always seemed to know beforehand. Weird.

As INSTRUCTED, I wore nondescript colors and fashions, instead of my ususal bodyarmor. I wore all light brown, the most common color in this part of the world. All tan except for *the socks.*

I wondered about that for a moment and then resumed looking out the window. I usually wear the light and very baggy pants favored by the natives here on Mirren. When standing still, the pants are so baggy they look like a full length skirt. I hate looking like a girl; the things I put up with trying to find work. Damn.

*Geez. There isn't anyone here but me and this lady with her bawling, ugly kid. I hope she's not my contact...*I looked around some more.

Waiting was never my strong suit.

Hell, I don't even know if it's a "he or she" I'm waiting to meet.

There was a slight jar and then the tingling...We're moving again. Finally. We'll be in Kino in less than an hour. What if he doesn't show by then? There were no contingency instructions as to what I should do if that happens. That would be bad. I don't think I even have enough for the return trip....It's damn tough making a living 'way out here.

I hadn't even brought anything to read. The message had said to come empty-handed. So even though I could easily have left a reader on the train, I came empty-handed as I had been instructed. This might be a good paying gig. I didn't want to blow that over a fecking reader.

THE DUN COLORED countryside whisked by the window at

400kph and what little I could see was more of a washed-out looking impression rather than anything in detail.

My *sightseeing* was interrupted by the lady and her fussing brat again. I looked around to glare at them for making so much noise. It was then that I saw a tall man wearing much the same outfit as me: a doublet and panatloons. He was standing in front of me, just looking.

I wasn't in the mood. There were five cars. I looked up, pizzed off and tired.

"What? Can I help you with something?"

The man put his foot up on the opposite sling, exposing a red sock. He began tying his laces. Then he looked at me pointedly.

"Oh, I was just wondering, I was, if you knew if the train will be on time. Got an appointment, I do."

I looked him up and down as he settled into the sling opposite.

Odd unplaceable accent...Earther, but removed...Mars?

"So far as I know, it is."

"That's blest. Thank you."

Kino was a medium sized town near the frontier. It was where the maglev was spun around for its eventual run back to Cape City, the Capitol. I watched the tall guy for a clue, and when the train stopped, he looked pointedly at me, then got up to leave. So, I followed at a discrete distance.

I followed as if I were trailing him, but not bothering to be subtle. I wasn't concerned if the tall guy glanced back. I looked around to see if anyone remarked on our passage though.

We passed the muni-center and continued toward the outskirts of town. The weak sun was already low in the

Western sky as we rounded a corner and came upon a long, wooded grove. There was a dual row of very large green-dun trees with thick trunks, receding into the distance. These trunks and the leaves hiding everything in the area from prying eyes from above; housing a small bazaar.

As we drew nearer, I could see that one side seemed to be guys selling drugs.

Illicit drugs no doubt, way out here.

The other side...seemed to be a sort of *anything-goes* lover's lane. I could make out various people in various stages of undress.

Oh hell, what the fuck is going on? What weirdness have I tumbled onto?

The tall guy had stopped. He was obviously waiting for me.

Meanwhile, two burly looking guys came out from a hollow in a nearby tree to block our way.

As I came close I heard the larger of the two ask: "What kin' o fun you after? Left fun?" He gestured with a quick tilt of the head to the left side; the sex side. "...or right fun?"

The tall man who I arrived with said, "Neither. Talking only we are. He and me."

This was not the answer either of the two giant meat roadblocks had been expecting or wanting.

The tall man turned to me.

"The MirrenGov watches and listens to everything. All places in this god forgotten metro are fully covered with cams and buggies...All places except here."

Meanwhile, the two burly guys had reached a decision:

"You gotta go, you no buy something."

"Yeah!" the other agreed

So, the other one had a tongue after all.

The tall man smiled ingratiatingly.

"I can pay. We'll stay away from both sides. We just need a *quiet* place to chat."

The two guys looked at each other, momentarily confused.

The tall man extracted a debit voucher from a fold in his doublet and handed it over. The second roadblock brother produced a scanner and after passing the card over it, he smiled and nodded.

The two guys backed away from their gate; doors, swinging wide. Each gestured to go right in.

"Nothing weird tho, you hear?"

The big man on the left whispered as I passed.

A few steps further on we got some strange looks from "vendors" on both sides. I tried to open my mouth to say something but with a sharp wave of a long fingered hand, the new guy cut me off. Instead, the new guy spoke: "I am Abbot. You are Bishop."

"Wait a second, my name's…"

His eyes met mine and flared a bit. Then, he restated himself more firmly.

"I am Abbot. You are Bishop. No real names. From now on until we're done and we part ways. This is the only name we use. Understand?"

"Yes."

"Good. I did some back checking on you. You've got a very strong reputation on Homeworld. Tell me why you're on Kino?"

We walked.

"There was a misunderstanding…" I started.

"Yes, I heard."

"I felt that it was *expedient* to leave rather than try to sort things out, at least until tempers had cooled a bit."

I looked around and doing so, I noticed the two road-block brothers giving us the stinkeye.

Abbot followed my eyes, noted possible trouble, nodded and continued.

"I see. So, are you finding a lot of work way out here. Is there much work for a man with your unique skills?"

"No. To tell the truth, I'm pretty amazed at how expensive everything is here, considering what a flyblown waste tract this whole planet is."

"And?"

"And, your ad sounded like something I could excel at and make enough gin to get off this damn rock."

"Well, that maybe so. I'm putting together a team of specialists. We're going after something that will set us all up for life. However, I must tell you, that I seriously doubt that *all* of us will return alive."

I stopped walking.

"Hmmm. How dangerous?"

His smile was as cold as a reptile's.

"No moreso than Taranga Straits...."

I gritted my teeth. *Taranga Straits. Damn.* I thought back.

"We lost half the division taking that feckstick Taranga. Then, we had to dash out because the bastards booby-trapped it. We lost even more when the entire island sank!"

That was the last place I wanted to remember right now.

"As I say, risks, there are."

"Understood."

I was weighing my options when the roadblock brothers came up behind us. Each was hefting a long fat dowel with lots of *divots* in each.

Lots of use in that bludgeon, I thought.

Abbot turned to the two big guys. I noticed that he'd deftly palmed an *out-of-a-pocket* a small round device. From out of the device, I could see twinkling "string" playing out. Abbot stayed cool and calm and the brothers didn't seem to notice the string, but I did! I slowly backed away scanning for something I might use as a weapon.

"We t'ink you no pay enuff to hang aroun'. You no buy no-ting."

The other moved to my side, gently tapping the bludgeon in his ham-like hand.

Then he added: "We tink you should pay more. You pay right now!"

I guess the brothers thought I was getting ready to run, because they moved fast to cover the space between us.

At this, he raised the small tree in his hand, but Abbot had activated the "policeman's friend" in his hand.

The "string" froze into a diamond studded and very efficient cutting device four feet long!

Abbot sliced diagonally shoulder to hip across the guy about to strike us, and when the other assailant saw what was happening, he swung at Abbot's head.

He neatly sliced through the wood and continued his swing carrying away the top of the second guy's head.

I stood there poleaxed by Abbot's over-the-top reaction.

"Feck….me!" I breathed in shock and awe. I expected him to cut the bludgeon and scare the piss outta them. I wasn't expecting...*this!*

I wondered at this overreaction. Does he have Loastacin? The spacer's disease? That would explain...*this.* I looked for an escape from this crazy dek.

I saw him press the small orange third stud, which vibrated the blood off the line and retracted it. He turned off the tiny sabre and pocketed it as we made to leave.

"Come on!"

The people having sex were otherwise engaged, but the drug vendors looked to be armed.

I was no longer sure I wanted what Abbot was selling, but I followed, such was my desperation.

"Come on, damn you!! Time to leave here, it is!"

As we ran, I considered what I'd just seen. Simple weapons...small weapons aren't that difficult to obtain, *But how*, I wondered, *How are there any weapons at all on a world where they are so illegal? Who is this guy?*

The grove was well behind us, but we didn't stop, instead we walked briskly, not talking, but glancing behind every few steps to see if there was anyone pursuing.

With a weapon like that against a damn cudgel, I guess not, I thought.

* * *

KINO WASN'T BIG, but the walk to the other side of town and halfway back to see if we were being followed took the better part of a deci-hour.

Eventually, and without any other speaking on Abbot's part, we arrived at a grimy looking hotel. He gestured up the stairs and then to the right.

The door looked to be some sort of metal. Not that surprising when you consider that this place is covered in trees but the lumber from those trees isn't worth a tinker's cuss in a snowstorm.

He knocked three times, then two, then four. The door opened a crack, then wider to admit me and Abbot.

Inside, seated around a dingy room were two women and two men.

Abbot pointed to each in turn, the two guys: "Deacon, Priest" and then the two females: "Pope, Saint...Meet Bishop. I believe that we have our quorum. Have a seat, get a drink if you want one...."

He looked at Pope, "Swept the room recently?"

She nodded confidently, "We good..."

"Excellent, thank you."

She nodded in acknowledgement, as if it was her due.

Pope was lithe, thin...looked to be in good shape and literally about half my size. She wasn't pretty in the conventional sense, but she had a look that made me want to look more. *Sexy...independent.*

Deacon was very tall and very thin; balding with long fingers and a long face; Priest was big, a bit bigger than me, and with muscles that strained his clothing.

Saint was stocky, with short-cropped dark hair, and a no-nonsense look about her.

All wore more or less what Abbot and me wore. Not a uniform, just the same colors and styles.

"No servo for the drinks?" I asked.

"Not in a hotel this cheap. You'll need to go get a beer yourself, or you'll die of thirst."

Saint, Deacon and Priest thought this was funny and laughed at Abbot's joke; Pope just watched everything.

I got my drink and *saluted* the others before taking a swig from the small square-ish container. I resolved to find out if the others were recruited in the same manner I was, but figured that could wait. Instead, I sat and waited to be told what the gig was.

Abbot sized everyone up and then started. "Specialists we are. Each of you will fulfill a valuable and essential function. And if you do so, then, there is a chance, just a chance that we will all make it out of here and off world, wealthy people."

He paused and looked pointedly at each of us in turn before continuing.

"The leader I am. What I say goes. Any insubordination will be met instantly with a minigun. Clear?"

Nods all around.

"That's blest. This is my score, but I brought all of you along to do what you do best: Saint, here, is our ordnance and explosives expert."

"Deacon is our marksman. He can shoot any gun and hit almost anything anywhere. If it can be shot, Deacon can kill it."

"Priest will handle the ongoing logistics, planning, subject to my approval, of course, and will be second-in-command."

"Bishop, you're our workhorse. After your experiences dealing with the fiasco and fallout of the Taranga incident. That proves to me that you can handle yourself in a tight situation."

I tensed at that mention of my latest failure again.

"What about Pope?" I asked, missing out the only person not introduced.

Priest said, "Oh, she's coming along as eye candy, the randy little doxy…."

Pope said nothing but saluted with but one finger.

Abbot interjected, "She's an expert finding, diffusing and developing countermeasures for traps…Booby and otherwise. Good with a scanner, too. Supposed to be the best hereabouts."

Let's hope so, I thought.

Saint plopped down next to Pope and hugged her.

"She's gonna keep us safe!"

"Uh, excuse me," I started. "I understand that this will not be a normal para-military operation, but what are we doing…To worry about bombs and booby traps?"

Abbot sat down and looked at each of us in turn.

"Once I tell you the beginning you have to decide if you're in or out. After I tell you everything…You're in. Understand?"

Everyone nodded.

"All right, first, the good news: Extraordinary is the amount of money that comes to all of us if we are successful, and I wouldn't even consider going if I didn't think we'd succeed. It will split seven ways – one for each of us and one to fund this little vacation jaunt. Since this is all on my shoulders and since I will be paying for everything, and since I have the map…I get the extra share. Any objections?"

Pope languidly put her hand up. "I got no problum, but I gotta know whut I'm agreein' to."

Abbot's face clouded over with a brief flash of anger at her impatience.

"Patience…"

She made a gesture with her eyes and hands that said: "Go ahead."

"Fair enough. Anyone ever heard of the Roc of Petra?"

"The mythical bird, out in the scrub?"

"I hear it's ten times the size of a man and ferocious!"

Abbot held up a hand.

"No…The idol. Thousands of years old…Made from a fortune in terranium with precious stones inset all along the base and with two serra-diamonds, diamonds as big as your head, inset as its eyes!"

"Terranium?"

"Just how big would this *Roc* thing be?" I asked. "And, where are the people who worship this idol? Won't they object?"

I spoke up above the general babble.

"And why, for frake's sake, has no one ever gone to steal it, that's what we're talking about, right? Stealin' this precious idol? Why hasn't anyone done it yet?"

Abbot stopped and smiled.

"Again. Now you know. Before I say anything else…In or out?"

He pointed to Pope: "In," she replied.

Then Deacon: "In." In one syllable Deacon's basso filled the room.

Then, me: "Aw…*In*… I got nothin' more promisin'…"

Then Priest: "In, baby! Waaay in!"

"Saint?"

"I'm with him. Waaaay in, too!"

Abbot smiled.

"Well, then. Congratulations. That's blest! Blest it is! We are bound together until we succeed or we die."

He got up to get a bottle of local wine that had been chilling in the refrig unit. He poured a bit in each glass, holding his aloft.

"To success and all of us enjoying it!"

"To success!"

Then I choked a bit on the wine.

"Oh gods, this is bad wine!"

"Yeah, Abbot, where did you get this swill?"

He grinned. "It was the best the bodega at the corner had. Imagine if I'd cheaped out!"

* * *

POPE and I inspected the gear.

"All terrain quad and Corvini six-wheelers, cases of guns: slug and energized pulse tech, bombs and bomb making stuff, the biggest block and tackle I've ever seen... field dampers? *Why do we need field dampers?* Special blades and saws for clean-cutting terranium, rebreathers, gas masks, oxy: in, one, two, three...uh, five forms for our use... Night vision, IR vision goggles, radiation detection and protection, radiation scanners, shoulder mount lasers, mini rail-guns...*gods!* Plus enough food for a month of feasts, all outfitted onto this flat bottomed boat, with a crane built onto the stern, no less!"

She smiled at me.

"Im'pressed?"

"Yes, and more than a little scared that he thinks we'll need half this stuff."

"Scared, too?" she toyed with me.

"Shit, lady. With all this stuff, the six of us could hold off a division of troopers."

She looked at me as if to say: "Don't exaggerate."

"Think about it. What are we strolling into that we need all this firepower?"

I suddenly found Abbot behind me.

Damn! The man moved so quietly!

"I believe in going in…what was the old Earther expression? 'Loaded for bear?' Yes, I believe that was it, though I confess I've no idea what *'loaded for bear'* actually means. Nor any idea of what a 'bear' might be…or might have been. However, in this sense it means taking everything to cover every contingency. I'm paying, so why worry? Think of all this as a cautious man's insurance."

"Not none of us *are*… cautious men… or women."

"Too true. Indeed," A slight indulgent laugh, "Too true, but humor me."

"Yeah…Okay…Where did you find all this stuff on a planet where even owning a little popgun is illegal?"

"Special orders."

"Yeah?"

"Very special orders, they were."

I guess…

Pope laughed a bit at my concerned face, before she slinked away.

I watched her perfect and beckoning ass hungrily, and I'm certain she knew it.

* * *

THE KINOTAL RIVER took us in the right general direction, according to Abbot. It was seldom more than a man's height deep, but it was usually over a hundred meters wide. Hence the flat-bottomed boat was invaluable.

I was struck, I supposed at the river's bright aqua color that became more pronounced in the middle where it was deepest. The contrast with the tan-green of most of the vegetation was remarkable.

I wondered how much that much terranium weighed and if bringing it back on the boat would swamp it or worse. I looked over the side watching the foam flecked blue-green water lazily flow past.

How will we ever unload all that cargo of valuable minerals anyway? Will we melt it down into ingots? Just cut it up? Can I even carry one seventh of our score?

All these things were floating through my mind when I noticed a commotion approaching.

Abbot was pushing Priest in front of him, Priest's arms magna-lock'd behind him. For all his size, he looked helpless, but still defiant.

Then I noticed the pulsegun in Abbot's hand.

"What's goin' on?" Pope demanded. She'd been eyeing Priest during the meeting and smiling that *'I'll see you later'* smile. Things didn't look so good for Priest now.

"I found this, *and this*, in his tackle." He tossed out what looked to be a MirrenGov ID and what might have been a tracking module, onto the scuffed deck.

Then, he hit Priest on the back of his head, forcing him to his knees.

"Somebody give me a second opinion. Is that ID legit?"

Deacon picked up both items and presently whistled in awe.

"He a big deal in Cape City coppers." Then, Deacon put his face in Priest's, "You a fuckin copperhead?"

Deacon suddenly had a small pistol in his hand held up against Priest's jawline.

Priest clenched his jaw and looked defiant.

*Look tough all you want, bitch. But you should also be pra-yin'
to your diety!,* I thought. *That's bad luck, bad planning, bad
everything....*

Abbot shoved Deacon out of the way and dragged Priest
to his feet, standing him at the edge of the boat.

"Anything? *Skinny* bitch? You send the fucking skinny to
the gov on me? Bitch!"

"What you're doing is illeg-"

Abbot shot twice into the air then shoved the superheated
barrel of the gun roughly between Priest's legs.

Priest screamed in pain and alarm.

Abbot stomped down on Priest's feet and Priest's eyes
went wide.

"You're being tracked! I'm your only hope!"

Abbot shot him in the forehead, and a small hole opened
up in the back. Then Abbot lifted his foot and pitched Priest
overboard. Priest leaked the red, red that flows in us all and
the aqua waters briefly turned a ruddy brown, quickly left
behind.

Abbot stood up, trying to collect himself. He grimaced as
if unhappy with himself. He positively *vibrated* with
displeasure.

"Checked, I did. I tried to be as thorough as I could... Still,
I end up with this undercover scum. Damn."

He shook his head. Then he looked at each of us in turn.
His gaze made me want to tremble. I stifled it, but I knew the
burst of violence that he was capable of, wondering if, this
time I'd really 'stepped in it.'

Abbot shook his head sadly, seeming mystified. "I was so
careful. But not enough...Do better next time, I will."

He then turned to us, smiling again.

"Well, we'll have to do without him. More for all of
us, eh?"

"Blest! Blest! Instead of one seventh, now you're all in for One sixth! That difference will buy you a second island on Jondirira, for when you get tired of the main island!"

He tried to sound jolly, but we all were quiet, considering how fast we'd just been whittled down to a party of five instead of six.

Just then, I caught the scent of something *impossible*. I turned to Saint, "Is anyone cooking something?"

She grinned derisively. "On this tub? Where would we even try, hey?"

"Umm hmmm. I guess..."

I could swear that I smelled garlic. Just a whiff carried on the breezes and then gone. *It can't be. Not way out here, so far from Earth. I've not had garlic in ages...*

Then I remembered stories I'd heard, rechecked my weapons, and I began watching the skies more as we moved on.

* * *

"WELL, any loofa salesman can look at the river and track us, eh?"

Abbot looked at a map tacked out on a gunwale. Deacon and Pope looked over his shoulder. Saint sat nearby, but was quiet. The murder disturbed her, as it did me. At the moment, I was as far away from Abbot as possible; at the stern, watching the water swirl in our wake.

"So, now we fool 'em, we will. We go to land sooner than we were gonna. Then we approach from more South-like. The tracker is in the drink with the traitor so all's they know is where we were; not where we gonna be. 'Sides, they got spy satellites. Now they lookin' for us, track us they won't be able to – not if'n we go inland...'Kay?" He looked around briefly.

"'Kay!" He'd answered for all of us.

* * *

WE FOUND a suitable spot to beach our *whale* and set up a *ping'a'pong* to alert us to where we'd left it. It changed *freqs* every second, so no worries on unwanted ears listening in...

When we were finished pulling the flatboat ashore I began taking off my clothes.

We'll need the boat to ferry us back if the score is as big as Abbot says...We'll need to find this damned thing for the return trip, and hope that the MirrenGov types aren't so patient as to wait for us. I was thinking about the equipment we stowed ashore. I tried to guess what would be the most valuable things to bring; what we'd be forced to leave.

Not much chance of backin' out now...I thought. *He's serious enough to murder someone in front of us all. A Gov'ment someone, too. He made his point...and now I've begun to wonder if that was all planned: Get rid of a troublesome hitchiker and make us all afraid; afraid to question him.*

DEACON STRODE over to the area where equipment was being off-loaded.

"What are you doing?" He articulated carefully, as if Earther wasn't his first language.

I looked up. I was stripped to the waist and the ties on my shoes had gotten knotted.

"I figure if we're going into the forest, this is my last chance to wash off. I figure to take it."

The shoe finally came off, then did my pants.

I noticed Pope and Saint watching with interest. *So what?* I dove into the water and then stood up. The water was up to my chest.

Saint called out to me. "You wanna be real careful-like. I hear they got those little chiggers in these waters that go up your willy and make a nest."

"Aw, I won't be in here long enough for them to find me. Just a few deci-mins washin', swimmin' and then out and dry," I replied.

Pope stripped hurriedly and dove in off the boat. Her supple form sliding by me, almost touching. I wanted to reach out for her, but something told me not to.

Saint jumped in a moment later with the air of a chaperone at a party.

Eventually Deacon and Abbotstripped and washed off as well.

When me and the others emerged, we dried off. I changed into clothing better suited for a lot of walking: heavier pants, shirt, hat, special boots and gloves.

I pulled some tape from supplies and taped the place where I'd tucked my pants into my boots. Then seeing interest in the others' eyes, I tossed the roll to Saint who did likewise.

* * *

IT WASN'T EASY, but the quad-bikes found their way through the trees. Sometimes they had to back up for as much as a half-kilometer, but even though the progress wasn't any faster than a man walking, bringing the bikes made it easier to bring a lot of gear. And Abbot was *all about* bringing gear.

Birds high in the trees protested the intrusion and the minimal noise that the battery-powered bikes made, but we saw few land animals. We'd been warned about small, but ferocious 'cats' that were hungry for fresh meat, so each of us had a sidearm loosened in our holsters.

Far, far above them I thought I caught my first glimpse of

the rare and dangerous Mirren Roc. I'd heard a loud call that came from far above, and looked up through the spindly branches and pale green-yellow leaves to see a bird-like figure fly by, but the view was so transitory and the bird apparently so high up, with the trees as cover, that I wasn't certain how much I'd learned.

Pope noticed me looking up.

"They's big, cowboy. Bigger'n a Earther house, I'm told. Eat a lot, too, they says. Eat a whole man in one gulp..."Saint shouted from behind them.

"Yeah, whereas it takes Pope here, a couple-three!"

Pope flipped her off and rode ahead.

I sniffed the air.

Garlic. Very faint, but there for sure.

Abbot sat brushing off crawling insects as he tried to eat. Land animals weren't the real problem. There seemed to be precious few of them hereabouts, but insects, they were the real problem. As you walked, you went through pheromone nets, webs and so forth. Then, you got popular with the insect locals.

"I think they've gotten worse in the last few minutes," Deacon announced swatting another bug.

"Yeah, the ones who found us first, went and tol' their friends."

"They want to get into my eyes, and ears..."

"And your nose and mouth and any other warm, damp place too."

"Any idea of how far away we are? In other words, how much more of these bugs we've gotta deal with?"

"Yeah! I'm getting' ready to just eat them along with my

meal. They're everywhere anyway. 'Sides, they look nice and crunchy."

Saint looked up from her plate. The bugs didn't seem to be drawn to her as much as to the rest of us. "I wouldn't go eatin' anythin' I wasn't ab-so-sure of. I hear from natives that some of those buggies will give you a pretty serious case of the runs."

"So?" Deacon smiled quizzically.

She smiled back, knowingly. "Out here, the *runs* can kill ya..."

She let that information fall like news of a groom with venereal disease at a wedding service and quietly went back to eating.

Eventually Abbot explained that the SatTrack and the map didn't agree. He knew the direction, but not how far.

Swell. I thought. *How can that be? SatTrack can nail your position down to a meter most days...But not today.*

"Figure a week...Maybe a more..."

Saint perked up, alarmed.

"A week? And then the same back?"

He looked over at Saint before answering her. "You know a way to teleport back?"

"No..."

"Well, walk in we do; walk out we do. Oh yes, you'll be earning your payday. Assured. Assured."

AFTER THE FOOD was put away, we were able to set up the bug repulser. It did weird things to food, so you want to be finished eating; drinking, too. But it does keep the bugs away. Ultrasonics. Never been so happy to have a piece of equipment.

· · ·

A FEW DAYS LATER, early on, Saint slipped, fell and cut her hands on the rhino grass.

"Damn!"

Abbot looked at it.

"Did I mention, I've been to Med School, I have. Almost made it to doc, but ran out of funds…Ages ago, it was. Still I can see the wound isn't bad at all. Just annoying and bloody… First off, let's get it cleaned, sterilized and wrapped; secondly, that blood scent will make things busy here in a few, so let's move out. Away from here quickly, we should."

He looked at Saint as he hurriedly wrapped her hands.

"Gloves. A life saver they might be. I provide. You wear. 'Kay? 'Kay!"

We hurriedly left the bloody grass behind, the bikes making little noise.

A SHORT WHILE LATER, I heard grasses and bushes being trampled behind us. The sound was gaining on us.

We bein' tracked by somethin'. I pulled up the bike, setting the brake. I signaled to Deacon with my hand; fingers indicating what and from what direction we might expect followers.

"We got comp'ny. Deacon, you and I should hang back. If you ride with your safety on, take it off."

Myself, I never use the safety. I want to be ready.

Good thing, too. A huge dark glistening reptile with a long snout and lots of snaggle teeth emerged from the bushes behind us. It was obvious that he was gaining on us and had we not stopped he would have run down the hindmost.

That'd be me…

I shot. So did Deacon. Nothing much happened. He kept coming. We shot again and again but with little effect. He was closing now. He smelled a kill; easy meat to be had.

Suddenly from behind me I felt the distinct prickling of the hairs on the back of my neck. It was a railgun warming up.

Abbot stood panting and flushed, wearing the dull metal-colored half helmet that was required to use the damn things, aiming the cannon at the giant lizard.

Then with a deep, and important-sounding *pop*, it fired and there was a distinct rushing sound. A split-second later, the reptile's head opened up as if hit square on the top of its head with some massive meat cleaver; deep, deep reddish blood spraying everywhere.

Then a gout of steam escaped the chamber. Hence, the helmet.

I made a mental note to remind Abbot to replenish the H2O reservoir for his gun, so it'd be ready if we needed it again. *Wouldn't do to fry something so...useful.*

WE STOPPED and looked at the monster in a kind of awe.

"Must be over a thousand kilos..."

"Three...maybe three and a half meters long..."

"Now we know why we haven't seen any small animals."

"Yeah."

Abbot took Deacon aside.

"Deacon, surprised, I am that someone like yourself wasn't better prepared. It shouldn't happen again. If you're stopping next time, I might not hear."

"C'mon, people," I said. "If this guy was following the scent of blood, he might not be alone."

"And now there's even more blood," Pope chimed in.

"Yes," I concurred. "Now there is. More."

She looked at me and there was something in those eyes...I could fall into them and never come up for air. Time seemed to slow down and many of the important things in my life suddenly seemed over rated.

Saint shouted from point, "So? We go now?"

"I, uh, yeah...Let's get out of here."

THE NEXT DAY WAS HELL. We backtracked three times trying to find a way through the overgrowth. That night, amid the sounds of the nocturnal critters in this part of the forest, we figured that we had progressed less than three klicks all day.

Abbot announced that we'd park the bikes. We'd discuss what was to be brought along and what might be left.

If we bring everything... I thought, *we'll never be ready in time for another of those giant lizard things; if we don't...*

I didn't even know the rest of that equation; not knowing only made me more anxious.

After we finished eating and putting food away, Abbot set up the bug repulser.

I hurriedly untied my boots before doffing them and crawling into my little personal enclosure. It was a little thing of special fabrics and a network of little bended rods to keep the dew and whatnot off. You could wipe your hand on the inside and it would go from opaque to clear. I wiped it and watched the stars as I drifted off.

Go to bed early; get up and goin' early...

I slept. At least I slept until sometime in the middle of the night, I felt someone slipping into my one person *tent.*

"Who...?"

"It's me, Pope. I'm scared, and I'm cold..."

"Darlin'..." I shook my head in the darkness. "I don't b'lieve you've ever been scared once in your life, but cold? I guess I'll b'lieve that one..."

I confess, I felt like a kid again trying to nail my first piece of ass, tryin' to be all quiet and still snickering...fumbling in the dark, two people in a decidedly one person space...Eventually though, we found a system that worked.

Afterwards, she went to sleep before me. I looked up and saw a shadow. It might have been Saint, looking in the clear spot I'd created to watch the stars and night sky. It was full-on dark, but I'd swear she was watchin' though it was even darker in my enclosure than it was outside.

"I'll loan her to you, but she's mine. Don't forget that." Was what the shadow whispered before it disappeared.

The next day, Pope was gone before I woke up.

"Hmmm," I wondered if I'd seen and heard what I thought I had, or was I just dreaming?

I looked at my boots again before putting them on again. The slanted light accenting the striations and micro rips in the boot's uppers.

They seemed even more worn than yesterday.

How can that be? I wasn't out walking in my sleep. Could the grasses contain some degenerative chemical? Something that eats the boot materials? They're made here. FOR here. They can't be ignorant of this happening...how will we walk back if our boots are thrashed? Shit.

My blood ran cold.

"ABBOT. LOOK AT MY BOOTS." He did. I held them out for him to see.

"You're showin' wear already? That's weird. Not good weird. You been rubbin' them with tincture of rogue horned beetle?"

"What's 'tincture of rogue horned beetle'?'"

Abbot looked disgusted. Went, you did, and bought boots, the best you could find, yet no one did tell you to wipe the boots down? Each night, that is to be done. Each night. Shameful! Shameful!"

He reached into his pack.

"Here is Priest's supply. Guessing that he'll not object…"

THREE MORE DAYS OF TRUDGING, carrying far too much gear (and two more nights of having an exciting visitor) and we were…there.

I guess.

All I really knew was that Abbot called a halt. He had an air of: *'This is it!'* about him.

I'll admit, I was tired lugging all that gear, so I was glad to have arrived.

THE AIR FELT…ODD. Like there were vibrations happening just out of my ability to sense them. It seemed to make everyone edgy, especially Saint.

Abbot wanted to talk, but after we ate, no one wanted to do anything but bed down.As for myself, I thought about how *comfortable* I was on the maglev train just a short while ago.

Was it really so bad on Mirren? I wondered. *I feel like complete crap now…*

Then, I noticed a smell: Garlic again. *Burnt* garlic. Faint, but definitely there.

Damn.

Garlic? I thought. *Garlic is too expensive to bring out here to waste. It won't grow anywhere but Earth…Garlic costs…out here… It costs a fortune!*

A giant bird-shape glided above brushing the treetops and screeching like the end of days. He'd not made a sound as he approached, and erupted while just above us, this thing the size of a small Earther commercial air transport.

"Damn!" I looked up.

Deacon was already pointing a large gun into the sky, but not sighting yet.

The 'girls' were hastily digging through their packs. Pope for a gun; Saint for a bomb she could throw, I'd bet. By the time each had something in their hands that comforted them, the bird was gone. We all, well almost all of us, stood, shaken and flat footed, looking resolutely at the sky, waiting...waiting for the bird's return, frowning; panting in fear or excitement.

Abbot stood there, gun in hand, his eyes burning, as if daring the bird to return.

The bird didn't come back that day. That was 'Tuesday'... Mirren-time, I think.

Now I know where that smell came from. The stories I'd heard while wasting time in a bar were true. *And that's not good.*

'Wednesday' was the day things started to really go sideways...

THE FOREST GOT UNEXPECTEDLY CHILLED each night, but moreso that particular night. From hot and dusty in the daytime to, 'Damn, I need a coat,' after the sun retreated.

Abbot turned up the central heating emanator sitting in the middle of our campground. We'd used weed-eater to clear the ground of grasses right where we were bedding down and each of us had personal light sources.

"We can have the emanator or we can have the repulser; we can't have both," Abbot announced.

The repulser sets up a field that while making it uncomfortable for bugs, curdles milk in a heatbeat, spoils food in a hurry and completely fucks with most other foodstuffs. So

Bugs, no heat; or…heat with bugs. We voted and opted to be cold, but without bugs.

Big surprise.

We had questions; wanted to plan our *campaign,* but Abbot begged off until "Tomorrow… 'Kay? 'Kay!"

I SLEPT ALONE THAT NIGHT, though I thought I could hear Pope and Saint arguing, whispering, fighting. *Dissention.* I shouldn't have slept with her. I know better, but hormones win out most times. They did the last few days, that's ab'so'-sure. Damn.

I hope that's them trying to work out who's supposed to be where and when. Don't jerk up the mission…Damn. She was so pretty, so sexy, but all I had to do was say: "Get lost, girl. You b'long to someone else." I didn't.

I didn't sleep well that night. Prob'ly 'cause of the vibrations. They seemed to get stronger the closer my head got to the ground.

I didn't like the feeling I got the next morning when I joined the others, either. Maybe the vibrations kept the ladies awake, too.

* * *

IN THE MORNING, Abbot was up cooking; cooking for all of us. Unusual. He was nearly finished by the time I rolled out of bed and rolled up my tent.

I got dark looks from Pope and Saint; Deacon seemed oblivious, nursing his hot caffeine.

It was all meals ready to eat stuff, but cooked instead of just heated and someone else did it for me.

Nice.

I checked my boots again. I didn't like what I saw. Then I

thought about the tires on the bikes. I'd seen wear on them as well.The tires were manufactured specifically for work on this awful rock, and the boots were the best I could buy. Unfortunately, the grasses were winning. I hoped salving my boots each night would slow down the progress of the deterioration.

I got no other way outta here...

"LISTEN UP. Today, reconnoiter we shall. No progress, only see the lay of the land. 'Kay?"

"Why, Abbot? We're here, right?" Saint was impatient to get in, get out and be gone from me, I gathered.

"Oh yes. Here we are, but we are careful going in, yes?"

I pressed my lips together slowly figuring out a few things as the fog in my brain evaporated.

"So, this giant Roc... It's just a bird, but near an ancient temple, is it? – And, it's got something to do with this weird vibration; this feeling I have, right?"

Deacon stopped nursing his liquid stimulant. He was suddenly interested in our conversation.

"Ancient, it is. Yes, yes..."

"Is it a native temple?" I pressed on.

Everyone was paying attention now.

"No. No, it is not...Though it is ancient, quite ancient..."

"Is this the thing that the MirrenGov was trying – *and failing* – to keep under wraps? That weird *something* that was recently found in this tan-green hell...by the surveying sats?"

Abbot looked at me as if I'd spoiled the surprise.

"It was all hush-hush, but someone leaked a few details... then a few more...no one had the complete picture...Until us, right?"

Abbot frowned. Clearly he wanted to dole out the information, not have all of it dumped in our laps at once.

Well, hell, I'm a professional. I thought, looking at his sour face. *D'you expect me to not read the pubs? There's all sorts of valuable information there for free every day.*

As Abbot was about to explain, the damn bird appeared right above us – screeching again. It scared the crap outta me!

A few of us started shooting in the air, but the Roc was already gone. The air stunk of garlic. The Roc...this bird's musk must mimic that smell naturally.

Weird.

Then I looked back at him after the excitement quieted, "And let me guess...the vibrations attract these giants, so they are essentially guarding this...*alien artifact*, right?"

"Yes, and yes...Alien it is, they think."

"So, there's no treasure?" Pope was angry now; before she had just been simmering, *at me I guess*, or Saint. Who cared? Now she was hot!

Abbot's hand reflexively went to the sidearm at his waist. I wondered if anyone noticed besides me. My hand rested on my sidearm in case things spun outta control.

Abbot talked fast, "Oh, yes! Treasure is there. Scanned and catalogued from space, it was. Made from terranium... Treasure...Yes, more than you can imagine. This is why the MirrenGov tried to keep it under wraps; to keep it for itself, but also alien tek as well likely there is. There for the taking, if we can get in."

That brought me up short.

"Whoa! Wait. *If* we can get in?"

Abbot nodded to Pope.

"She's the best in the Four Worlds. I checked. "She will find the booby traps, solve the puzzles, prevent ambushes, snares...She is here so that we can go forward."

"So that's why all the detection devices. You expected to have trouble getting in. You knew from the start that this was no ancient caveman shite; you knew that we were dealing with true ancients who pro'bly crashed and some survived. They built this...as a monument? A beacon? What the hell is it, Abbot? What else do we need to know? What the fuck else should you have told us in that cheap hotel before we committed?"

Abbot scowled. I really think I had spoiled his surprise. He wanted to *tell,* not have it prised outta him.

"Dangerous, it might be, yes. But we don't know this. Pope will ascertain same for us, yes?" he looked over at her.Pope made a gesture that said: "I guess..."Abbot nodded, smiled and continued, "If nothing else, we will have all the terranium we can carry; if we're skillful and lucky, alien tek might be gleaned. If they were here thousands of years ago, mustn't *advanced* be our assumption? Very advanced?"

He paused, gathering his audience in. "And, advanced tek might not weigh much of anything and be far more valuable than terranium."

Well, I for one, no longer wanted to shoot this lunatic in the head...not just yet anyways... I'll wait to see how this plays out first.

Deacon had been watching for the bird again. This time the cannon that he'd been carrying since getting chewed out by Abbot was already aimed in the right general direction. The bird swooped and again began its blood curdling cry, but it was cut short by the thunderous boom of Deacon's gun.

The bird shape flinched, flapped its wings hurriedly and was gone. The garlic smell was even stronger now. Something splatted loudly in the underbrush nearby. Shite no doubt.

The garlic smell is a factor in its blood? Is it a phermone it exudes? Or something it absorbs from the ancients?

"Blest Shot! Deacon, a wonder you are! Truly!"

. . .

AN UNMARKED BOX we'd carried produced little probes on wheels and more that were drone shapes about the size of my boot.

We sent a probe on wheels up the *driveway*, for that was what the approach looked like: an access for large wheeled vehicles.

The wheeled probe was about a hundred millimeters tall with four articulating axels. It rolled blithely the entire way, slowly getting smaller in the distance.

We all watched hopefully with all spec distance glasses.

"It's still okay..."

"Blest! Blest."

There was a single large indentation. That was where I'd go if I were gonna knock to be let in. I steered the probe into it. The ambient light dipped radically, and we all switched to IR. Then we all saw the probe melt.

"Shite!"

"What was that?"

Pope looked into a spec analysis. "Without warning or ramp-up, suddenly there's a highly concentrated beam of what looks like microwaves, and our little rollie is a meltie! It's a puddle. Damn!"

I withdrew a flier and sent it off in the general direction of the cavity. I was intending to control it carefully and slowly once it got close to the artifact, but a hundred meters out, it was sliced into three pieces!

By what, I couldn't see. It, too, was around a hundred millimeters tall. The pieces fluttered to the ground like broken little parts of some child's toy.

The rollie went under the sensor, I guessed. None of us are less than a hundred millimeters *tall* while on our bellies!

So, sneaking in under the sensors isn't Option One. Just walking in upright is a no-go.

Glad t'know that, goin' in...

Abbot took charge: "Five sides there are on this prize. Four we've not seen yet. Each of you take one rollie and one flier and try to approach from each side. Report what happens. Be back in a deci-hour. Go."

As we left carrying our probes, I saw Abbot unlimbering the rail gun.

Okay...so that's how it's gonna be, I thought glumly. *We blast our way in? If we do that, what happens to all that advanced alien tek?*

He saw me looking and guessed my concern.

"A test shot is all. Testing what will be."

He smiled benignly.

I'd seen the crazy beneath. That smile means nothing.

I needn't have worried. The first railgun slug melted before hitting the *door.*

WE GAVE the building a wide berth, sneaking up on it at a right angle to the side we each faced. And, we eventually returned, after tramping through the undergrowth with our toys, and watching them each die from something. I looked at my boots. They were noticeably worse than yesterday.

Pope and I reported for us all.

"What now?" I demanded.

Abbot looked perplexed. "Thinking...thinking, I am."

I WASN'T USED to being denied by machines, alien or not. I pulled out one of the shoulder mount laser cannons and began denuding the entire approach; first one side, then the other. I found nearly a dozen devices, any of which might have killed us.

Might have been what killed the original probes. A few fought back. By the time the laser had overheated, the approach was three times wider than it was a few deci-hours earlier. Ozone hung in the air, and my arms and hands ached from controlling that beast of a weapon.

One after another rolling and flying probes made it to the monument, if that was what it was. We *dared* the thing to take them, but all returned unscathed.

Pope and Saint tentatively went forward; Pope with a number of sensor/flux receivers on a little home-made cart. It had a shield for them to crouch behind. They pushed it in front of Pope. Both wore pulse armor and Saint had a pulse bomb launcher at the ready.

While they were inching their way up the driveway, Deacon, Abbot and I put on pulse armor as well. If Saint uses one of those pulse bomb things, I don't want my insides turned to pudding.

Deacon and I *covered* them though, since we didn't know what to expect, if anything. I wasn't certain how effective we'd be if we needed to lay down fire for their emergency bugout.

No emergency retreat happened, though. We were all nervous as hell, but I admired Saint and Pope. They were doing the really dangerous work right now.

They slowly rolled right next to the left side of the opening, where Pope began scanning the insides. Saint produced a pry bar and pried loose one of the precious stones inset along the edge. It came off easily.

She grinned and held it up triumphantly.

"That will pay for some of the equipment," I heard Abbot intone distractedly. "Blest…"

I wondered if now wouldn't be an excellent time to cut

our losses. I'm no coward, but I know when to call for a tactical retreat. I said nothing, though…Just like hormones, greed *also* usually wins an argument.

ABBOT PICKED UP THE INTERCOM: "Saint? What's the range of your launcher?"

"With the big bombs or the little cuties?"

"A big one, I'm thinking…"

"Around thirty meters…"

"Then withdraw you should, twenty-eight meters."

"Doin' it."

Then Abbot had Deacon and I readied the laser cannons. I hoped that the one I'd used had cooled off enough to be effective.

Abbot donned the half helmet of a rail gunner.

"On my mark, concentrate fire on the center of the door. Pope watch the door, if you see any wavering in the field, signal Saint to launch at the same target."

I gulped, hoping pulse armor would be enough.

"Ready?"

"Yes," times four.

"Fire!"

Deacon and I concentrated on the center of the indentation, hoping it was a door of some sort. The lasers first hit the microwaves, but eventually pushed through! I could feel the weird tingling in the air get more pronounced.

Then, I saw wavering in the fabric of the door.

So did Abbot.

He fired the railgun, and a second or so later the pulse bomb exploded.

Despite the armor, the pulse felt sickening, but I was alright.

We all stopped firing at once.

Saint and Pope made their way back to us. The blast had been 'shaped' by the indentation to pass by them, but Saint had a bloody nose just the same.

Damn lucky that's all! I thought, smiling. I admired the two ladies all the more now!

We all sighted on the door, for that was what it was. We knew that because it was open now.

"The base is almost two meters thick! And it's all terranium!" Pope exulted, producing various scans from her close up peek.

"Amazing! I didn't know there was that much in the entire system, much less here in one spot on a backwater planet like this."

That was the most Deacon had said all at once, in the entire time we'd known him. It was made all the more striking and strange by his odd accent.

We all looked at him.

He looked uncomfortable at all the attention.

"And, there are over thirty of these…" Saint held up a gemstone the size of her fist.

I was feeling a bit better about my decisions then.

That good feeling wasn't to last.

We were standing around feeling happy that we'd succeeded, at least as regards this step of the journey, and wondering what we might do next. We weren't prepared for an attack. We should have been, but we were tired and felt great that we'd *won*…at least a bit.

Suddenly, the entire area – the spot in the middle of our group was full of feathers that reeked of offal and feces…*and garlic.* We were all knocked down and blown back by the huge bulk that had just landed amidst us! All of us, save Deacon.

A split deci-second later, that same huge tree-colored bulk lifted off. We were pressed us to the ground as the wings beat the air to get aloft. And, when it did, we were four, not five. Deacon was gone!

Then it hit me: The area I'd cleared in the last few hours to make us safer, wasn't so safe. I'd cleared an opening that had allowed the Roc to swoop in on us. The wings had made no noise at all. And all that was left after Deacon was gone was a blood spot on the trampled ground. Though, the blood didn't look like human blood...it looked thinner, very, very dark, but somehow less dense.

The Bird's blood? I wondered. *Deacon hit him. He shot at him...He wounded the great Roc! And so, if that's true...Did the animal know which of us to take his revenge on? Were these birds that smart? Oh shite. Now we're fighting the aliens and the birds?*

We beat a hasty retreat. The sun was failing anyway, and we needed the cover of trees to stay safe from the Roc if it returned.

Abbot tried to cheer us up.

"An even 20% each. That's something, it is....Poor Deacon, but his was the responsibility to watch and shoot if the bird returned..."

Pope was incensed.

"*Poor Deacon?* You don't care a whiff of smoke for him; for any of us! Poor Deacon! You hid information from us, you *doozer!* Information we might have used to decide...*better,* if we wanted this thing...this fucking quest. You cheated us! I should kill you now!"

At this, Abbot's hand appeared with a sidearm in it as if by magic.

"Calmly...My dearest...Most calmly. Truly, Deacon is missed, but what can I do to assuage your grief...?"

He spread his hands, one still holding the pistol, but he'd spread them anyway, as if to say, "I'm as bereft as you, *you who only met him a week ago!*"

"I know...Instead of 20%. I'll share my stake money. Now we'll all split equally. We all are in for 25%. Blest?"

He looked around, and seeing the indecision in our faces, holstered his weapon as a sign of leadership and confidence.

"Blest!"

We sat around, most of us introspective; none of us talking over dinner.

Then we bedded down, posting a well-armed guard, which we changed every few deci-hours.

It was still dark, though not long 'til sunrise when we arose.

We donned the all spec visors and scanned the area for any unfriendlies.

Nothing.

"Pope, my dear..." Abbot began, whispering in the chill and dark.

"Could you please send some probes, and affix some smoking pyrotechnics, to see if we're still cleared?"

She said nothing, but soon, two rollies and one flier were doing their work, smoke trailing behind them. They got all the way to the doorway and...nothing happened.

"Good. Call them back."

She did, still not speaking.

We scanned the area on every freeq we could access; sub viz, visual, near viz, ultra viz... Nothing. It was still and quiet between here and the doorway.

After that, all bets are off, I thought. *I wish we could have brought the field dampeners...*

One by one, we made our way to the side of the monument. We leaned against the cool and very valuable metal, armed and ready to fight, panting and tense.

Yet nothing happened.

Saint went off by herself for a moment, just to test a theory, and returned with another fist sized jewel.

"Lookit! Ain't it binkie?"

Abbot looked at her with disgust.

"Focus, please. Put it down. That's the little shite, it is. Bigger and better awaits."

He turned to Pope.

"Now what?"

She thought for a moment. "We don't know what to expect...What the floor's like. We sent fliers in, with scanners...cameras...we check and prep. But mostly, we wait."

She looked at Abbot: "...'Kay? 'Kay! Blest it is!"

He didn't think her making fun of his speech patterns was funny; she seemed to be making a point however obliquely. She didn't think that Deacon was expendable... Because if he was, we all were.

IN A LITTLE WHILE, three fliers were outfitted. In that same time, we donned the pulse armor, and Abbot added the railgun helmet and charged the gun itself. Even if I hadn't seen him ready the gun, I'd have felt it.

THE AIR VIBRATED AND SHIMMERED, more so now, it seemed. Just a bit and just out of visual range or acuity.

My skin itched. And, I wanted to shoot something. Almost anything. All this tension could only be dissipated in one way: Killing something that was threatening me.

Give me something to kill! I thought.

The fliers went through the charred hole of the doorway and began sending back pics and scans of the inside.

"It's bigger than Caracol, on Pentalume!" Abbot gasped.

Myself, I'd only heard about that, and heard about the ancient treasures that were found there. Part of the reason I was interested here... I smiled. I took a deep breath and lowered my laser cannon a trifle. *Things were looking up.*

"Abbot," I said. "I might have an idea..."

"Yes? What is it...Tell..."

"What if we use the lasers to slice off huge sections of this...thing? We'd leave enough so that it wouldn't fall over or become unsteady, but we'd open up a lot of it – we could see in, without getting into the hot-hot of danger..."

Abbot smiled. The smile said: "And that is why I brought you!"

IT WAS SLOW WORK, but we sliced off sections weighing far more than we could carry away quickly. It soon became apparent that we must cut pieces that were manageable sizes. Sections fell upon the dirt, cut away from their...*home.* Then, they were cut up, again and again. It was slow, hot dangerous work, but we were putting money in the bank! Sections made of solid terranium! In time, we were cutting them into ingot sized pieces and stacking them off to one side.

I began to feel hopeful.

The lasers were replaced by the special saw. We might need the laser yet again.

"Let's not wear out the battery," I offered. I got dirty looks because the laser was a lot faster. *But the saw isn't as important as the laser...*

The stack grew but the view inside the monument didn't improve much, though now we did have easier ways to send in probes to gather even more information. It was almost as if the darkness inside was fighting the light that tried to get in.

. . .

AFTER TWO DAYS of intense work, we'd substantially opened up two sides. We all agreed that it was time to go into the monument. Abbot wanted to see if the treasure that was the monument, contained something else; something better. So did we all. We didn't need prodding. That was why we were here, right? *Or was there something more...?*

However, since the two sides we'd opened up were contiguous, Abbot wanted to open up a side as far away from the initial cut as possible, "To see if light will travel through it."

Since it was so dark *in there*, there'd been talk that perhaps the artifact was partially in another place, and was a nexus for transportation for the builders. That *dark* could be the transition area...That would explain why it was so dark inside this...thing. That would be a good thing to know before, just charging in discharging weapons.

THE NEXT MORNING before dawn and after we'd sent the smoking probes out in front of us again, we started cutting away at the other side of the artifact.

This time we didn't cut up the pieces, we just opened the side.

We shone a light from our position to Abbot, who'd walked to the other side.

"See the light, I can't. Wave it around."

We gave up eventually. We couldn't shine the light all the way through. Was that a reason to give up? I didn't think so.

"Time, it might be, to send probes again..."

Pope readied two and two. We each had a controller and by plan, we stayed as far away from each other as possible.

I had a little flyer and I dove it into the dark that still persisted in the center of the monument. I knew that if I lit the area up with all spec, I'd kill my batteries pretty quick, so

I opted for a quick look around and a hasty get out, before my flier ran outta juice.

I captured some pics of the interior...It was kind of disappointing. I half expected a starship comm. station or something, but it was mostly empty inside.

Saint had a flyer also, and after a quick spin around the interior, daring them to shoot her, he used up the rest of her reserve batt taking pics, backing her way out.

All the probes returned unscathed, and ready for recharge and reboot.

We poured over the pics and motion feeds looking for anything that might be threatening. Since it was mostly empty...it looked like a covered and protected meeting place more than anything. There wasn't anything that was overtly threatening; no gun emplacements ...nothing obviously set up to deter the likes of us.

Also there was nothing inside that looked like alien tek; nothing we might cart away and reverse engineer. So the terranium was all there was...Well, that's okay, too, I guess, I thought.

We waited all day, thinking there would be countermeasures, and when the sun was dipping in the West, we decided that tomorrow would be the day we went in.

THE VIBRATIONS SEEMED to more persistent and they kept me up most of the night...I can't speak for anyone else, but I heard nearly everyone stirring or talking in my one, point five deci-hour watch shift.

Anyway, the night passed uneventfully and with four of us, and a six deci-hour night, it wasn't tough duty.

THE NEXT DAY after eating some MREs, we resumed the protocol from two days earlier. Pulse armor, and Pope and

Saint, on one side with sensors; Abbot and me, on the other with a laser and railgun. Now that the sides were partially opened up, we figured we could shoot anything that moved inside.

The hours spent moving slowly were well spent, I guess. Nothing happened. We finally, all of us, went inside. It looked empty, with alien writing on the interior walls that glowed slightly, but nothing else.

I took pics with a handheld, just for fun. *They might be helpful as a memory device later,* I told myself.

Abbot and I searched one side, Pope and Saint, the other, eventually we met in the far corner and walked back.

Pope searched and scanned.

She was methodical. The three of us searched, and she scanned every freeq she could find, methodically and carefully. She was good.

"Talented she is!" Abbot grinned.

"Correct you are! Indeed!" She laughed.

This time he did smile at someone hijacking his speech patterns.

We all were feeling a bit better.

Pope was diligent and thorough. Each scan came back negative; each time her grin went from tentatively happy to slightly more relieved and joyous.

I couldn't speak for anyone else at that time, but my breathing had quieted a bit, having not run into any traps. After a bit, we resigned ourselves to salvaging Terranium only. And walking back to camp we began planning how to take sections out to make the structure fall in a controlled manner, so we could cut it up completely.

We'd relaxed considerably and I consider it my fault.

Suddenly, there was a rushing or buzzing sound from behind us. Before I could put a threat to the noise, dozens – maybe *hundreds* of anti-personnel flechettes were launched from inside the structure at our retreating forms! The damned thing sent little spinning sharpened arrows seeking us. That was the buzzing. Hundreds of projectiles coming downrange at high speed! The projectiles caught us unawares; and each of us numerous times, in the back, the legs... One took off Saint's left hand, and crippled Abbot, burying a flechette deep in his right leg. I caught two in my back, and one in the arm just below the shoulder.

We hurried to cover around forty meters from the maw we'd created and licked our wounds.

There were three of us. Abbot, me, Saint...all injured... *Where's Pope?*

I saw her just outside the structure with a projectile half-protruding from the side of her head, not moving. She lay there in the dirt.

The pulse armor didn't stop these things! It sent hundreds of Lo Tek weapons after us...Lo Tek that our armor wouldn't protect against!

I shook a bit.

Her scans; my experience were worthless. The thing suckered us!

The damnable thing was waiting to get us after we'd left! It was intelligent ...sentient...waiting, and guarding...

And I'd decided: *It was evil...*

"Feck..."

WE HURRIED as best we could to our camp. Saint was ambulatory, as was I, but she looked like she was going to puke, or go into shock, or both soon. Abbot's leg was useless until we splinted it. I supported one side.

He might walk with an exo skeleton, if one o' them is in the med kit...

I pulled out all the flechettes. A worry was in the back of

my mind…On Earth, they used to coat them with nastiness like carbamate and saxitoxin. I doubted that I had antidotes to that stuff in the med kit, much less whatever poisons an alien bio chemist might think up.

Oh well, it is what it is. I sweated profusely, hoping that we all didn't get very sick and die in the next few deci-mins.

Working off the hope that we might live a lot longer than a few more heartbeats, first order of business was stopping Saint's bleeding. I put a cap on her arm and cinched it. You always hope to never use the damn things, but if you need one, they're life savers.

Then, I gave her a stim. In a few deci-mins she was lookin' less pale; less like she was gonna keel over on me. I may need all the help I can get soon.

ABBOT'S WOUND WAS PERSISTENT. The coag mixture I dug out of the med kit washed away *twice*. He was too excited and his heart was poundin' like mad. I could see the fear in his face.

Seen that look before…He may be mad but he understands this.

My eye fell on my boot. And then, an idea hit me right between my eyes.

There's nothin' t'lose. Why not?

I ripped Abbot's pant leg completely away. I flinched and he saw my face. *Looked bad. Very bad…*

I dug out the tube of rogue beetle and squirted a bunch of it into my hand, then I just placed my hand over the wound and held it there.

The blood stopped flowing almost immediately.

He looked down at his leg, visibly calmer.

"Amazing…that is…Blest!"

If it sealed up a leather/skin boot from rips, why not skin torn open by an arrow?

After he was calmed and no longer bleeding, I looked to

my own wounds, applying the rogue beetle as I had on Abbot to my shoulder. It worked just as well. I also wondered if Abbot was bleeding internally. From the look of the bright bright red, I think they'd severed an artery.

I flexed my injured shoulder.

Nothing broken...just hurts like hell. That'll be my reminder: Never take these bastards for granted!

I gave Saint something to do, to keep her mind occupied: "Saint, would you rub this stuff on the wounds on my back?"

She just nodded. I spread some in her good hand and she applied it as I had.

We sat there looked around and nervous, but slowly calming and getting our bearings.

I got up and took a quick walk to the edge of the driveway, just to see if Pope somehow was moving...Maybe she'd wave or call out.

"Pope! Pope! Move, call out. Wave a hand...anything. I'll... we'll get you out."

Her body was still and quiet.

Shite...

I turned and re-entered our camp.

The air smelled like burnt garlic. *Burnt Garlic?* I thought. *It'd cost a year's salary to burn that much garlic...Is it coming from the artifact? And the Roc is attracted to it...Of course...maybe. That's why the Roc smells as it does!*

After I checked on both my wounded compatriots again, I fixed up some MREs. Everyone seemed to feel a bit better with a full belly.

I thought about posting a guard, and discarded the idea. Maybe Abbot was up to it, but Saint needed rest. If I did it myself, I wouldn't be ready for whatever we decided tomorrow. I lay awake for a while listening for noises of something approaching and trying to figure out how to get all three of us back to the boat. Before I knew it, the sun was creeping into my tent and I heard Abbot and Saint already awake and talking.

"They had thought pattern sensors trained on us. That's the only way it would have known that we had let our guard down; that we weren't watching it," Saint whispered.

I lay there listening.

"True that is, I believe...So disable the structure, we must, eh?"

"I still have lots of pulse bombs...I say we bombard the thing... degrade its ability to fight us. Eventually, it will become inert."

"And then, the terranium....."

"For us...Yes. After all this, I'll use some of my money to have them grow me a new hand."

I climbed out of my tent scratching and feeling like I'd been run over by one of our Corvini six-wheelers.

"Saint, why not just leave the stump to remind you, *and all of us* how fucking greedy and stupid we are?"

They both looked at me as if I'd slapped them.

"How is it, that revenge is not topmost in your mind?" Abbot was bewildered and angry.

Saint sneered.

"He lost the least. You can't walk without the exo steel."

It was then I noticed him standing without any help. *So there was an exo kit in the med unit...*

Saint continued building steam, getting really angry.

"And I lost a hand ...*and a lover!*"

She turned to face me, fuming.

"All you got was a few puncture wounds. I saw them up close. That's *nothing!* You'll heal in no time!"

At that moment, I realized and thanked my gods, that there was no bio toxins on the flechettes. They were bad enough without *embellishments.*

I looked from Abbot to Saint and back.

"You're kidding, right? We're lucky to be alive. And I would like to stay that way. If you're staying, I'll just take the first gem, and you can consider me paid if full."

"You can't leave."

"Abbot, this is even worse than Taranga, in terms of numbers lost and having no support possible!"

Abbot was livid. He wasn't listening; nor was Saint. He actually seemed to vibrate, he was so angry. He wanted blood. Not my blood; *alien* blood. I could see it in his eyes: "They have to pay!"

"We can't stay. The three of us might make it. But we need to leave now; now before any of us is injured; degraded further."

"Not goin' yet. I can still hold a bomblet launcher."

Saint gritted her teeth.

Abbot nodded sagely, suddenly eerily quiet.

"Nor me...nor you. Agreed, you did when we started. Agreed, you did that my word was law. You will stay. Helping. Us. Kill. It."

"Come on. The thing, *whatever it is*, beat us. We're still alive. After everything, isn't that enough?"

"After everything? After everything – all we lost?" Saint spit, "No...It's not enough. Even if we melt down that entire mountain of terranium, it will *never* be enough."

Unhappily, I took all this in, sifting the facts for the true nuggets of worth:

One: I didn't like my chances of getting back alone.

Two: I didn't like my chances of turning my back on Saint and Abbot, either.

Three: We have learned a lot. We won't make those mistakes again.

And Four: They used flechettes. Old tek. Very old tek. They might not be so different from us. They use the some of same sorts of technology as countermeasures. Maybe we might think like them and beat them at their own game…Maybe.

I THOUGHT BACK TO "NUGGET ONE" and "nugget two"…*What choice did I have? I may as well put a smiley face on it, in case I get a chance to bug out, then they might not be watching me so hard…*

"Okay. I stay for a while. We see how this plays out. What's the plan?"

They relaxed a bit and we ate, planning the next assault. My head swam. The audacity; the stupidity; the…anger. The madness. He's infected Saint now.

Never go into battle angry, if you can help it. Anger makes you do dumb things; dumb things can get you killed. I thought that rather than saying it out loud. Nobody would have listened to me anyhow.

SAINT OUTFITTED all of our fliers with bomblets. Abbot figured to snug them all up all along the upper reaches of the monument. We didn't see anything on the floor, so Abbot's thinking was that they hid everything up high.

"So, hit them there, hard, we will!"

We had just under a dozen, but each needed one-on-one control.

Apparently the module that would have controlled any number of them existed, but waited for us on the boat.

So we flew them into the structure in waves.

The first wave slipped right in. And using the onboard cams, we found little structures here and there that clung to the ceiling, like Earther wasp's nests or Mirren bees. I snugged my flier up to the one, and waited for the others to get ready. Of course we coordinated all three and detonated the charges.

I'd swear that the vibrations I'd been feeling for almost a week...was it only a week? I felt those vibrations ramp down a bit...Then slowly they ramped up again.

There was more of that garlic smell in the air; carried on an errant breeze.

The fucking bird is nearby...

I TOOK the next flier in alone. We'd taken pics of the hives clutching the ceiling and I knew where I needed to go. I got about halfway there and a huge shower of flechettes came buzzing out of one of the holes we'd opened up. My flier was cut to pieces.

No surprise there.

We next went to the far side and input the hives we wanted to hit into *guidance* on our controllers. We crept up as close as we dared under the circumstances and went in, *dodging and weaving*, all the while making for the three targets. Once we each got there we didn't hesitate: one-two-three explosions racketed off the inner walls and tumbled out into the forest. I heard a bunch of nearby birds leave in a hurry.

We waited a little while and did the same thing from the other side: One-two-three *more* explosions.

This time, the vibrations stopped altogether!

We looked at each other wondering if we should hope to feel triumphant. Then we hurried back to camp. To plan.

"There's no way we get away with that three times, people," I said. "We need to think of another line of attack. We hurt it this time. I know we did. We've just gotta press this damn thing home!"

"Truth, I feel he is talking, though tired, I am. This exoprosthetic is heavy and it takes a lot of work to make my leg move. Sit for a while, just for a short while, I must."

Saint was still up for blood, even if it was unlikely we'd ever actually see any of the designers' blood…unless it was them living in the hives…?

Everybody's gotta be somewhere, right?

I tried to calm her, and finally did by handing her an MRE and pointing to the sun.

"Time enough for revenge; for treasure. Do you want to go in there in the dark? I don't."

She sat down next to Abbot and began eating.

I LOOKED at my boots again. Even slathering the rogue beetle crap on them wasn't keeping them from starting to really fall apart. I guess I started too late. They were worse now than yesterday.

Not good.

I peeled the presstape seal off another MRE and handed it to Abbot. He devoured it as if he'd not eaten in days.

I opened mine…and I just wasn't interested. I was hungry, but …I don't know…I didn't feel like eating. I know, *I know…* Tomorrow would be a strenuous day and I needed to eat to stay sharp, so we could beat these fuckers…But I just didn't feel like eating. I ate a few mouthfuls and set it aside. I laid down to watch the stars.

In a couple of deci-mins, when I sat back up, the tray was empty.

I looked at it and thought: "Who cares?"

We all slept sitting-up, with a weapon across our thighs.

Nothing much happened though. I awoke clear-headed and ready; appreciative of the fact that nothing came in the night to eat us or bite us…or shoot us. Except, of course the bugs.

The bugs are a given.

.   .   .

THE NEXT MORNING was completely spent doing prep.

We decided to cut the bottom of the artifact between holes *one* and *two* on the left of the *door.* We figured that if we did that, the artifact would become unsteady. If we were lucky enough to be able to cut another portion off – like between the *door* and the hole we cut in the right side – we might make it really unsteady. It might fall over; if it fell over it might make it unable to send any more flechettes downrange.

I could think of a few flaws in this plan, but since Abbot and Saint were still in *murder mode*, and since I figured that we could do all this from the relative safety of the end of the driveway, we'd be okay.

They figured to use three big guns: Two Laser cannons and one railgun, two mounted on tripods. I wanted to hold mine and not be locked in to a site and style. Tripods are great. You can be accurate; you can be steady, but at what price? You become a stationary emplacement to be knocked out. Right? Of course. Any military person knows that.

The plan was *to concentrate* on the *leg* between holes one and two, to see if we could elicit a panicked response from the monument.

In which case, we were ready: Field sensors, bombs, bomblets, proximity sensors with built-in triggers. We even set up a shear wall of upshooting lasers we'd hoped would protect our position. We'd rigged them to fire if we discovered any incoming projectiles.

THE FIRST PHASE started out by the numbers: We set up and began wave-cutting with the lasers at the portion of the support we decided upon. Abbot stood ready with the railgun. He was well off to the left, behind an embankment. His tripod peeked over the top. I looked over at him. I could easily see that he was itching to shoot something.

I knew the feeling.

Abbot's good leg was bent and the other was splayed out to his side, because it didn't unbend easily, and, if we had to move quickly, he might have gotten caught by the folded leg not opening up fast enough to run.

Saint was behind another dirt mound with a laser cannon. She also had a bomb launcher and a cache of bombs and bomblets ready to go. She was toward the middle of the driveway but behind a tall berm. – Safe from fire.

I was opposite Abbot, in a dense stand of trees, ready to fire upon the support with my mostly used up laser cannon on Abbot's signal. I didn't know how long my battery would hold up. It had already had a lot of use.

We were tense. Ready. I couldn't speak for them but my trigger finger wanted to close with the actuator button and begin raining some retribution upon this...*thing.*

WE'D CUT AWAY another huge section in the support when I heard, then felt, a shockwave bursting through the place, and tossing us around as though we were leaves before an autumn storm!

The uncomfortable buzzing picked up again in earnest. It was annoying in that it was almost within my hearing. I hated it; I hated them. It intensified. I picked myself up off the ground, feeling bruises and scrapes that would become more pressing and insistent later, when I wasn't stressed.

"Shockwave!" I shouted.

"Ultrasonic..." Abbot shouted back. Saint was in the middle and she just hunkered down trying to keep on living.

The buzzing suddenly grew more intense.

For some damn reason, Abbot stood up to run and he was

almost cut in half by flying circular serrated cutting wheels, around 200 hundred millimeters across traveling at nearly supersonic speed! Suddenly, these wheels were coming for each of us!

The blades, I counted a dozen or more that went after Saint, imbedded themselves hotly in the berm.

The ones that came for me with ass-puckering speed and ferocity, ricocheting off all the nearby trees, scaring the crap out of me until they settled down, dented and buzzing slightly, lying all around my position. For just an instant, I debated whether shooting them would be a good thing, but since they held still, I nervously looked downrange

Then, the Roc appeared and swooping in, settled noiselessly and remorselessly upon Saint. The huge thing made eye contact with me, maybe 100 meters away, as if *daring* me to do something about this new attack. One great red-brown eye on the near side of its head fixed upon me and dilated repeatedly. Was it anger? Fear? Territorial behavior?

Unknown.

This caused me to hesitate, seeing that in a great alien creature.

In a second, he was lifting off again. Saint was no longer there!

I took aim with my cannon, hoping there was enough of a charge left to do some damage, when the Roc exploded! My finger never touched the trigger.

I covered my face. The blast was impressive.

Oh...Birdie. You picked the wrong meal!

The huge burning feather ball and a smaller burnt thing tumbled slowly to the ground not far away.

PANTING, I went to check on Abbot.

Abbot was in bad shape; dying.

"Well, friend..." He choked a bit. "Too bad that is, but more for us, there is. Blest. *Blest!* Half and half, eh? How's *that* for a payday, eh?"

I wondered: Was he in shock? Did he not know there was no way this side of a full-on field hospice unit that he was going to survive? Was it shock? Was it bravado? Was this the Loastacin speaking? Was it just wanting to "win"?

Who knows? Who cares! All this is well past my pay grade, I thought, breathing heavily and angry. *My boots are trashed.*

I looked down. Abbot's feet...Abbot's boots might fit me...

I took them. He didn't protest.

The air reeked of death, offal, piss and shite. Just like Taranga.

Damn. Just like *Taranga! Except for the garlic. That's new.*

Oh, at that moment, that's when a new and troubling wrinkle occurred to me: *Aren't birds usually in pairs?*

I wasn't certain I could make the best strategic decisions possible in my exhausted condition, but I figured to try.

I put Abbot's boots on, tossing my boots away.

I stood up. *Ready.*

I sniffed. By now, I'd almost gotten used to the burnt garlic smell. My mouth watered. I thought about how much garlic that would take – to make this whole ...*theatre*...smell like garlic.

It'd cost a fucking fortune! My mind reeled...*Shock, exhaustion, bloodloss, pain...*I ticked them all off on a list in my brain.

Abbot was dying, nearly dead, bleeding out; Saint was long gone by now, as was Pope, Deacon, and Priest. All gone. Except me.

Abbot called out to me: "Bishop. Bishop!" His voice was an urgent croak.

I ignored him. I got up; started walking.

I kept moving toward the monument, my laser cannon at the ready.

He called again. "Bishop!"

I turned and shouted over my shoulder: "I'm not Bishop. My name's Linklattar…"

I faced the devils who had tormented us and shouted again: "Linklatter!!"

I DIDN'T CARE if the aliens knew my name, so I shouted it out for any to hear. I figure you ought to at least know the name of the guy who's gonna kill you.

Copyright Zaslow Crane
ZaslowCrane.com

ONE THING

One thing that I've always hated is when I'm getting towards the end of the book and I notice that there's only three pages left.

I think: *Dang! The book is almost over. They're gonna have to wrap it up fast, now!*

I hate this because it tips the author's hand and tells me (You?) where the climax is.
   I have always felt cheated by that.

So the last few pages and the next few pages are there to keep you from figuring out how and when "The Roc Of Petra" is supposed to end, and to make you wonder what's still to come. There is a bit more. Scroll down.

I hope that you have enjoyed the stories; I hope that they made you think, shudder, laugh or …call your accountant in the middle of the night.

I hope that I entertained you…And I hope that you'll pick up

"The Future Is Closer Than You Think…Book 2", coming soon.

Be well
    Be happy

Z

Drive safely

Be nice to one another

14

PERELANDRA'S BOUNTY

Preliminary notes on flora, fruits and vegetables of Perelandra; Perelandra's Bounty.

By Jefferey Wannamaker, lead exo biologist, Sam Cho, lead exo chemist, Lara Potemkin (posthumously), lead exo nutritionist

PLEASE NOTE: This is by no means definitive, nor a complete compendium of our findings on this, our first colonizable planet.

The livestock and personnel are too rare and valuable to risk unnecessarily, and so our aim is to disseminate information as quickly and thoroughly as possible to forestall any further injury--either to an individual, any of our breeding animals or the new colony as a whole.

Careful screening in the laboratory can, of course save lives, but the laboratory is not always available, and so, a good solid general knowledge is something to be fostered throughout the colonists.

And, while a number of indigenous fruits and vegetables and grains have proven to be edible (but with mixed nutritional benefits) there are some varieties that bear some caution, even avoidance.

(More information will be added on an as learned basis.)

P **APPLES**. (*Please see appendix 4 through 14 for pictures, both whole and dissected, P Apples in their natural state and further findings regarding their seeding systemization.*)

This is a perfect example of a fruit that can be perfectly safe and nominally nutritious, if handled properly; carefully.

The P apple looks like a rather large, robust Macintosh apple. Underneath the off-red skin however is another membrane that takes up nearly half of the insides. This membrane is inert and if cut away the fruit can be enjoyed safely. If ingested, the secondary membrane, the outer hypanthium (as opposed to the *inner* hypanthium) is rather dangerous, at least in human bodies, as found out by those rash enough to try some of the fruit without thorough testing.

The secondary membrane seems to serve a reproductive purpose, as we believe that it provides more protection for the ovaries and ovule, from predation. If an unwitting animal were to simply bite into it without foreknowledge, it might learn the hard way that this was not something it should eat.

That is: In the human intestines it simply congeals, unmoving, eventually causing a complete blockage if enough of the outer hypanthium is consumed.

Note: The outer hypanthium looks and tasted more or less the same as the inner hypanthium, but has a different texture and chemical structure. We've been forced to perform two emergency bowel resections so far (one on our teammate Mr. Cho) and while not dangerous, nor difficult, one feels that it is an operation that might have been avoided with a trifle more prudence and care; less enthusiasm and familiarity.

The stem, or pedicel is to be avoided completely by man and beast because it is devoid of nutritional benefit and holds a concentrate of the tree itself. More on 'trees' as follows:

WALLY TREES and as near as we can determine all trees to varying extents, on Perelandra – are peculiar. We surmise that this must present some evolutionary advantage, but our team is at a loss to explain why the following traits are a benefit.

The ground around trees on Perelandra seems to be exceedingly acidic; so acidic, that lying in the shade of a tree under the sometimes oppressive heat of Sol 2, people have been burned. In truth, they have been burned right through our day-to-day, light non-protective clothing, (*not* the lite-enviro suits that we recommend for daily wear outside of the compound) and it doesn't take very long to *scald*, such is the type and strength of the acid. More tests are being run to determine if there are simple ways we might neutralize this acid. (*Please see appendix 16 through 44 for pictures, specs, graphs on acidity, photos of burn victims, more...*)

Local fauna, similar to squirrels and very small monkey-like animals have been documented climbing in these trees, standing with no ill or obvious effects on the ground adjacent to trees, and even doing cursory digging in the soil. Again, with no apparent ill effects.

We chopped down a few trees in a stand to see if the ground would revert to its normally mostly benign characteristics. We've been waiting for nearly six weeks, and while the soil acidity has abated somewhat, it is inconclusive so far as to whether a tree 'damages' the soil permanently or, if in time, it reverts.

It should be noted that while preliminary scouting and surveys have been done of the other two continents (Across the Timour Sea), no extended study has been undertaken. However, there is no evidence to suggest that conditions are substantially different on Maleldril or Tenindril, the other two landmasses on Perelandra, so where and when we do explore, care is warranted.

ARTICHOKES--NAMED because they resemble artichokes of old Earth before the Change, though if our records from Old Earth are correct our measurements put these artichokes at approximately three times the size of the largest Terran artichokes.

(*See appendix 45- 61 for "Chokes" growing wild, "Chokes"*

cultivated in our test garden and for an anatomical cross section. Note: the "thorn" section should be discarded immediately. It makes good compost and is not – I repeat <u>not</u> edible.)

These plants are so far, our greatest find, in that there seems to be no ill effects for those, human or animal, consuming them. Moreover they seem to be quite nutritious if not particularly savory. (This last observation is a personal one. There are quite a few colonists who eat the P-Chokes with gusto.)

The choke itself is a rather benign afterthought with a huge tasty heart that is easily accessed by cutting the stem and going in through the bottom.

The vitamins and minerals in these 'chokes could easily sustain a human long term.

THE PURPLE SOLANACEAE

High altitude, Hi Rez surveys show that this plant grows wild throughout the entire planet, except for at the poles, where nothing much is seen to be growing. However, again, we have been busy "putting down roots" so to speak. There has not been time for true exploration beyond our meager boundaries.

(Please see appendix 61-79 for mapping, density, growing photos and growing season information. Further see appendix 80-89 for (mostly) *anecdotal information regarding this seemingly ubiquitous fruit.)*

This fruit is edible by all the local fauna. There is documentation aplenty both visual, digital, and through fecal examination.

However, there is no mode of preparation thus found that will allow terran species to consume it.

No one has perished, since it is everywhere, it was one of

the first potential food sources that we examined. There is a compound that is poisonous to us, but seems to pass right through the Perelandran animals, like a package that was left unopened. There is something in their chemical makeup, particularly in the makeup of their gut that allows "this package" to stay closed and for them to derive sustenance from the meat of the Solanaceae.

As for how they accomplish this miracle, we, to date, have no clue.

All one can advise at this time is to avoid ingestion. Contact seems to present no problems, which is lucky indeed, as avoiding contact with this plant would involve, denuding by fire great tracts of land, which we are, of course loathe to do in light of our Terran experiences.

How strange and terrible that the most prolific food source on the planet is so far most definitely beyond our reach.

BUNDLEBERRIES

Additional notes provided by J Wannamaker: (When I was growing up on Earth 1, my father told me an aphorism that he said had been passed down from his father and from his and so on. It was no doubt intended to be clever, even funny. It goes: 'Blackberries are red when they're green.')

While no one for generations has seem any food that is not hydroponically grown, I can discern (as I hope you can as well) the kernel of truth in that saying.

The saying in its relaxed, homespun way tells you that blackberries are unfit to eat if they are not black. If one spies red blackberries, they are in fact 'green,' and not ready to eat.

While on Earth, this mistake would only (presumably) result in a mouthful of quite sour berries if one were to fail to follow the directive; on Perelandra and all of "Earth 2" for as much as we know, not following a very similar directive could have consequences far beyond a simple inconvenience."

Bundleberries grow quite prolifically on Perelandra and lie in little bundles, close to the ground, each berry up to 52 millimeters in diameter, and not unlike pictures of strawberries that we've all seen from the 20th century, with enslaved workers picking them so that the overlords, our great, great grandparents, could enjoy the fruits planted on the stolen lands.

(See appendix 90 through 119 for pictures, graphs of growing stages, and the all important color renditions of the berries when they are "green" and when they are ripe.)

It is important to examine these berries before ingestion.

When the berry is 'green,' it is an appealing red overall. Special care is warranted! While handling them presents no problems that we are aware of, ingestion by man or animal can be painful, even fatal. We've lost one person who did not adhere to this dictum, and while she was out surveying for the colony, apparently forgot to check for the blue tinge on the underside.

All we have is her frantic calls for help and her vids of her anxious anaphylactic injections.

The underside of the berry, where it is in contact with the naturally very acidic soil, turns a light to medium blue, with the rest of the berry looking for all the world like an appetizing bright red. The bundleberries have an unusual 'freshness/readiness to eat characteristic,' that is, when the berries are blue on the underside they are fit, even delicious and nutritious to eat. However, that is a small window indeed. Perhaps as small as a couple of "Earth 2" Days.

In a couple of days after achieving the bluish tinge, the

tinge is subsumed by the overall red and is unfit to eat. *And of course, they are not fit to eat before the blue tinge appears.*

If one were to eat the berries while they were in this state, severe anaphylactic reactions would occur. We believe that the more one might eat, the more severe the reaction in humans. There is no documentation of the adverse effects it may have on terrestrial livestock, though a few have died suspiciously and autopsies are pending.

(For more, please refer back to this report which will be appended as more information becomes available.)

As for Lara Potemkin, she was given a posthumous partial credit on this report as it was her death that taught us a great deal about the 'freshness/viability' cycle of a potential local food source. Ironic, that our lead nutritionist was the first to succumb to poisonous foodstuffs. This points out the need to follow directives and avoid the hubris that breeds casual practices. We are not welcome here. Not yet.

However, local foods must be embraced if we are to survive here long term. Oh certainly, there will be the occasional shipment of colonists, which will of course also include livestock and some foodstuffs. However, the supply of MREs will not, and can not be inexhaustible. The Earth is crumbling. That is why we are here, as the vanguard of the quest to find a new place for the teeming millions to live; a place that with our better, cleaner technologies will not sully the new Home as badly or as quickly as we did the old one.

WE CAN ONLY HOPE.

ZaslowCrane.com

Perelandra's Bounty is an introduction to another upcoming book of short stories.

This book will focus solely upon the 182 human "settlers" on a new exo-planet. It will focus on their trials and their experiences. There will be no monsters, or super villians…Only the mundane, day-to-day normalcy – if you can call it that while colonizing a new World.

Because, sometimes, the mundane will transform and surprise you.

"Perelandra's Bounty"…watch for it.

❀ Created with Vellum

15
EXCERPT FROM UPCOMING SERIES

Excerpt- from an upcoming series.

The First is called "Stairway To Hell", coming soon.

There will be five stories total, starring Ansel Mulligan, Prefect of Mars.

16
STAIRWAY TO HEAVEN EXCERPT

Chapter 7 Math, Force and Velocity

. . .

I LEFT.

I walked the crowded pedways.

As I walked, I slowly noticed that I had comp'ny. In my rearviews I saw a lurker; a follower... Following m'self and creating a danger...

Glosser's decs...?

I...

Felt my teethbuds grind.

I slowly increased my stride and looked for an indent where I might lie in wait for this Glosser employee; this feck-stick following...

Eventually, I found a likey waitspot and did'so...

It didn't take long...

I KICKED at the side of his knee as he passed my hideyhole, and swatted the back of his head with my baton cradled in my arm, making it an arm-long cudgel.

He went down. *Hard.*

That knee's is going to need attention before he walks anywhere. I was gratified to notice it veer off at an unusual angle.

He shouted in pain and then moaned clutching his leg.

I repositioned, standing on the balls of my feet, then leveling my gun at him. "Move and I shoot. Understand?"

The dek nodded, sweat beading up on his high, scuffed forehead, his buzzcut hair standing up moreso than usuaya-like, I'm guessed.

He moaned in pain and held his bustified knee.

"You fecking *burakugado! You broke my leg!"*

"What I did was tear your MCL. If you're lucky, the damage won't be perm-like."

He panted, realization dawning.

He looked into mine eyes and I localed his despair!

"Spread your legs."

Hesitantly, he did, panting and anxious.

I stood between them making sure he had eye contact with the barrel of my gun.

Now...*some* peace officer-types like the newer seed/pulse weapons, because of their ability to control where the round goes...Seed/pulse weps are stopped by the infrastructure in every wall...They won't continue through a wall to hit an *unintended*. So, no collateral damage, that's a good feature, but they look like plastic toys regardless of how potentially lethal they are.

They simplamentally do not intimidate like a real slug.

I still use an oldlike slug wep. A round is forced through a chem reaction out the front of this ...*antique.*

I guess that's more evidence of me being some sort of throw back. I don't know a handfull of officers who still pack these old style...guns.

"Once the slug leaves the barrel, it's all math, force and velocity...*and irreparable damage.* So, there's no mistaking the intent of this wep".

I was counting on him noticing; counting on him real-izing that he was true-like in danger from a-like o'me, here'n now.

From this angle it must look like a protocanon to this sweating dilbo.

I looked deeply and meaningfully into his eyes.

"Now...there are some things I need to know, and I'll bet you could tell me if you wereso inclinated. Suchwise, to that end, I will supply the inclination. Remembering that if you move, I kill you; if you won't talk, I will emasculate you."

"Emasculate? What's that?"

"Basically, I might shoot your dick'n'balls off...That's

emasculate. You won't die, but you'll never feck again...so you'll wish for the dying."

His eyes bugged.

I took a deep breath. I made certain that he stared down the barrel of the gun.

"Still benno?"

The dek nodded, panting.

Then I began to step on his nutsack, exerting more and more pressure.

"Keeping in mind...You're going to think that you could surprise me. You can't."

I paused and stepped a bit harder.

"Or take me and get the gun. You can't. I'm that good. You're not."

All the while slow-like applying more pressure...

"Now keep this in your feeble brainpan. Try anything and I'll not only kill you, but I'll sleep like a bav t'night."

I paused looking deeply into his eyes. I wanted him to see that I spoke true-wise.

I think I recognized that bit in his eye, and so with that handled, I continued:

So... let's begin the quiz..."

THE QUIZ WAS QUIZ-SHIZ.

He was a lo lev dek knowing not, and following orders that no one thought would be fulfilled.

I left with finding out nothing for certains, I glommed that he was a part of an org...probably the Glosser Org, because he denied it so...*vo-ciferaously.*

You deny what you want not to be true in the face of a knowledgeable accuser.

I know.

An' he did.

But…he didn't seem to know anything. Really…*nothing…*

Not even when I squashed his privates under the steel toe of my boot!

Was he such a lo-lev op that he wasn't prizzy to *any* details?

Unlikely.

This led me to thinking that he was a common thorothug…*Had I again overreacted? Again threatened a dek's life unwarranted?*

Locstatin again?

I whispered to him: "If you come at me again, I will prevail, and I will make your life as fucked as I can. If you believe me then keep running. I will take no action unless I see you again. At which time, I will cut your dick off and shove it so far down your throat that it will come out your azz."

He actually seemed to believe me and shudder.

That warmed my heart.

Maybe I believed me as well.

"Claro?"

He looked shocked and tried to avert his eyes, his eyes were hidden by his shoulder. But eventually I saw them, and they spoke eloquently: "Please gods…Allow me to escape from this crazy's dek's control!"

"Claro!" He blurted as he struggled to get up, up and away.

I kicked at him.

He managed to wobble out of sight. He hop/walked as fast as he could.

Sometimes… I really am a crazy dek.

STAIRWAY TO HELL synopsis

EARTH, Mars, Titan Calisto, Ceres, Pluto, Charon, Europa...
All these and more are settled by "Hoomans".

Earth is The Center of Things, beyond Mars are the
Outers; those who dwell in the far reaches of the SolarSys,
mining and drilling for minerals and "vaasa" (Water- the
most valuable commodity in the system).

The Inners (Earth) hate the Outers because they are
rough-hewn and uncouth; the Outers hate the Inners
because they are coddled and safe and because Earth dictates

all the terms for the entire system. The Outers feel screwed, and Mars is caught in the middle.

A murder takes place with a weapon that can't be explained (or even found). An ex Special Ops officer with a past and a disease he is trying to hide and "manage", is dispatched from Mars to solve this murder. To say that he's unwanted on Titan Colony would be the understatement of the year. This is a back-handed attempt at revenge for a beating that he gave to an out of control youth. However, this youth was the scion of the wealthiest man in the entire solar system.

This is the first part of a three-story arc that tells how the worlds will develop and how humanity probably won't ever change. There will be some who will steal or kill; there will be others determined to bring them to justice. Huge vistas and tight underground corridors throw disparate groups together causing friction that will cause a conflagration eventually.

Ansel Mulligan must find a way to navigate, not get "cleared", and get back to his family in one piece.

WELL, *two out of three ain't bad.*

MUCH, much more is coming soon.

www.ZaslowCrane.com

AFTERWORD

There will always be more "Future" (until there isn't), so there will always be more opportunities to explore that in fiction. This is what I hope to do for quite some time.

ACKNOWLEDGMENTS

And, Many thanks to:

My Writers critique group (especially Steve and Sarah Boshear, James McMann, and Reggie Johnson) who were a constant source of constructive criticism and always tried to show me ways to make the story better.

My Mom and Dad -neither of whom lived long enough to see this happen.

My many beta readers- thank you for your thoughts and encouragement. Enthusiasm is contagious. For that, I am grateful.

Dede Utzinger, my editor- who made this possible, and who was my main "cheerleader"; chief "grammar cop".

The CCWC (Central California Writers Conference) who got me started out on the right foot and gave that essential kick in the butt in that general direction.

All my friends' encouragement -(even if Sci Fi wasn't "your cup of tea").

Also, Thank you very much to:

Elise Night- The author of the "Chronicles of the Common" series

Anne R Allen – Author of the "Camilla Randall Mysteries" and much more, for showing me the way, sharing what they knew, to help this book become a reality. You both barely know me and you helped anyway. THANK YOU!

And anyone else deserving, whom I may have forgotten in the whirlwind of getting ready to publish.

Smoke and Mirrors, which pointed the way "forward".

And the many writers and musicians who influenced me along the way- advising me, entertaining me, and teaching me, without whom I wouldn't be "here."

This is BY NO MEANS a complete list.

Also -In no particular order:
ALFRED BESTER
ROD SERLING
Umphrey's McGee
Philip K. Dick
A.E. Van Vogt
Ray Bradbury
Tangerine Dream
Steven Roach
Alistair Reynolds
John McLaughlin
Jethro Tull/Ian Anderson
Yes
Ozric Tentacles
Disco Biscuits
Alistair McLean
Vivian Stanshall
Nancy Kreiss
Philip Jose Farmer
Damon Knight
H.G. Wells

Joe Haldeman
Michael Moorcock
Ursula K LeGuin
Weather Report
Ray Bradbury
Robert Heinlein
Clifford D Simak
Fritz Lieber
Larry Coryell
Harlan Ellison
Cordwainer Smith
L. Sprague de Camp
Jack Williamson
Colliseum
Harry Harrison
Lester del Rey
Poul Anderson
Cream
Andre Norton
Paul Zelazny
Chick Corea
Joe Zawinul
Frank Zappa
Roger Zelazny
Jules Verne
John Brunner
William Gibson
Alan Moore
J.G. Ballard
Alistair Reynolds
Philip Jose Farmer
Harlan Ellison
Pink Floyd
Hawkwind

Neal Stephanson
Paul Butterfield Blues
Marcel Duchamp
Klaus Schultz
Nancy Kriess

And... my Uncle Gerald , who *turned me on* to real Science Fiction by giving me a "Charmin" case/box FULL of paperbacks of the old Masters when I was a kid.

Uncle Gerald, thank you!

You never know who you will influence when you go out there and give of yourself.

www.ZaslowCrane.com

ABOUT THE AUTHOR

Zaslow Crane has contributed to numerous magazines over many years, and has been an editor for a national magazine, ran an award nominated podcast and written perhaps 300 short stories and a handful of novels and novellas.

He lives in a little house on a hill, overlooking the Pacific Ocean with a parrot who is too big for her feathery britches and a dog who, everyday gives new meaning to the word: "omnivorous."

He teaches at a local college whenever he can get his valium prescription renewed.

The Future Is Closer Than You Think
Book 1

Book 2 ...In "The Future Is Closer Than Your Think- Tales From The Day After Tomorrow" BOOK TWO is coming soon.

In it you may find-

* A simple Med Tech finds that the fate of all Humanity is in his hands. Is he up to the task?

* Most people in the Future have nothing to do. No job. No responsibilities. No aspirations. Humanity is at a cross-roads. Evolve or...?

* "First Contact" The love of Music brought *Them* from across the Galaxy. Now that they're here, what do they really want?

* Superfood to breed and to feed super animals to augment the World's food supply. What could possibly go wrong?

* In a post-apocalyptic cattle drive there is both more and less to the day-to-day grind of a cowboy.

* They came. They sat "up there". They destroyed all of our lines of communication. Humanity's last days? Perhaps…

* In an alternate present, colossal dirigibles transport goods from West to East. They leave on a regular schedule transporting the goods that this country wants. Just a delivery service really, until things begin to go wrong. Then things go *really* wrong.

* The world has collapsed. Is there a place for love…is there even time?

* The buying and selling of fake holy artifacts is reprehensible…unless it's not really fake.

And more …

Plus I'll be releasing a few novellas that might turn out to be Summer Movies.

Stairway to Hell -Book 1 (an "Ansel Mulligan, Prefect of Mars" story). … Coming soon

Two more Ansel Mulligan books are coming "soon".

www.ZaslowCrane.com

ALSO BY ZASLOW CRANE

The Future is Closer Than You Think- Book 2 Tales From the Day after Tomorrow

Coming soon-

In "The Future Is Closer Than Your Think- Tales From The Day After Tomorrow" BOOK TWO.

In it you may find-

* A simple Med Tech finds that the fate of all Humanity is in his hands. Is he up to the task?

* Most people in the Future have nothing to do. No job. No responsibilities. No aspirations. Humanity is at a crossroads. Evolve or…?

* "First Contact" The love of Music brought *Them* from across the Galaxy. Now that they're here, what do they really want?

* Superfood to breed and to feed super animals to insure the World's food supply. What could possibly go wrong?

* In a post-apocalyptic cattle drive there is both more and less to the day-to-day grind of a cowboy.

* They came. They sat "up there". They destroyed all of our lines of communication. Humanity's last days? Perhaps…

* The world has collapsed. Food is running out. Winter is coming on. Is there a place for love…is there even time?

* The buying and selling of fake holy artifacts is reprehensible… unless it's not really fake.

And much more …

THANKS

Thank you for buying this book I hope that you enjoyed it.

You can always reach out to me at:

Zaslowcrane.com

facebook.com/people/Zaslow-Crane

Zaslow Crane, writer

"I'd much rather attempt the risk, than not risk the attempt"

Made in the USA
Middletown, DE
23 July 2022